ICE ANGEL

ICE ANGEL

An Alex Turner Thriller

MATTHEW HART

PEGASUS CRIME

NEW YORK LONDON

ICE ANGEL

Pegasus Crime is an imprint of
Pegasus Books, Ltd.
148 W. 37th Street, 13th Floor
New York, NY 10018

Copyright © 2021 by Matthew Hart

First Pegasus Books cloth edition September 2021

Interior design by Maria Fernandez

Library of Congress Cataloging-in-Publication Data is available.

ISBN: 978-1-64313-811-4

10 9 8 7 6 5 4 3 2 1

Printed in the United States of America
Distributed by Simon & Schuster
www.pegasusbooks.com

For Mich and Mez

They fought last year by the upper valley of Son-Kan,
This year by the high ranges of the Leek Mountains,
They are still fighting . . . fighting!
They wash their swords and armor in the cold waves of
      The Tiao-Chih Sea;
Their horses, turning loose over the Tien Mountains,
Seek the meagre grasses in the white snow.

                —Li Po, "The Long War"

PROLOGUE

ate came looking for Jimmy Angel on an August morning on the shore of a little bay a mile above the Arctic Circle. In Canada they call that region the Barrens, a treeless landscape of water and rock and bushes already turning scarlet. In the Barrens in August, winter was in the air. The frost on the tent glistened in the early light. Jimmy stood with his eyes closed and his face tilted up, his lumpy, grizzled features arranged into a grin so broad it could only have been put there by the fusion of two ideas: Jimmy and a large sum of money.

He tossed back the dregs of his coffee and took a bite out of a twelve-inch salami sub with Swiss, olives, peppers, dill pickles, and honey-mustard dressing. Smell-wise, it packed a punch undelivered by any other food likely to be found between Jimmy and the city of Yellowknife, where he'd bought it two days before. A sub has a pretty good shelf life in the Arctic, as long as you leave out things like lettuce and tomato, which Jimmy hated and would have left out anyway. He had twelve subs—a three-day supply. After that it would be freeze-dried meals like chicken à la king and beef stroganoff that he would boil on his camp stove. When cooked, they looked like wads of newsprint, and that was what they tasted like. Anyway, this is academic, because it wasn't Jimmy who was going to eat the rest of the subs or the freeze-dried chicken à la king.

A breeze ruffled the bay. Jimmy's floatplane creaked against the lines that tethered it to the stony beach, and wavelets slapped the pontoons. In his head Jimmy was writing the press release that would send his share price skyrocketing. He tossed back the last piece of sub. All that now remained of the sandwich was the swarm of gaseous molecules saturated with its scent that swept up the gravel slope behind the tent and spread downwind. In a single cubic centimeter of air there were twenty-seven trillion trillion molecules to smell. To the right nose, a lot of information.

Jimmy strolled around the site, admiring his handiwork—the grid of squares marked by twine, pegged out in a professional way. The ground had been scraped clean of surface minerals. Mostly clean. Here and there a few grains winked in the sunlight like tiny gems. Jimmy crouched by the grid and fingered them lovingly. Ilmenites as black as coal, and the brilliant emerald green of chrome diopsides. Best of all, the garnets. Some of them bloodred. Others a scarlet that edged toward orange. And most tantalizing, most irresistible—those that throbbed with a deep-purple pulse.

Eight miles downwind, the bear was snuffling among the Saskatoon berries when the first molecules of salami sub arrived. Eight miles is not far for a bear. A bear can pick up a scent twenty miles away. It can smell seven times better than a bloodhound—and a bloodhound can smell three hundred times better than a person. A bear is really a smelling machine that eats. The part of a bear's brain that manages the sense of smell is five times larger than the same area in a human brain, even though the bear has a much smaller brain. The sensing surfaces inside a bear's nose are hundreds of times greater in area than those in a human nose. So never mind the Saskatoon berries and never mind the stinking bits of scale and bone that clung to his fur from a dead fish he'd found on the side of a stream. Those salami molecules sailed in loud and clear. They hit the bear's nose like a freight train. His big shaggy head went up with a jerk, and he made the bear noise that translates as: *whoa!*

And then that bear went loping out of the bushes on a beeline for Jimmy's camp. A grizzly bear. *Ursus horribilis.*

Jimmy sat down on a boulder and began to fill out a series of plastic sampling tags. The tags would be affixed to the sampling bags that were already loaded in the plane. Jimmy took pleasure in the task, checking the GPS coordinates and inking them onto a tag with his Edding field pen. He had beautiful lettering. His mapping instructor at the Colorado School of Mines had been a scrupulous calligrapher, and Jimmy's charts were works of art. He was neat in everything he did, and his sampling sites were meticulous. Where he did sometimes nudge things out of kilter was in the way he disclosed information to the stock market. He would include this data, but not that. Whether this made him a felon or not, people could argue. *Had* argued. That's not to say Jimmy deserved the bear.

They are not pretty things, bears, unless your personal aesthetic relies entirely on regard for function. In that case, sure. Bears are more efficient than they look. They get where they have to get, and you'd be surprised how fast. A loping grizzly bear looks like an animal wearing an animal suit that's a size too big. They look like they will trip on their own skin. However, they don't.

The last obstacle between the bear and Jimmy was an esker, a kind of gravel ridge. The bear hit the side of the esker and tried to gallop up. The esker got steeper toward the top. The bear dug in, spewed loose gravel out behind it, and then just slid backward down the slope on its ass. Without even stopping for a second to have a think, it flung itself back at the hill and went pounding up again, except this time madder.

Jimmy tucked the sampling tags into the pocket of his shirt. The wind was starting to gust, so he carefully buttoned the pocket flap. He strolled back to the tent for a last look around, checking inside to make sure everything was in order. It was. He went back outside for a last good look at the site.

It was perfect. No two ways about it. Jimmy put his hands in his pockets and pressed his top teeth against his lower lip, rocking back and forth on his heels with a feeling of deep satisfaction. He walked one way and then the other, studying the shore. The cove where the plane was moored and where Jimmy had his camp was called Clip Bay. Its shoreline formed a perfect arc that looked as if it had been clipped out of the side of a circle. Another thing that attracted Jimmy—the drop. The water didn't shoal away gradually. It plunged straight down. There was the shore, ringed by a narrow band of shallow turquoise water, then black. An inky impenetrable depth. Jimmy knew what had caused that shape, and that knowledge was going to help make him very rich. Such were Jimmy's thoughts when a ticking sound—the sound of pebbles and larger stones colliding—made him turn around.

The bear was already halfway off the esker, storming down the steep side in a cloud of dust and gravel. "Fuck," said Jimmy. "Fuck fuck fuck!" And he ran for the plane. There was a loaded pistol in the cockpit, clipped under his seat. A pistol doesn't sound like much, but it was a Ruger Redhawk. A .357 slug in the face will take the sparkle out of even a grizzly's day.

The straightest route from where Jimmy was standing to the plane lay through the pegged-out grid with its mesh of sturdy twine. Understandably, he forgot it was there. He galloped into it, caught his boot on a line, and sprawled headlong onto the hard ground.

He flailed at the tangle of cords that ensnared his arms and legs, finally yanking the whole grid out of the ground. He hobbled to the plane, trailing a line of stakes, and scrambled onto a pontoon. A single metal step like the rung of a ladder was fixed to the fuselage below the door. Jimmy got a foot on the step and yanked the door open. He was reaching in for the pistol when something struck the side of his foot and made a loud metallic bang as it hit the rung. Jimmy's boot flew from its foothold. He was hanging from the door, trying to hoist himself in, when the bear arrived.

The grizzly hurtled off the beach, smashed into Jimmy, took off the airplane door with a swipe of rage, and cannoned into the water—Jimmy and the bear all mixed up together. The bear thrashed at the water and dislocated Jimmy's shoulder with a blow that opened a gash down to his elbow. With his good arm, Jimmy flailed at the water and managed to flounder away. The bear swam to shore and hauled himself out. It stood roaring at Jimmy, rocking from side to side. It shook its head wildly and smacked a paw on the end of a pontoon, tearing the metal with his claws. Gasping, Jimmy made it to the far end of the pontoon. He looped his good arm over it and looked at his wound. The bear's claw had sliced the leather of his jacket as neatly as a sword cut. Blood leaked into the water. A pink cloud curled against the silver metal.

Then the bear recaptured the scent of the salami. It lost interest in Jimmy and went roaring into the tent. The tent collapsed, and the grizzly got tangled in the canvas. In a demented rage it reduced the tent to shreds. Five minutes later the bear was lying on its stomach in the ruined camp with the smashed food locker clasped in its massive paws and bits of olive in its fur. Its big red tongue raked around in the splintered plastic for pieces of salami.

Jimmy was still in the water.

The temperature of lakes in the Barrens is never far above freezing. Jimmy got cold fast. When a human body loses heat faster than it can replace it, hypothermia sets in. As body temperature drops, the nervous system and the heart fail. Unless you get out of the water fast, you lose consciousness. At the temperature in the lake, Jimmy had about fifteen minutes before blacking out. But although the bear roared on the beach for only five minutes before it headed to the tent, Jimmy couldn't pull himself onto the pontoon. The first thing the cold takes is not consciousness but coordination. In that water, Jimmy had three minutes before he would lose the ability to control his limbs, and those three minutes were almost gone.

A ribbon of blood wound through the shallow water by the shore. Jimmy noticed how beautiful it was. He would have liked to slide into the curling stream of color. Then he thought of his daughter. He fixed her image in his mind and stretched his good arm along the pontoon. With the last of his strength he dragged his body half out of the water. The stones and gravel were warming in the sun. He laid his head against them. He tried to push away the shadows gathering in his mind. To keep his daughter there. Had he told her about the garnets?

The bear roared, followed a split second later by a sharp report. Jimmy tried to turn his head to see. His chin dug into the gravel, and he couldn't move it. He listened for the bear. Instead he heard the crunch of footsteps.

1

A dirty wind came off the river. I turned my back to shelter the flimsy pages. They had the usual heading. Department of the Treasury: Financial Crimes Enforcement Network—FinCEN. A line of red type warned that it was a federal crime to read the document without authorization.

In a few terse paragraphs, the document described Jimmy Angel's life as the government saw it.

Born 1952, Fort Collins, Colorado. Geology degree, Colorado School of Mines. PhD, University of Utah. Married 1990. One child: a daughter, born 1994. Widowed 2000. Then came what they really cared about.

Jimmy Angel hadn't led a blameless life. To finance his mineral explorations in the Canadian north, he'd formed companies and issued stock. Sometimes the people who bought that stock came to believe that Jimmy cheated them. Once, a court agreed, and once was enough. He was in our files for good.

"OK," I said to Tommy, "he cut a few corners. It's not like he brought down Lehman Brothers. Why do we care about this?"

Tommy put a ball on the tee and placed his tree-trunk legs wide. His lime-colored bowling shirt snapped around him. He brought the clubface to the ball, gave an irritating wiggle of his ass, and drove the ball in a perfect, soaring arc that cleared the netting at the end of the driving range and dropped it into the Hudson River.

At six-two and pushing 240, Tommy was overweight. But fifteen years ago, when he was still a New York Jet, he'd been the fastest cornerback in the NFL. There were men still limping today from hits they got from Tommy when he could cover forty yards in five seconds flat. Pro ball was the route that had taken a lot of Black kids out of the Bronx, but Tommy could pick up any sport. He just had that gift. That's what I kept telling myself as he teed up another ball and launched it into the river. Tommy was my boss, a circumstance I found even more irritating than the ass wiggle.

He stepped back and held the driver out to me. I ignored it.

"It's your meeting, Tommy."

He shrugged and tossed the club aside. "Did you see the breakout?"

I found the page he was referring to and turned my back to the wind again.

The driving range was on the roof of a pier that stuck out into the Hudson from the west side of Manhattan, a reminder to the glittering island that it once had to work for a living. The river sucked at the ancient pilings and slapped against the seawall. Hydrofoil commuter ferries from the New Jersey side flew by on their way to the downtown terminals. The wind groaned in the netting, and the windows in the little pro shop set up a constant tinkle of loose glass. Good luck with the parabolic mike if anyone was trying to listen in.

Tommy had an arrangement with the man on the gate. When we wanted the range to ourselves, we got it. Not that we needed it. For sensitive discussions, we had an acoustical "dead room" two steps from

Tommy's office. It provided total security. What it didn't provide was the opportunity for Tommy to demonstrate his alpha status.

I studied the breakout. It showed the usual tangle of ownership of a small company that had to raise capital from multiple sources. Angel Minerals was traded on an American stock exchange. That meant Jimmy had to disclose the identity of important owners in public filings. One of them stood out.

"The numbered company," I said.

We wandered down the range. Tommy limped a little as we made our way toward the river. That was another opportunity not offered by the dead room—demonstrating how to suffer without complaint.

"If you're going to stumble around like that," I said, "maybe you should think about a walker."

When we got to the end, we stood for a minute watching the river traffic.

"We pulled that numbered company apart looking for who owned it," Tommy said. He flexed his leg and rubbed his right knee. It always gave him trouble in the damp, but it had made him who he was. When his knee blew out, Tommy went to law school. He became an ace crime-busting prosecutor, handled a few top-secret cases for us, and now here he was, running our clandestine agency.

"Jimmy Angel," he began, but we were interrupted. Minnie Ho came tripping down the range, the sunlight flashing on her silver jeans.

"Hi, boys," she said, splashing us with her thousand-watt smile. "Don't let me bust up the powwow." She gave Tommy a peck on the cheek and plucked a fold of his rippling rayon shirt in her slender fingers. "Just wanted you to know I'm here. Take your time. I'll be outside." She glanced at her watch. "The show doesn't start until three, so we're good."

"Outside" meant Minnie would be waiting in the parking lot in her vintage Bentley, a car that looked stately but hummed with enough communications equipment to run a war. Minnie was one of New York's hottest fashion designers. Her shows drew buyers from London, Paris, Milan, and Hong Kong. She was never out of touch with her global business. I knew because my daughter worked for her. Minnie had taken her on at a bad time in Annie's life, mostly caused by me.

"Five minutes, Min," Tommy said.

"Hey," she said, tilting her head at my blazer. "Is that Etro?"

"Annie," I said.

She grabbed a lapel and twisted it this way and that to examine the seam, then shook her head. "Man, that girl can sew."

She blew Tommy a kiss from her fingertips and was taking her first call before she'd gone three feet.

Tommy did his best to conceal how knocked out he was by Minnie, but I could see him struggling to remember what page we'd been on.

"You were going to tell me why we're suddenly interested in Jimmy Angel," I prompted.

Tommy looked at the water and frowned as he pulled his thoughts together. Just upriver, a stack of gleaming decks slid away from a pier. The cruise ship's passengers packed the rails as the liner turned its bow downriver.

"Jimmy's disappeared."

I let a little silence seep into the space between us while I mulled this over. "And you know this how, exactly?"

"We were keeping in touch."

I would have laughed, but I could already see where things were headed, and for sure the joke was going to be on me.

"Let's see if I'm getting a handle on this," I said. "Since you're all up to speed on Jimmy Angel, to the point where you know that he's gone missing, I'm going to take a wild guess that you were running him as some kind of agent. You were running Jimmy Angel, and now you've lost him and you don't know what to do."

"Sure I know what to do. I call you. You're the big-time spook on the payroll. You put on those phony glasses of yours with the mustache and false nose and go find him."

If you nicked Tommy with a knife, sarcasm was what would dribble out. It didn't fool me. He was worried, or he wouldn't have called me in.

"He's missed a reporting date, hasn't he?" I'd been here before. Tommy's predecessor had tried to run an agent too. They get hooked on the undercover side of the business and decide it looks like fun.

Formally part of FinCEN, our small and secret agency had a lot of independence. We investigated the kind of financial crimes that couldn't be solved by a subpoena for bank records. The people we dealt with were at a level of bad where it was sometimes necessary to put a gun in their ear to promote cooperation. Put into a report and read over coffee by people with too much time on their hands, it looked easy. They'd decide to give it a whirl themselves.

"And that numbered company," I said. "Tell me how that fits in."

"It's registered in British Columbia. FinCEN's computers flagged it when there was an exchange of wires between the numbered company and a private bank in Singapore that we were watching. The Singapore bank has only one client. That's what set the alarm bells ringing. The client is a private fund called China Hard Asset."

"Oh boy," I said.

We made our way back up the range.

"You know about it, then?"

"What do you think I did for a living before you joined the department? *Yes,* I know about it. It's the foreign investment arm for top officers of the People's Liberation Army. It's where the Xi twins get their money."

We reached the tee line.

"Jimmy Angel's a smart guy," I said. "In his own field, he's brilliant. But that's one of the richest diamond fields on the planet. If the Chinese brass and that pair are targeting it, and they think Jimmy's in their way, it's very bad news that you haven't heard from him."

Tommy took a deep breath and blew it out slowly. He jammed his hands into his pockets and kicked a ball that was lying beside a tee. It rose in a surprisingly graceful arc and dropped back onto the range twenty-five yards away. We watched it roll to a stop.

"You'll have to go up there, Alex," he said.

"What do the Canadians know about this?"

"Beats me," Tommy said. He glanced at his watch and yanked open the door to the stairs. When we reached the parking lot, Minnie was waiting in the Bentley, windows rolled up against the noise of the traffic on the West Side Highway. She was swiping through pages on a computer mounted on the dash and talking nonstop into the tiny mike attached to her headset.

"China Hard Asset is there to provide a retirement for men who expect a comfortable lifestyle," I said. "Xi Fan and his sister have built some of the biggest companies in China using their money. Their holdings include iDragon, one of the largest telecommunications companies in the world. I'm assuming you know that, since our government is trying to destroy it. Our latest move was those phony fraud charges we cooked up against Fan's twin sister, Mei. Then we convinced the Canadians to arrest her on an extradition warrant when she was changing planes in Vancouver. She's still under arrest, and Fan and his high-ranking friends in the Chinese government are breathing fire."

"Let me tell you how this works," Tommy said. "We didn't *convince the Canadians to lock her up.*" He scratched in air quotes. "We tipped them off that she was coming through Vancouver and made a formal extradition request. It's called a treaty obligation."

"Tell it to the Chinese. They've been waging all-out war on Canada since then—locking up Canadian businessmen in China and charging them with spying. They're in a rage, demanding her release. Fan was dangerous before; now he's a blood enemy of the United States."

Tommy stopped with his hand on the door handle. "Is that so? Listen, champ. We've got his sister. Let's see how much fire he breathes when the penny drops and he understands how long we could put her away for."

He opened the door and got in. "There's a plane waiting for you at Teterboro. Go tonight. Try not to rely too heavily on your wide network of criminal friends."

He slammed the door. Minnie shot out through the gate, still talking. I paced around in the lot for a minute, then faced the music and called Lily. She heard me out, and let an icy silence settle in my ear.

"If that's how it has to be, darling," she said at last, "I'm coming." And she hung up.

2

I looked out the window of the little jet. Below the wings spread a thick, unbroken layer of cloud, pale white in the moonlight. The flight tracker at the front of the cabin showed our position: north of Saskatchewan, heading west.

I told the steward we were fine on our own, and he went to sit in the cockpit with the pilots.

Government executive jet: not my usual ride. This was the one normally used by the secretary of the treasury. Leather sofa and a pair of easy chairs. Huge desk. Of course I looked through it. Some habits you never shake.

The steward's log was in the left-hand bottom drawer. My flight was the most recent entry. Mostly it was just a list of hops between Washington and New York, where the secretary's family lived. Couple of flights to London. An overnight to Montreal caught my eye because I'd been spending time there. Not really thinking much of it, I snapped a picture of the entry with my phone. Other than that, nothing more scandalous than a few winter weekends in the Bahamas. I tossed the log back in the drawer.

The cabin felt more like a stateroom on a ship than an airplane. Lamps with shades. Real china cups. Lead crystal glasses. Not to mention the food. That network of criminal friends Tommy had mentioned: the main one was perched at a table, devouring a platter of sashimi.

"For God's sake, Alex," Lily said through a mouthful of raw fish. "Eat something. Do you have any idea what this costs?" She tapped her chopsticks on a deep-red lump of fish. "Bluefin tuna belly. Excellent protein, plus a rare chance to rip off the government."

With the tip of her chopsticks she spread wasabi paste onto a jewel-like tuna roll, added a thin, coral-colored slice of ginger, deftly plucked up the roll, and popped it in her mouth. She rested the chopsticks on the little china stand and chewed contentedly, leaning forward to examine a parcel of rough diamonds.

Slav Lily had porcelain skin and dark, lustrous hair cut short. It looked as if a typhoon had just blown through and plastered her head with a mass of jet-black curls. She had pointy, elvish ears that poked through the storm of hair. The shape made her look like a Vulcan, except Lily's eyebrows weren't pointed. They curved above her gray eyes as if they'd been painted on by Leonardo.

She stirred a finger through the diamonds. "This is lovely rough," she said. "Very white. Nice sizes. Very cuttable." Lily was Russian. She spoke English with a mid-Atlantic accent, too polished to be American but too slick with Russian vowels to be British.

"Where are the stones from?"

"Canada," she said. "It's rough from the Ekati mine." She gave me a playful look. "We're going to the Arctic, darling. Alex gets sudden urgent assignment," she said, spreading her hands in mock alarm. "Assignment has to do with missing diamond explorer we both know. A delightful man, but a fraud." She pinched a few diamonds between her thumb and forefinger and let them drop back into the little pile. "I thought I should familiarize myself with the kind of goods people steal up there, because I'll probably be offered some."

She was still a little mad. I didn't blame her. We were supposed to be living a new life. She'd bought a huge apartment in Montreal, the only city in North America she considered European enough to live in. I prefer a place where people insult me in my own language. But it's a forty-five-minute flight from LaGuardia, so we sawed it down the middle: I kept my apartment in New York. That gave me a place to spend weekends with my daughter on those rare occasions when she felt like it. The rest of the time I lived with Lily.

Then the call from Tommy. Technically I'd been on what the department called temporary long leave—a vague acknowledgment that they'd screwed up my life and put my family at risk in the business of the Russian Pink. What was not so vague about the agreement was that they could snap their fingers and I had to come. That's the problem with a new life; it's still attached to the old one.

I got up, rummaged around in the galley, and checked out the fridge. "Ever heard of a vodka called 'Spirits of the Tsars'?"

"Two hundred and fifty dollars a bottle," Lily said. "Is it cold?"

"It's in the freezer."

"Pour me one too."

I splashed some into crystal tumblers and put one in front of her. I stretched out on the sofa with the laptop on my chest and scrolled through the background file.

Until the US government cooked up the fraud charge and engineered Xi Mei's arrest in Vancouver on an extradition warrant, the twins were always pictured in places like Cannes, sharing the steps of the Carlton Hotel with movie stars, or stepping out for the night in London or Macau. They had an exotic cachet that beautiful and famous people liked to bathe in.

Their father was a "princeling," the term for the privileged son of a Chinese revolutionary hero. He was the fabulously rich governor of a province until he backed the wrong side in a dirty fight at the top of the ruling clique and found himself impoverished and in jail. He'd lived like a monarch, and his downfall filled the world's papers with lurid stories of orgies and corruption.

Suddenly pictures of the twins were plastered all over the world's front pages—the cossetted offspring of the fallen titan, members of a "red aristocracy" enrolled in elite universities in the United States. There were photographs of Fan at Harvard, a pair of stoned, topless girls sprawled across him as he sat in his Ferrari snarling at the camera. In another shot, he gaped drunkenly from a sofa, his shirt unbuttoned and his tie askew, as another pair of girls, or maybe the same ones, brushed makeup on his cheeks. His rosebud mouth blazed with scarlet lipstick.

"Remember him?" I said, holding up the laptop so Lily could see the screen.

She stirred a finger in her vodka and tilted her head at the picture. "Should I?"

"Yes. He's one of the Xi twins, before they got serious. Now they're trying to bust their way into Canadian diamonds."

I dragged the photo back into the folder and opened the file on Mei. She was studying business at the Wharton School, a CEO production line that fed a stream of graduates into Wall Street banks and America's top companies. Unlike her brother, Mei didn't wear lipstick. She wore blue Converse sneakers and powder-blue chinos and drove a VW Golf. Also blue. She was often pictured with a tiny cat peering from her purse. She wore thick glasses with blue frames. A pair of lapis lazuli clips pulled her hair back from her face.

"Weren't there rumors she was sleeping with the brother?" Lily said, leaning over my shoulder to gaze at the picture. Her breath smelled of fish and vodka. Suddenly she clamped her teeth on my ear and gave it a tug. "Sinful," she murmured.

She went to get another drink. I put the pictures away and clicked on the file with the yellow band across it that the FinCEN archivists used when the information inside came partly from outside agencies. Like the FBI and the CIA. Well, not *like* them. Them.

The twins' money dried up fast. Two gorillas from the embassy in Washington went up to visit. There were transcripts, so somebody'd got a wire in. The twins sat still for an icy lecture about enemies of the people and the values outlined in the Chinese Constitution. Ferrari back to dealer. Goodbye lipstick. Brother and sister met once a week. For lunch.

Fan hired a tutor and managed to scrape out a C. Mei graduated top of her class. She would have anyway. At the end of the academic year, the twins flew back to Beijing to begin the round of groveling that saved them from following their father into prison.

I clicked back into a bullet-point file of a type that FinCEN called a "scope." It listed the careful alliances the twins had built with influential people. They bought a small factory that made knockoffs of expensive Western handbags. Then they bought another factory. Then a small gold mine. Then not so small. Soon they had a condo in Chaoyang Park, a leafy central Beijing enclave full of young millionaires. Then they made the move that separated them from mere millionaires and launched them into the stratosphere. Their masterstroke. They went to see the generals.

In China, no one had more power. The FinCEN scope included a list of the companies owned by the military, including the gargantuan state monopolies on railroad construction, shipbuilding, and aircraft manufacture. Salaries and bonuses from these enterprises made the generals rich. Wisely, the twins stayed away from sectors already controlled by the brass. Instead, they pitched them on what amounted to a private hedge fund. The fund would invest not only in China but, more importantly, abroad, gobbling up companies that were both profit-able and strategic. Lining the pockets of its investors while at the same time providing them with economic crowbars they could use to influence other countries.

Inside five years, lipstick boy was back in the papers, the master of the rosebud sneer, his hair cut close on the sides and brushed straight back on top. He was the hood ornament of modern China. Mei was always at his side, a pace behind. Sometimes she held her little cat. The file said it was a breed called Singapura. Mei still wore her hair fastened back with the bright blue clips. Sort of dreamy smile. I airdropped a picture onto Lily's phone, where it landed with a *pong*. She flicked her eyes from the diamonds.

"He'd better sleep with one eye open," she said.

"You think?"

She spread her fingers to expand the image. "Pay attention to the cat."

I looked more closely at the picture. Its ears were flat as it peered at Fan.

I went to the latest pictures. The glittering twins—not so glittering now. Fighting their way through the press that swarmed the Vancouver courthouse where Mei was battling extradition. Fan's face a mask of fury. One hand was clamped like a vise on Mei's thin wrist as he dragged her through the crowd. His black eyes burned with hatred.

The Canadian judge had allowed Mei to stay at a house they owned on the ocean while the court decided her fate. She wore an ankle monitor. A court-approved security company kept her under watch 24/7. Paid for by the twins.

I closed the file and opened the one on Canadian diamonds. Canada produced more than twenty million carats of rough diamonds a year, mostly from the Arctic mines. In terms of value, it was the third largest diamond producer in the world. The question seemed to be, were there any mines still left to be discovered? Apparently Jimmy Angel had convinced the twins there were.

"Did you pick up any rumors about what Jimmy was finding?" I said.

Lily had folded the diamond parcel away. She was reclining in the black leather executive chair, her gray suede ankle boots resting on the desk while she blew on her fingernails. I didn't know who the secretary of the treasury took along when he traveled, but Lily had discovered a pullout compartment full of expensive French cosmetics. She'd been engrossed in her nails for the last ten minutes. Lily could vacuum up data by the terabyte. She'd finished the entire report before I'd made it through a dozen pages. She wiggled her fingers at me.

"This one's called Carnal Red," she said in her husky voice. "Don't tell me you're not struggling to control yourself."

"Jimmy Angel," I prompted.

Lily held out her hand at arm's length, the fingers splayed, tilting her head as she swiveled her wrist to examine the nails.

"I made some calls before I left Montreal," she said. "He's been showing around some fantastic garnets."

"Pyropes?"

"Yes. G10s. Beautiful colors. Deep red, purple. Dazzling." She wiggled her fingers again.

Pyrope garnets were what diamond prospectors called "indicators." If you found them, they indicated that diamonds were nearby.

Lily knew Arctic diamonds. She'd grown up in Mirny, a small city in the Siberian diamond fields. She became a top sorter and diamond grader for the Russian state diamond company, Russgem, before she was twenty. Her career hit a snag when the crooked oligarchs who controlled the diamond business discovered she was siphoning 140,000 carats a month out of their pockets and into hers. It was an ingenious system that took advantage of the way Russgem rounded off decimal places when it weighed the rough, leaving fractional amounts uncaptured. Russia produced forty million carats a year, so the fractions added up fast.

The oligarchs almost killed her. They didn't, because Lily had something they wanted more than revenge: the secret of how she'd laundered the stolen rough into US dollars. The deal she worked out made her even richer than she'd been before. She gave up the details of her laundry, and they put her in charge of their Antwerp operations.

That's where she came to my attention. When she started buying African contraband. I laid a trap, and caught her at Brussels airport with a few million dollars' worth.

I turned Slav Lily on the spot, flipping her against her Russian gangster bosses. It was a triumph for law and order and the forces of good in the world. Except for one thing. It detonated into a love affair. And not the kind where you gaze into each other's eyes and sigh. The other kind. The kind where you try to outwit, use, and deceive each other until your hearts are black and blue, and shame is the measure of your tenderness. Tell me that's not love.

"Here's what I'm wondering," I said. "Let's assume Washington really is afraid that Fan and Mei and some Chinese generals might score on a long shot mineral play. They make a diamond strike. Why is that a problem? What could the Chinese be getting that we don't want them to get?"

I unzipped the bag that operations had packed for me. Military-grade first aid kit, including painkillers; selection of high-tech hiking gear; and at the bottom, under the wick-away socks and thermal gloves, a SIG Sauer MPX Copperhead submachine gun with three extra thirty-round clips. If you were going to pack a submachine gun in your luggage, that's the one you'd pick. Not much more than four pounds. About fourteen inches long. Still, it's not like remembering to put in the underwear. Field-grade meds and a SIG with extra mags. Makes you wonder what they know that you don't.

"The Chinese are diamond crazy," Lily said, flashing her scarlet fingernails in the light of the desk lamp. "They buy more polished diamonds than any other country in the world. They have no mines, and other countries have managed to keep them out of the rough business. That means they can't buy directly from mines. They have to pay large markups to those who do. They were always trying to buy direct when I was in Mirny."

"Did you sell to them?"

Lily put the nail polish back in the case and took out a magnifying mirror. "Once you start with the Chinese, there's no way out."

"That's not an answer, Lily."

She unfolded a metal stand from the back and stood the mirror on the desk. She uncapped a lipstick and leaned toward the mirror. "Christian Louboutin," she said, applying a smoldering scarlet to her lips. "Ninety dollars a stick."

"So a Chinese investment in Jimmy's company could be part of a larger plan."

"*Mwa.*" Lily smacked her lips at the mirror. "*Mwa, mwa.*"

"The Chinese," I prompted.

Lily tossed the lipstick on the desk, folded the mirror, and put it away. She swung the big chair around and parked her suede boots in my lap. She splayed her ruby-tipped fingers on either side of her beautiful mouth and gave me a wicked smile.

"Investing in Jimmy," I plowed on. "Part of a larger plan."

"Alex, they're Chinese. *Everything* is part of a larger plan."

3

Somewhere over the north the sky cleared. The moon slashed a silver stripe across the black sheet of Great Slave Lake. Here and there on the ragged coast, the light of an isolated cabin stabbed a pinhole in the darkness of the forest. The small jet shuddered as it dropped through a layer of turbulence.

We banked for final. Yellowknife appeared in the window, glowing on the shore. From the air it looked like a toy city unpacked from a box and set up in the wilderness—a cluster of office buildings, some traffic lights, suburbs, and a mall. Everywhere else, pressing at the edges of the town, the dark unbroken forest.

The undercarriage unfolded with a thump. A river glittered in the trees. A thread of gravel road wound along the shore of a long bay. A pair of headlights bored a tunnel through the night. We scraped in across the city and landed.

At that hour the airport had a desolate appearance. A single jet with the logo of a diamond-mining company on its tail waited at the passenger terminal. Miners heading out to start a rotation at a distant mine trudged from the departure gate and made their way across the tarmac. The intercom clicked on.

"Directed to the RCMP hangar," the pilot said.

We turned off the main runway and headed to a far corner of the airport. On the way we passed a floodlit parking ramp where a pair of Canadian F-18s stood with their canopies open. Cockpit ladders hung against the sides. The network of cables that keep a fighter jet ready to scramble coiled across the pad. Just past the jets, in the shadows beyond the lights, a soldier in camo stood beside a military truck and watched us taxi past.

The engines whined down as we turned off the taxiway. A woman wearing ear protectors and a reflective vest stood in front of a white hangar, pointing her orange batons to guide us in. Above the hangar doors, a buffalo wreathed in maple leaves lowered its head at the world. But I didn't need the official crest of the Royal Canadian Mounted Police to identify the guy waiting for me.

A shock of hair fell across his forehead, almost hiding an ugly scar. He had a satanic smile, dark eyes, and a feral restlessness, like a wild animal pent up in a cage. He paced back and forth on the oil-stained pavement, hands shoved deep into the pockets of a dark blue trench coat. The fury of his movement almost disguised the slight limp. His mouth twisted into a crooked grin as he daggered glances at the plane.

We rolled to a halt. The steward wrenched up the handle and pushed the door open. As the seal broke, the inrush of cold air filled the cabin. Lily pulled on her red leather jacket, pocketed the lipstick, and slipped on her Akris techno-fabric shoulder bag. Thirteen hundred dollars at Bergdorf. Easily big enough to hold the makeup Lily had looted from the stash on the plane, with plenty of room left over for her Glock Slimline subcompact and the two extra clips she always carried. Talk about ready for an evening out.

"Yankee bastard!" the man in the trench coat roared when the stairs deployed and we left the jet. He strode forward and grabbed my hand in a crushing grip. "Where have you been hiding! Trying to sneak in without telling me, eh?"

"This is Inspector Luc Savard," I said to Lily.

He turned to her with his savage smile. "And the famous Slav Lily too," he thundered before I could complete the introduction. "This is a bonus!" He stepped in close and dropped his voice to a hoarse whisper. "You're much better looking than that Belgian mug shot."

He put his head back and roared with laughter at his own joke, then gave me a thunderclap slap on the back.

"Belgian mug shot," he repeated, still laughing. When he was through he took me by the arm.

"We have a car for you," he said to Lily. "I'm going to borrow Alex for an hour and beat him up in the basement." He flashed his evil grin. "I'll return him later."

"Make sure you wipe off the blood first," Lily said. But she didn't like the way Luc was deciding who went where any more than I did.

I wasn't surprised to see him, but not this soon. He was based in Ottawa. The regulation notice Tommy had sent to the Canadian government just before I left was supposed to make my trip seem like a bureaucratic errand. Also, it was as long a flight to Yellowknife from Ottawa as from New York. Yet he'd been there ahead of me. And never mind the laughing and kidding around. When a cop decides where you're going next, you're in custody.

"I don't remember asking for a ride," I said.

"Hospitality is in our blood, Alex. We're a warm and welcoming people. It says so in the tourist ads."

A constable held open the back door. When I was in, he slammed it shut. Something I couldn't have done myself because there were no handles on the inside. When considering how warm and welcoming Canadians are, remind yourself that they invented hockey.

The constable got into the driver's seat. Luc climbed in on the other side. A Plexiglas panel separated them from me.

Every cop car smells of vomit. The stench kept me company while I thought about Luc. By referring to Lily as Slav Lily, as she was known in the diamond world, he wanted me to know he'd run her through the files.

Another thing. The Belgians hadn't taken a mug shot of Lily that night at the airport or at any other time. If the Canadians had a headshot of Lily, they'd taken it themselves.

It was two A.M. We drove to a small building close to the passenger terminal. We parked, got out, and entered a shabby gray room with scales and a baggage-inspection counter. Luc sat behind a metal desk and motioned me to a chair.

"Remind me of the official reason for your visit, Alex?"

"Routine inquiry," I said. "Didn't the office send an advisory? Just checking up on an American-listed company. Dot some i's and cross a few t's."

He carved a grin into his hard face, but his eyes weren't joining in.

"You flew in on a government executive jet. Unless your bosses are treating you better than they used to, I wouldn't call that routine."

He made a gesture with his hands. They were large and badly scarred. When Luc played semi-pro hockey in Quebec, his blistering slap shot had earned him the nickname "Boom." But it wasn't the slap that gave him the scars, it was his temper on the ice. That's how he'd picked up the limp too. He'd had an opponent's top scorer against the boards and was hammering away when one of the guy's teammates skated up and cut a two-handed slash to Luc's right knee.

"The notice came from Tommy Cleary," he said, "so I guess he's running things now."

I tried to think of a clever remark about two guys with bum knees but decided maybe not.

"Here's where I'm having a problem," Luc said. The chair creaked as he leaned back and laced his thick fingers behind his head. "You work for FinCEN. FinCEN is a bureau of the US Treasury. Its *mission*," he said, clearly reciting something he'd just read up on, "is to protect the financial system, combat money laundering, and promote the national security of the United States through the strategic use of financial authorities and the collection of financial intelligence." He studied the ceiling. "OK so far?"

The constable came into the room carrying my bag. He dropped it on the floor beside the desk. It made a loud clank. The constable gave me a look, but Luc ignored the sound.

"And then there's you," he continued. "FinCEN added your department, Special Audits. There's a short clause somewhere in the legislation that describes your task as 'enhanced data capture.' What it comes down to is: you're spooks. When certain people use the American financial system to further a crime, and they're not the kind of people bothered by court orders and threatening letters, it's you who shows up."

He slid the chair forward and splayed his hands on the desk.

"That's why you're here, Alex. Something is fishy, and probably dirty. And bad enough to scare somebody high up in Washington."

He held out his hand, and the constable gave him a thick blue folder with the RCMP crest stamped on it in red.

"We're supposed to be allies. You and me—we've worked together before." He held my eyes with an unwavering stare. "So I'm going to show you something."

He took out some glossy eight-by-tens and laid them on the table one by one. While I was looking through them, he continued.

"A week ago, a hunting party arrived in Yellowknife. They had licenses for the Barrens. They're allowed to bring in their own weapons. The fish-and-game guys check the luggage to make sure they're not bringing in prohibited weapons, such as assault rifles or anything that's fully automatic. This one"—he tapped a picture—"is semiautomatic, which the hunting regulations allow, as long as the clip holds no more than four rounds."

I put a finger on the corner of one of the glossies and turned it so I had a better view.

"Care to guess where the hunters were from?"

I took my time with the photograph, but really, there was no mistaking it.

"The rifle is a QBU-88. People's Liberation Army," I said. "The Chinese military's go-to sniper gun. Gunsmiths call this the bullpup configuration, where the magazine is behind the trigger. Rated accurate to a thousand yards. But it's got a five-round clip."

He nodded. "If they show a modification, they can get it in."

"Sure," I said, "and then restore it to the full five later."

He pointed to the other picture. It was the top-line spotting scope from Kunming Shunho Optics.

"And they were cleared to go ahead?" I said.

"They were."

"Then you've got a Chinese kill team in the Barrens, Luc."

He raked the glossies into a neat stack and put them away.

"So you can understand why I wonder what you're doing, turning up here to investigate a company with recent Chinese investment, just at the very moment that we ourselves are trying to find the right answers."

"Or even the right questions."

"Just so."

"Yes," I said.

"Yes what, Alex?"

"Yes, I can understand you wondering."

Luc had already erased any sign of friendliness from his expression. He had a message, and he'd delivered it. He knew about Jimmy Angel, and he knew about the Chinese. Agreements between our countries meant that he would let me operate. He would give me the rope. If I hanged myself with it, that was going to be OK with him.

Luc shot me a sour look. He nodded to the constable, who grabbed the material from the desk and followed him outside. I grabbed my bag and followed too, but they were already driving away by the time I got outside. Somebody turned the lights out in the terminal, and I heard the door lock snap.

4

Veils of mist rose from the forest. I made my way around the abandoned terminal. A direct-line phone to a taxi company hung on the wall outside the exit doors, but before I picked it up, a cab with a yellow roof light pulled to a stop and flicked its lights. I walked over and stood by the driver's door until he rolled down the window.

"Somebody call you?" I said.

"Mister, this ain't Chicago. They ain't a lot of air traffic at the moment, case you didn't notice. I seen that little jet come in." He had a reedy voice and a greasy ponytail held together with an elastic band. "I figure, hey, maybe some guy needs a ride."

Fine, I thought. Somebody knows I'm in town and sends a mutt to get me. Let's see what they have in mind. I tossed my heavy bag in the back, climbed in, and gave him the name of my hotel.

He took the main road into town, but after half a mile he turned off. We passed a few houses, a single-story building that advertised tours to see the northern lights, then nothing but woods.

"What's with the back road?" I said.

He shot me a mean little glance in the rearview. "Shortcut." He shrugged, not caring if I believed it.

So I already had my bag open and a clip snapped into the SIG when I heard the motorcycle coming up behind us. I lowered the window. The cold air blew in.

The rider coasted alongside and backed off on the throttle. His big Harley made that *potato-potato-potato* sound that's part of what you pay for. The predawn light was seeping into the sky, and the small round lenses of his sunglasses flashed pink.

If you typed "mean biker dude" into your request to central casting, the guy on the Harley would be who they sent. Black T-shirt torn off at the shoulders. Black jeans. Leather vest. One of those small, token helmets that doesn't mess with the flowing hair. And of course, the flowing hair.

His powerful arms were covered in tattoos. He pulled a Walther PPK from his belt and waggled the barrel at us to pull over. The cabbie shot me an ice-cold glance.

"Hey, bud," he said. "No choice here. I gotta stop."

"You bet," I said, snicking off the safety.

The tires crunched on the gravel shoulder. Harley guy gave me his killer look, the Walther held loosely in his hand. We were just rolling to a stop when the rider flicked his pink lenses at the road for a second, and I hoisted the SIG and blew away the back end of the bike. The tire exploded, and the saddle dropped backward. The frame hit the road in a trail of sparks. The bike shot sideways into the ditch, and the rider snowballed along the pavement like a load of laundry.

"Holy fuck!" the taxi driver screamed. "Holy Jesus Christ!"

"Put your right hand up where I can see it and open the door with your left."

"I never seen that guy!" he screamed. "I never seen him before!"

I poked him in the back of the head with the barrel. "Open the door. Then both hands up. Get out of the car and lie facedown on the road and lace your fingers behind your head. Or I'll kill you right here."

He gaped at me in the mirror. "I had nothing to do with this, man."

I gave him another jab.

When he was on the pavement I got out and patted him down. "You got a piece in the car?"

"Under the seat, man," he said in a pleading voice. "It's for protection. I swear, I never seen that fucker."

He had a Baby Browning .25 under the seat. Tough guys call it a mouse gun, but it can kill you, and so could the .38 I found under the dash. I shoved them both in my belt and came around and yanked his head up by the ponytail.

"Listen," I said. "Don't move until I say. I have a fresh clip in the SIG."

I banged his face into the pavement and went to check the biker. He lay motionless beyond the twisted motorcycle. Road burns on his face and arms. His right foot stuck out at a bad angle. The helmet had shattered. Blood was seeping into his hair. I felt worse for the Harley.

I made the driver drag the unconscious biker to the car and load him in the trunk. Then I told him to climb in too.

"Mister, so help me God, I had nothing to do with this. Them guns is just for personal protection."

I emptied the pistols and wiped them down and dropped them in the trunk. I kicked the Walther into the ditch. Give the cops something to play with when they find the Harley.

I drove into town. Near the floatplane dock, a public boat launch slanted down into Yellowknife Bay. I backed down until water was lapping at the rear bumper, put the car in park, and set the emergency brake.

I opened the trunk and let the driver have a look. A breeze was kicking up, and waves licked at the bottom of the concrete ramp.

"I need to know who you work for," I told him. "Otherwise I shut the trunk, put the car in neutral, and release the brake. Your call."

It didn't take long. The cabbie and the biker dude were pretty far down the criminal food chain. He was a low-grade mule for a local gang, and the Harley guy was muscle for hire.

I locked the trunk, left them there, and walked uphill to the hotel. It was six o'clock when I checked in and went upstairs. Lily had the covers pulled over her head. I stepped out onto the balcony and slid the door closed behind me.

The rising sun was spilling crimson light onto the bay. A tug was coming slowly up the channel, towing a massive barge. A woman in overalls came out of the wheelhouse and walked back to check the tow.

Tommy answered on the first ring. I filled him in on what had happened.

"Were they pros?"

"As opposed to what?" I snapped. "It was a cash contract. Local gang."

"Who hires clowns like that for a hit?"

"You're the mastermind with the big office. You tell me."

"Did you find out how they knew when you were getting in?"

"Aren't you skipping a step? Isn't the first question: How did these jerks even know who I was?"

Tommy grunted. He knew where this was going.

"But they did know. Then all they had to do was watch the airport. US government jet comes in. Not hard to guess that's me."

"And you obliged by getting in a cab you didn't call for."

Lily slid open the balcony door and stepped out, wrapped in a blanket. The thrum of the tugboat's diesels reverberated in the air. A sharp breeze came off the water.

"I got in that cab, Tommy, because the sooner we can all get used to how totally your masterful Jimmy Angel operation has been blown, the better. What were you using for your secret communications, Facebook?"

"You don't know who put those guys on you. Maybe it was the Canadians."

Tommy liked to demonstrate the dark depths of his mind. But if the Canadians had wanted to put me on ice, they wouldn't have needed a pair of yokels to do the job. They have people on the payroll. Even easier—they turn the jet around. But they didn't. They let me in. I had a feeling the Canadians had front-row seats for whatever game I'd been sent to play.

"This is bad, Alex," Lily said when I was off the phone.

"I'm all right."

"No!" she said in a fury, yanking the blanket tightly around her shoulders. "You are not all right. You were betrayed and marked to be assassinated." She was shaking. "Don't think that because this is a bush-league Arctic town, it's not dangerous. I grew up in such a place. Once you add diamonds, it's not bush-league anymore. Because the men who tried to kill you were pathetic doesn't mean the people behind them are pathetic."

Lily had ears like a bat. She'd heard every word when I told Tommy what had happened.

"Don't pretend you're not angry," she said. "You are. You're angry because Tommy controls you. And the people above him. You can't get free. They have you by the throat."

She thrust out her arms to demonstrate how to clutch a throat. The blanket slipped from her shoulders. She was naked. Her pale skin glowed pink in the early light.

"The department blackmailed you into working for them. They took advantage of you."

This was one of Lily's articles of faith. But the department didn't even exist when I was recruited by the CIA. That was twenty years ago, and I was no innocent kid. I had an apartment in Cape Town with a view of Table Bay. In the garage, a cream-colored Mercedes 190SL. I lived by trading diamonds. My main supply was stolen goods. High-end rough from the Namibian diamond beach. I ran it up to Antwerp every month, timing my trips to coincide with the big London diamond sales, when Antwerp was full of disappointed traders who hadn't got what they wanted in London. The guys who came to my apartment that night in Cape Town knew all about it. They offered me a simple choice. I could work for the US government or take my chances with the diamond branch of the South African police, who were waiting for their call.

Lily was a collection of fierce beliefs. One of them was that I could go back to some truer past. I'd find the real me, the pristine spirit that existed before the government turned me into its instrument. But the government hadn't turned me into anything. They'd liked me just the way I was.

Lily was shivering. I picked up the blanket and wrapped it around her, and we went back inside. There were still a few hours before we were meeting Jimmy's daughter. I drew the heavy blinds on the bedroom windows and held Lily's cold, hard body in my arms.

"Next time it will be professionals," she murmured in my ear.

"Yes," I said.

"Then you will have to kill them."

"Try to get some sleep."

5

"What's a Beaver Tail?" Lily asked the waiter.

"Basically a large doughnut, except shaped like a beaver tail and no hole in the middle." She tapped a pencil against her teeth. "Deep fried," she added, holding the pencil straight up, as if in warning, "then dipped in sugar."

I handed the menu back.

"Bacon and eggs."

"You'll live to fight another day," she said.

Lily ordered zero-fat yogurt and muesli. When it arrived, she unscrewed a small bottle of protein powder mixed with chia seeds and cinnamon, and added it to the muesli. The cinnamon, as I'd heard often enough to be able to recite it in my sleep, inhibited the clumping of a protein called tau in the human brain, thus helping to ward off dementia. What signs of dementia had alarmed a thirty-two-year-old woman who spoke five languages, including Gujarati, and who could calculate the value of a diamond parcel at a glance, I had never learned.

I took out my phone and scrolled through the research on Jimmy Angel's daughter, Mitzi. There was always too much information. The NSA's supercomputers operate in teraflops. One teraflop is a million million floating-point operations per second. You enter the search terms, there's a big sucking sound, and every grade she ever got in school comes pouring out. Every visit to the orthodontist. The names of her mother's cocker spaniels and of the Irish wolfhound (Finbar) Mitzi had rescued from the local pound and who'd slept in her bed every night until a snowy winter's day when he'd fought and lost his last skirmish with the City of Boulder number 14 bus.

The report ran more than a hundred pages. In a rare act of mercy, someone in research had put it through a filter that selected the most relevant data and placed it in a separate table. That was where I learned that she'd just finished her geology degree at the Colorado School of Mines in Golden and was a director of Jimmy's company. She had a boyfriend named Pete Parson, a Dogrib Indian and bush pilot.

I studied the photograph of a tall girl with a crooked nose and a gaze that could penetrate steel plate. The phone pinged to announce a text. I closed the document, changed to the secure setting, entered my password, and read the message.

"We have to be at the floatplane dock in an hour," I told Lily.

"You should change that password," she said. "It wouldn't take a genius to guess it's your daughter's birthday."

"It's supposed to be something you won't forget."

"You remember the date, Alex, but you're never ready for the actual event. Unless Pierrette reminds you, I have to."

Pierrette was my ex. She and Lily had worked out some elaborate truce. I'd liked it better when they were enemies.

"Is this flight a search for Jimmy Angel?" Lily said as we made our way to the elevator.

I finished scrolling through the details. "We're going to check the known places Jimmy was exploring. You're sure you want to come? I thought you were going to use the trip to build up contacts here."

"I want to see where the diamonds come from. But what do you mean by "known places"? I thought part of the problem was that people didn't know where he'd been looking."

"His daughter knows."

"Mitzi Angel is in Yellowknife?"

"She's been here three days. This will be her second flight to look for him."

Lily screwed the cap back on her little bottle of powder and shoved it in her pocket. "Why would she take us with her?"

"She's an American citizen and a director of a US-listed public company. I work for the Treasury. She doesn't really have a choice."

I didn't ask how she knew Mitzi's name, but I sure wondered.

I changed into beat-up camo pants and a long-sleeved tee and laced on my old hiking boots. We were supposed to be ready to stay out a few days.

Lily's main concession to a trip into the wilderness was to change from her white Ashland jeans to the equally expensive black. She slipped on a slightly older pair of the Gianvito Rossi suede ankle boots she favored. She wore a soft red leather jacket, perfectly tailored to conceal her little Glock Slimline. It was small gun anyway, but Lily made sure it packed a punch by loading it with Fiocchi Extrema, a no-kidding-around, nickel-jacketed hollow-point she liked. She had emptied the Akris shoulder bag and had just re-packed everything into a black-leather Prada zip-top when someone knocked. She seemed to expect it. She opened the door to a small round man in dirty jeans and motorcycle boots. He wore a cheerful expression that went well with his clerical collar.

"This is all I could find on short notice," he said, handing Lily a long, narrow parcel.

"Thank you, Father," Lily said. She handed him an envelope. "Please say a mass for your own intentions."

He sketched a cross in the air with two fingers before he left.

"Jesus, Lily. You made a gun buy before breakfast?"

"Someone tried to kill you."

Lily had friends wherever there were diamonds. She also practiced a form of Catholicism that involved a practical arrangement with the deity. She gave generous donations, and in return she expected God to look the other way when she did what a girl sometimes had to do.

That priest had more than a seminary in his background. The package contained a sawed-off Ithaca Featherlight twelve-gauge. Police called that weapon a riot gun. Lily worked the pump a few times to get the feel of the action, checked the three boxes of shells that came with it, and slipped everything into the Prada zip-top. It fit perfectly.

We went downstairs and out to the parking lot. She fished out a set of keys, pointed her arm, and pressed the unlock button. A black Ford F350 King Ranch gave a squeak and flashed its lights. In Lily's view, brand awareness was a form of prayer. God put things on the earth for his creatures' use. Prada, Ithaca Featherlight, F350. You gave thanks and climbed aboard.

At the floatplane dock, we parked in a gravel lot. We hauled our bags out of the back and made our way past a small operations building. Exhausted flight crews clustered around a fire map posted on the outside wall. A yellow water bomber ran up its engines as the crew cast off the mooring lines. The big plane pulled away and plowed out to the main channel. Forest fires had been burning all summer, from Siberia to Alaska and into Canada's northern territories. The closest fire was two hundred miles away, but when the wind was from the west, as it was this morning, you could catch the smell of smoke in the air, and the faint scrim of haze had turned the sun red.

Mitzi Angel stood at the end of the dock in front of a Twin Otter. She wore a faded denim jacket with the sleeves rolled up to her elbows and a pair of heavy work gloves. She was lobbing bulky pieces of luggage through the open cargo door as easily as if they were full of ping-pong balls. She had long, sunburnt legs in baggy cargo shorts. A tassel of chestnut hair, caught into a scrunchy, sprouted from the top of her head.

A man stood in front of her, bouncing on his toes and shaking a wad of papers.

"I'm warning you, Mitzi. If this airplane takes off, I'll have it impounded when you get back. You could be charged with theft and criminal trespass."

She slammed a bag down on the dock and swung to face him, planting her hands on her hips. "Jesus Christ, Larry—trespass? You don't even know where I'm going. How can you say I'll be trespassing when you don't know where I'll be? Goddamn it. I thought you were our lawyer. I thought you were supposed to help me."

"I'm the company's lawyer. As an officer of the company, you should heed my advice."

"*Heed?* Who even says that?" She grabbed another bag and flung it into the Otter. "Pete," she called through the hatch, "will you for God's sake get going!" A moment later the right engine coughed into life.

"You have no right to visit any place where Jimmy was exploring," the man called Larry squawked. His face was white, and a vein throbbed in his forehead.

The left engine caught next and roared to life. It made even more noise than the first because the cowling was open. A yellow ladder stood on the dock beside it. Another bag went sailing into the plane. A young man in greasy overalls appeared in the cargo door and just managed to dodge the hurtling sack. Thick black hair, stocky build, dark features. Just like the picture of him scanned into the briefing note. Pete Parson, the pilot, Mitzi's boyfriend.

He hopped onto the dock, ducked under the wing, and scrambled up to examine the port engine. He reached inside with a wrench, made an adjustment, then closed the cowling and fastened it shut.

"I'm warning you one last time," the man with the papers shouted over the engines. "Control of the company has passed into new hands. Any knowledge you may have about diamond properties belongs to them."

"Mitzi Angel?" I said, stepping close so she could hear me.

"If you're the Treasury guy, get in!" she yelled over the engine noise, snatching my bag and launching it through the door. She noticed Lily. "You have got to be kidding me. You're bringing, like, a *date*? Honey," she said to Lily, studying her clothes, "this is the north country. We're not going on a fashion shoot."

"Honey," said Lily, returning the inspection, "that much I could have guessed." She let Mitzi see how much Arctic air a pair of gray eyes could hold, then rifled her Prada through the door and followed it in.

Mitzi tossed off the lines and tumbled through the door and latched it shut. We taxied away from the dock. Through the window I could see the man brandishing his papers again, this time at a white RCMP vehicle with its roof lights flashing, just pulling up at the foot of the dock. The same constable from last night leapt out and ran along the pier, waving his arms. I saw Luc climb out of the SUV. He knew we weren't stopping. He watched with a wolfish grin as we taxied out to the channel.

"Mitz," Pete yelled from the cockpit. "There's another water bomber coming in. He's on final five minutes out. I'll have to take off as soon as we're in the channel or they'll hold me until he lands."

"Help me tighten down the load," Mitzi said. "Use that ratchet on the bulkhead."

A heavy wire net with straps at the corners lay across a pile of timber posts. Each post tapered to a lethally sharp end. As the deck trembled, the posts shivered against each other. If one came loose, it would shoot down the hold like a massive spear. As we taxied through the chop I ratcheted one side tight and Mitzi did the same.

The plane lurched hard as it dug through a wake in the channel. One of the posts ground its way loose from the stack and, still inside the net, slammed to the metal deck.

"Tighter!" Mitzi called. I grabbed the lever in both hands and ratcheted the strap another click. The Otter pivoted into the wind.

"Mitz?" Pete shouted.

"Go!" she yelled.

He reached up and grasped the throttle levers above his head, pushing them steadily forward. The Otter shook as the engines roared and the pontoons smacked through the waves.

The back end sank as the airplane bulldozed up the channel, slowly gaining speed. Two more posts slipped off the top of the pile and boomed to the metal deck. The strong net held, keeping the posts from shooting free. The powerful engines pulled the Otter up. It gained speed swiftly as it planed across the waves. The cargo deck leveled.

Mitzi threw herself into a seat beside Lily and gestured toward the cockpit.

"Quick. Sit up with Pete. You're the tourist."

I scrambled forward and just made it into the right-hand seat when the deck tilted, and the plane climbed steeply from the bay.

6

The city slipped away beneath us as we climbed. Off to the right in the direction of the airport, I saw an F-18 dart up into the sky. It flashed in the sun, then peeled away and vanished. The dark trail from its afterburners hung in the sky until it, too, was gone.

A thick hand reached in front of me and pointed to the headset hanging from the panel in front of me. I unhooked it and clicked the mike switch to show I was plugged in.

"Pete Parson," he said and stuck out a large, square hand. When I introduced myself, he nodded wordlessly.

The cinnamon disk of the sun flooded the land with a powdery light. We were flying up the long inlet that led from Yellowknife to the open lake. An archipelago of rocky islands clung to the eastern shore. A cluster of houses perched on a headland at the mouth of Yellowknife Bay. Beyond, the soft pink sea of Great Slave Lake stretched to the horizon.

"This is where I check for a tail," he said.

"Why would anyone be tailing you?"

A click sounded as Mitzi cut in. "Because the bastards tailed us last time we went out," she said. "They must be trying to find where Dad was exploring. They're Chinese. I think he did some kind of deal with them. Isn't that why you're here?"

"What kind of deal?"

"How would I know?" she said angrily. "You think Jimmy would tell me? No. I have to find out from that asshole Larry."

We flew out over the lake for a minute. Then the cockpit tilted as Pete made a long, slow turn to the left until we were heading back the way we'd come.

"Ten o'clock," he said.

I squinted at the sky ahead and to the left. It seemed empty.

"There's some spare sunglasses in that pocket on the side of your seat," he said. "Try to look into the distance. Let your eyes relax."

I saw it then. A tiny dot in the expanse of sky.

"Any idea who they are?"

His aviator glasses flashed as he glanced at me. "I think your guess might be better than mine." His tone wasn't hostile, but it wasn't friendly either.

"What makes you think that?"

"I'll tell you what makes me think that," he said. "Jimmy disappears. Then these guys show up." He jabbed a finger at the dot, growing quickly in size as our combined speeds collapsed the distance between us. "Then you arrive, and Mitzi gets a message from the US government to take you with us." He made a slight course correction to take us wide of the onrushing aircraft. "That's what makes me think you might know who they are."

He adjusted course again as the fast-growing shape hardened into a large single-engine plane hurtling toward us. Then the other pilot corrected too, and the gleaming black plane flashed by with a roar at a distance of about two hundred yards. I caught a glimpse of the pilot staring blankly at us, and could just make out another face peering through a window.

"I didn't see that plane at the dock," I said.

"They're not flying out of Yellowknife. They have a camp on the North Arm, where the Stagg River enters Great Slave Lake. There's islands there. Good place to moor a plane. Friend of mine found the camp. He was fishing up the river and heard them shooting. They'd set up some targets."

"Did he get close enough to see them?"

"He's a bird guy. Has a four-hundred-millimeter lens. He could see, all right." He reached in front of me and tweaked a few settings.

"Did he see the rifles?"

"He did. He doesn't hunt, but he's a Dogrib. He knows what a hunting rifle looks like. They weren't hunting rifles."

"So if they're not in Yellowknife, they have a spotter in the city who lets them know when you're leaving."

"Must have. I couldn't shake them last time. There's some hills where I thought I could peel them off, but they stayed high and stuck to me like flypaper."

"Could they have followed Jimmy?"

"No. He'd left before they arrived."

The tree cover thinned as we flew north. The film of haze from the distant fire melted into a clear blue sky. The last road wound through some lakes and stopped. The forest gave way to a cover of scrub and stunted spruce. And after that, the vast, lake-speckled sheet of rock that stretched to the Arctic Ocean.

The sun was higher now. It poured an amber light onto the granite surfaces below. In the Barrens, the basement rock of North America tilts up into the light of day, polished smooth by the glaciers that slid across it ten thousand years ago.

We made another slow turn to the left to check the tail. The black plane was still there.

"If you couldn't lose them last time," I said, "why would you have better luck today?"

Pete busied himself with the instruments, making minute adjustments.

"That smudge on the horizon," he said at last. "That's cloud. There's a thick layer sitting over most of the Barrens. It should last for the next few hours before it breaks up. I'm going to lose the tail in there."

The dense layer of cloud took shape as we flew toward it. Gray wisps were already sliding beneath the plane, like veils pulled across the land. As we flew straight at it, the cloud transformed into towering white cliffs that loomed above us, cutting off the sun. And then we were in.

The plane shuddered as it passed into the cover. The cloud wrapped us tight. Water droplets streaked the windshield. In the suddenly dim cockpit the dials on the instrument panel glowed orange and green. The drone of the engines seemed muted.

"I'm going to stay on this course for another minute," Pete said. "Then I'll make a sharp turn to the left and begin a descent. You guys all squared away back there?"

Mitzi clicked her mike in acknowledgment.

Pete unfolded a chart and clipped it to the yoke. It showed a large lake. The scale revealed it to be about fifty miles long—a ragged shape with bays and inlets and a bulge in the middle maybe twenty miles across. Between the inlets ran penciled lines with figures neatly inscribed along them.

"Turning now and starting down."

The plane tilted sharply. We nosed into a steep descent. The needle on the altimeter began a rapid counterclockwise sweep around the dial as it counted off the altitude.

"OK. Turning in five," Pete said. "I'm flying blind, so I'll keep my eye on the attitude indicator." He tapped the dial that showed the artificial horizon, with the silhouette of a plane with wings level. "It will help if you keep an eye on the altimeter. Call out every five hundred feet."

He made another hard turn, again to the left. The silhouette tilted to forty-five degrees. The plane shuddered as we went around. I watched the compass needle swing. We came out of the turn at a heading south southwest. The two turns had taken us around 180 degrees.

The Otter bounced hard. The altimeter needle spun.

"Two thousand feet," I said.

"We're cutting across a ridge," he said. "This time of year, the rock is still warmer than the water, so there's thermals and downdrafts where they meet. Expect a thump when we go over."

"Fifteen hundred," I said. "How low before we can see where we are?"

"You mean, where's the ceiling? That's the million-dollar question. It's not like flying down south, where there's data wherever you are. Here, there are only a few monitoring stations, mostly at the diamond mines. Out here"—he reached up and tweaked a dial—"you'd better know the terrain."

"And you're betting the plane behind us can't follow you."

"I disabled the transponder and changed course twice once we were in cover. He's blind to my position."

"Can't he track you on radar?"

"Small planes don't have that kind of radar."

"One thousand."

The plane jumped. I heard Mitzi suck in her breath.

"That was at the shoreline. Now we're back over Lac de Gras. It's fifty miles long. I'll come up into the wind, and even if this cloud is lying right on the lake, we're good. Give me the altitude in hundreds now."

The altitude peeled off. At five hundred feet he pulled gently back on the yoke, his right hand raised above his head to grip the throttle levers.

"Four hundred," I said.

The engines changed pitch as he eased the power back and pulled up the nose.

At two hundred feet we broke through the cloud. The dull gray surface of the lake leapt into view. An enormous sheet of waves and breaking crests streamed toward us. The ceiling seemed to press us down onto the tossing water. A gust banged against the plane, and the left wing dipped. Pete jammed the throttles forward and stamped on the rudder pedal. The plane leveled out as bursts of spray licked at the pontoons.

"What are we at?" said Mitzi.

"Two hundred feet," Pete said. "We're about forty miles east of Clip Bay. Should be on the beach in twenty minutes."

And then the Caravan dropped out of the cloud.

A hundred yards to our right.

A gleaming black airplane hurtling across the water.

Rifleman kneeling in the open cargo door.

7

Turn to the left!" I yelled, tearing off my headset.

"What?" Pete said, and then he looked across me and saw the plane, just as the first round struck the fuselage: *tap*. A second later four quick rounds—*tap tap tap tap*. Lily screamed in pain. I flung off the seat belt and threw myself out of the cockpit.

The four bright holes with daylight shining through were grouped tightly together. A marksman. But he should have led by a foot. Then he would have killed me with a head shot instead of gouging a crease across Lily's cheek.

She sat staring at the blood-spattered seat, blinking blood out of her eyes.

"Flesh wound!" I yelled at her over the engine noise. "It's clean!" I reached for the white first aid kit on the bulkhead. We were turning away from the Caravan, but not fast enough. *Tap tap tap tap tap*. The cockpit window where I'd been sitting exploded. Shards of Plexiglas sprayed the cockpit.

"Pete, crank it!" I yelled. This time the Otter stood on its wingtip as he carved a tight turn away from the attacking plane. I flailed for a

43

handhold and slammed into Mitzi's seat, sprawling on top of her. We tumbled into a heap against the windows. The first aid kit went cartwheeling through the air, spewing its contents through the hold.

"Climbing!" Pete shouted. The deck tilted steeply again. The engines screamed at full power. Shaking and rattling, the Otter clawed its way up from the lake. The posts shifted dangerously.

Lily was staring at me across the cabin, still dazed by the violence. Blood smeared her chin and neck.

"Tear off your shirt! Hold it against your face!"

Then the cabin dimmed. We were back in the cloud.

The plane leveled. Mitzi looked shaken. Shards of Plexi glittered in her hair, and a trickle of blood crawled down her forehead.

"Mitzi," I said. "You OK to check the straps? I think they loosened."

"Shit," she said, looking stunned. But she shook her head and pulled herself together. She stumbled to the ratchet and tightened the strap.

I scrambled to the back and found my bag. I put the SIG to one side and took out the medic's kit. I ripped open a pressure bandage. Lily was holding a piece of torn shirt to her cheek. I took her hand away and sprayed the wound with antiseptic and pressed the bandage over the gash. "Hold it there." I wound a strip of surgical tape around her head a couple of times to hold the dressing in place. Her skin looked chalky, but she wasn't shaking.

"Are you OK?" said Mitzi, sitting in the seat beside Lily and putting her hand on Lily's knee. Lily plucked at the bloody strip of cloth she'd torn from her shirt.

"Alexander McQueen," she said. "Seven hundred dollars. That was the sale price."

The two women stared at each other, their lips pressed very tight. Mitzi raised a knuckle and wiped a speck of blood from Lily's cheek. "Men," she said.

Wind was howling through the smashed window as I struggled into the right-hand seat and clamped on the headset. Pete's face was speckled with blood from the storm of shattered Plexi. He turned to me, his face dark with anger.

"Who are these guys?"

"I don't know. The shooter has a sniper gun. Where can we go?"

He twisted the radio dial to a new frequency.

"Calling Ekati strip. This is Twin Otter Charlie Hotel Bravo inbound with emergency. Request armed security and EMT. Repeat. Twin Otter Charlie Hotel Bravo inbound with emergency. Request security and medical."

"What's Ekati?"

"Diamond mine. Eighty miles on this heading." He ran his eye over the instruments. "Maybe half an hour." He looked at me. "I'd like to go straight in, but I'm thinking maybe not. These guys must have some kind of military-level radar. He came out right on my wingtip. If he did it once, he can do it again. I'm going to fly a zigzag course," he said, and made a hard turn to the left.

"Twin Otter Charlie Hotel . . ." came a faint voice, then a burst of radio noise and then silence. Pete punched a button on the panel.

"Ekati strip, come in Ekati." Nothing. "Radio's gone," he said. "Must have been hit." We flew on for another minute, then made another turn.

"If he comes up beside us again," I said, "what side do you think he'll be on?"

He thought for a second. "The left. He was on my right, and I turned left. Our planes are pretty close in speed. To stay on my right would cost him the time to fly a wider circle. He probably turned inside me. He's on the left, out there in the cloud."

"Is there a door on the right side of the Caravan?"

"Yes. The passenger door." He glanced at me. "You want to know if he can shoot from that side."

"Yes."

"Not as good as he could from the cargo door, but he can shoot from there."

"And our door's on the left. If I set up there, I'll be facing him if he comes up beside us."

I went back and dug out the SIG and the extra mags. I opened the cargo door. Wind shrieked into the cabin. I took up position behind the pile of staking posts.

"I've got a rifle," Mitzi shouted. She crept back to the luggage. Her topknot thrashed in the wind from the open cargo door. She pulled out a green canvas case and joined me behind the posts. The gun she took out was a Weatherby Mark V with a scope.

The posts would conceal us from the shooter and give us protection. I clipped the bipod together, fixed it to the barrel of the SIG, and positioned it just off-center to the door. We had two advantages: One, he wouldn't see us right away; and two, one of our weapons was a submachine gun. A sniper rifle was unbeatable for accuracy, but at that close range I'd take the fourteen rounds per second.

Then I heard the worst sound you can hear in an airplane.

An engine coughed, gasped back to life, then stopped. For maybe fifteen seconds we droned along on a single engine. Then that one cut out too.

Mitzi and I exchanged glances. She grabbed her headset. "Pete?"

"Mayday, mayday, mayday." I could just hear his steady voice above the rush of wind.

"Twin Otter Charlie Hotel Bravo. Mayday, mayday, mayday. Both engines out. Making forced landing. Lac de Gras." He read out the coordinates and heading. I wondered if anyone had heard.

Now there was no sound but the wind blowing through the cabin. We were losing altitude fast. I could hear the ignition system whine as Pete made another attempt to start the engines. Then the cabin brightened, and we slid through the bottom of the cloud into the clear air. A red scroll of hills rippled along the shore of the lake. The plane bounced hard as we went through turbulence. The wind had picked up. Gusts were tearing the cloud to shreds. Slashes of silver light pierced the cover. The low ceiling had been chewed into wisps. The Caravan dropped into view.

"Fuck," Mitzi said.

"Stay behind the posts," I said, and headed for the cockpit.

Pete was opening the starter switch again when I got in. The left engine coughed into life, and the plane surged as the propeller bit. The familiar, powerful vibrations ran through the frame like returning life. Then the engine sputtered again, caught for an instant, and cut out.

"Fuel contamination," he said.

The airplane jumped and shuddered.

"If the fuel was contaminated, how did we get this far?"

"An Otter has three tanks. The first one was fine. The problem came up when I switched to the second tank. I just tried the third tank. It's contaminated too."

He kept his eyes fixed on the array of dials while he made minute adjustments to the trim.

"How far can we get?"

"It's not a great glider. With this turbulence, even worse."

As if to drive the point home, the Otter tilted and slipped sideways, losing a hundred feet.

I checked on the Caravan. It flew through a cone of light, its black fuselage gleaming. The windows blazed like mirrors in the sun.

"Can we get down and beach?"

"There's no real beach on this lake. It would be a crash."

"OK. Just to be clear. There's a professional kill team in that plane. If we land out in the lake, they will land far enough away so we can't threaten them. Then they'll just take their time and shoot us to pieces."

I don't know what Pete's parents taught him as a kid, but they should bottle it. Bad news had been arriving fast. Pursuers he thought he'd shaken off dropped from the sky right on his wing. A killer opened fire at point-blank range. He had two wounded passengers. And now he was going to crash his plane. His expression never changed.

We made a turn to parallel the shore. It streamed by a couple of hundred yards to the right. At this point, bare rock fell steeply to the water. Waves crashed against the slope, erupting into sheets of spray.

"I need you to keep an eye on the altimeter again," he said. "There's a little inlet about a mile ahead. I might get in on a sharp turn. Mitz?"

"We're good," she said. I glanced back. She'd dragged some baggage up and wedged it around Lily and squeezed in beside her.

We were at six hundred feet. The air was rougher near the shore. Suddenly the plane tipped and skidded toward the rock slope.

"Four hundred feet."

We eased away from the cliff face. I glanced ahead and saw what I guessed was the inlet—a jagged promontory with water boiling at its base and a gap beyond.

"Three hundred."

The plane shook violently.

"Two fifty."

"Now!" Pete shouted.

I could feel the plane shudder as it banked hard and pointed its wingtip at the rushing water.

We came around the corner of the cliff. The control cables groaned, the airframe rattled, and the wind slapped sideways at the plane. A scarlet hillside hurtled toward us; at its foot a rocky beach.

"Fifty feet."

"Brace!"

He pulled up the nose, and we splashed down onto the waves. Seconds later we struck the shore. The plane banged across the stony beach. The impact dislodged a staking post. It pierced the netting and shot into the cockpit, grazed Pete's seat, and smashed out through the windshield like a missile. The metal pontoons made a high-pitched screeching noise as they plowed into some boulders. The aircraft lurched violently sideways and stopped.

8

After the shriek of tortured metal, there was nothing but the murmur of wind in the sheltered bay, the ticking of the engine, and the sound of water breaking on the shore. The plane teetered, then settled with a crunch.

"Lily?"

"Alex, Mitzi's hurt!"

I snapped off my seat belt and clambered out of the tilting cockpit. Mitzi lay sprawled across two seats. Her skin was ashen and her body shaking. The staking post had ripped open the inside of her thigh. It was a dirty, deep wound, but it wasn't pulsing, so the artery wasn't cut.

I grabbed the medic's kit, mopped up the blood, and sprayed the wound with antiseptic. Another aerosol contained an agent called Quick Clot. I sprayed it onto the laceration. Then I ripped open a compression bandage and bound it tightly into place with pink elastic tape.

The operations woman in charge of our field equipment was an Afghan vet who'd suffered battlefield wounds. She was the one who always packed the medical kit. I found a package of Actiq and took one out. Actiq is basically a lollipop made of fentanyl. Mitzi put it in her mouth. In a few minutes, her breathing looked easier. I opened a little case full of morphine patches and applied one to her hip. It would kick in before the fentanyl wore off.

"Is she OK?" Pete said when I leaned back into the cockpit.

"For now," I said. "You all right?"

The staking post had ripped his jacket, but he didn't seem to be bleeding.

"I think my shoulder's dislocated," he said. He was leaning to peer through the shattered window, scanning the lake for a sign of the Caravan. The cloud was almost gone, torn into strips and flung away by the wind. Sunlight glinted on the gunmetal water.

"Better get out of the cockpit," I said. "If the Caravan lands out there, they can sit on the water and shoot us up inch by inch."

He shook his head. "Listen," he said.

The rise and fall of engine noise on the wind, faint at first. The sound grew, amplified by the rocky slopes around us. They were coming. We watched the headland. The sound clattered among the rocks, yet no sign of the Caravan.

"Wind's blowing off the land," Pete said. "They're not coming from the lake. They circled inland. They're coming up behind us."

"You have to get out of the cockpit, Pete."

Before I could help him move, they were on us. The roar was deafening. The black plane flashed overhead, flew out to the lake, made a hard turn, and disappeared around the headland.

"They're coming around again," I said. "This time they'll shoot."

"I know. I'm caught."

Not only was his right arm immobilized, but the mangled yoke had pinned his left arm to his body. The arm was bleeding. If he tried to yank it free, he'd tear it open. I squeezed in front of him and tried to pry the metal away. It wouldn't budge. I stopped to listen.

"They're moving upwind now," Pete said. "I'll tell you when he's back around and starting his run." He managed a grim smile. "Ears still work."

I sat down beside his seat, put my boot against the yoke, and shoved. Solid. No give at all.

"He's back over the land," Pete said, cocking his head. "He's making a big loop. Then he'll come downwind on us again."

I got up and grasped both sides of the cockpit entry. "Can you lean left?" I said. "Just get your head out of the way." I tightened my grip, leaned back, and delivered a dropkick. The heel of my boot hit the yoke cleanly, and I felt it give.

"They've turned onto their approach," Pete said, and now I could hear it too.

"Lily, get Mitzi over by the posts. It will give you some cover if they shoot from the side."

This time when I yanked the yoke, the metal groaned and it gave an inch. "On three," I said, counted down, and heaved with all my strength. The arm slipped free. Now the engine noise was snarling into a crescendo. I yanked Pete from the seat, and we sprawled together into the hold as the Caravan screamed overhead at fifty feet. I couldn't even hear the shots. The cockpit erupted in a hail of Plexi as the remaining windows blew out.

The sound of the plane dwindled rapidly downwind.

"OK?" I said to Lily.

"She's shaking."

Pete crawled over and took her hand. "She's freezing. Mitz?"

"You have to keep an eye out for the Caravan," I said to Pete. I went back to search the scattered medical supplies. The Epipens were in bright red packs. I found one and came back. Mitzi's face was gray and her breathing harsh. The shock had caught up with her.

Pete crouched in the doorway to the cockpit, watching the black plane. "They just splashed down outside the bay."

"How far?" I took out one of the needlelike Epipens. Each one contained a dose of epinephrine—basically, adrenaline. I pulled off the plastic cap.

"Not far, maybe half a mile."

I leaned over and jabbed Mitzi's thigh. "Keep her warm," I said to Lily, and to Pete, "You got a gun?"

"I'll use Mitzi's," he said, keeping his eyes on the Caravan.

I got the Weatherby, found a box of ammunition, loaded a round.

"They turned into the wind," Pete called. "I just saw something flash in the cargo door."

That would be the shooter scoping us. He wouldn't see me. With the sun where it was, our cargo door was in shadow. I got behind the staking posts and took a peek. I saw him look out again, then disappear. After about five seconds, he looked out again. Testing to see if he drew fire. I thought about the range.

The Weatherby fired a 6.5mm bullet at a pretty high muzzle velocity. Nice flat trajectory. The bullet wouldn't drop more than eighteen inches in a thousand yards. The SIG would be useless at that range. Also, it would help later if the attackers didn't know there was a submachine gun on the plane.

I had no idea what the wind speed was or how the scope was sighted. The guy took another look through the door. I squeezed off two shots and dropped behind the posts.

He replied with a fusillade. The bullets chunked into the staking posts. Splinters flew through the cabin.

Then silence. He was watching to see where the next shot came from, if there was one.

"Do you think your last transmission got through?" I said to Pete. "Will the mine know where we are?"

"If they picked it up, they'll know from the coordinates I gave them. But it's not like a regular airport. They wouldn't have us on radar."

"Would they send out security if they picked up the mayday?"

"I doubt it. They'd call the Mounties."

"How long would it take them to get here?"

"If they came right away, they could get here in an hour."

Or the transmission had failed and no one would come at all.

Our only door faced the water—and the sniper. I was wondering if there was some way we could force an exit on the landward side when the sound of the Caravan's engine powering up came faintly across the water.

"They're taxiing," Pete said. "Can you see if they're turning into the wind?"

I put the scope over the posts. "Doesn't look like it. They're moving out of sight, around a point."

Pete leaned into the cockpit and watched the Caravan. "He's not getting ready to take off," he said.

"Then I guess we know what that means."

Pete looked at me. "They're coming ashore."

9

Think like the killer.

The wrecked Otter lay sideways to the shore in a shallow bowl of hills. The only door faced the water across the rocky beach. The attack wouldn't come from that side; it was too exposed to fire from the cargo door. They didn't know what guns we had, and they wouldn't want a prolonged firefight. The kill team would have heard the mayday. They had to assume someone else might have too. Their best bet: get ashore and kill us fast.

The black Caravan had disappeared around the point on the right side of the bay. The killer would come from that side. I studied the terrain. Closest to shore, the flat hillside offered no protection to a sniper. I could shoot him through the smashed-out front windows before he had a chance to set up. But if he went further inland, the slope was steeper and littered with large boulders he could use for cover.

"I hear an outboard," Pete said, his features set in concentration. "They're coming ashore now."

"Can you shoot with your left arm?" I said. He nodded. I handed him the Weatherby and tucked some ammunition in his shirt pocket.

"Set up in the cockpit. Scope the hills. If you get a chance, shoot him. If he finds cover first and starts to shoot, get back here behind the posts."

I threw off the straps that held the netting in place. Lily grabbed the edge and dragged it off.

"We have to make a palisade," I said. "Once the sniper gets into position up there, he can just start putting bullets through the plane."

I didn't know how much pain she was in. We worked quickly, stacking the posts up to just below the windows. In ten minutes, we had a barricade four posts deep along the bulkhead. It ran from behind the cockpit to the tail. It wasn't Fort Knox, but it would have to do. Chinese snipers use a special ammo they call a "heavy round"—a streamlined bullet with a steel core for increased penetration. So they had that. We had two feet of Canadian maple.

We helped Mitzi shelter behind the barricade. The leg wound was giving her trouble, but she wasn't shaking now. Lily got the sawed-off Ithaca from her Prada bag and loaded three shells of Number 1 buckshot. Pete came back from the cockpit.

"There's two," he said. "They scoped us from that first slope. They were fast. I didn't have time to sight on them."

We didn't have long to wait. The first alert was a high-pitched sound from the hill. "Arctic fox," Pete said, "warning other foxes." After that, the alarm calls of birds marked the shooters' approach. Then no more birds. They'd found a place.

The attack opened with a boom and a blizzard of Plexi as the rifleman took out a window. He made his way along the airplane methodically from front to back. Five shots as he blew the windows one by one. Then he paused, re-sighted, and fired a rapid group of five—*bam-bam-bam-bam-bam*. The bullets tore through the seats and chewed up the cabin and filled the air with a storm of flying debris. Terror tactics. Spatter the poor bastards with Plexi, and then pick your way down the plane with tight, fast, five-round groups.

Lily racked the pump to load a shell into the breech.

The marksman had already fired ten rounds—two full clips if he was using the Chinese sniper gun. I counted up to five before the next five-round group struck the plane. This time he was aiming below the second window, where the barricade began. The bullets pierced the fuselage and struck the wall of staking posts. *Chunk-chunk-chunk-chunk-chunk*. Bits of wood flew into the air. I counted off three seconds while he put in another clip, then fired another group.

Disciplined shooter. That's what I was hoping for: a guy you could predict. I took out the MPX and laid it beside me on the deck. I had one mag clipped in and a spare. Sixty rounds. It wasn't an accurate gun, but it would give him something to think about. And then we all heard the same sound. A click. I stopped breathing.

The sound had come from outside the plane. Not metallic. Maybe two pebbles tapped together. I snapped my eyes to Pete. He held up a single finger—one man. Then he walked the fingers slowly.

That explained why the sniper hadn't started to fire the next group. He was waiting for someone to get into position. When that shooter was ready, the sniper would open up again, delivering cover for the second attacker to come around and shoot us through the cargo door.

I put my mouth to Lily's ear. "Guy behind the plane. He'll wait for the gunfire."

Lily nodded. Her blood-soaked bandage had slipped across one eye. She looked like a demon thirsting for human blood—her smeared face, shards of window glittering in her hair. She thumbed the safety off and stationed herself beside the door.

When it happened, it happened fast.

The sniper opened up with another five rounds. The bullets pierced the plane and tore into the posts. Bad guy number two leapt into view outside the cargo door. Lily had the Ithaca raised and pointed, and she fired point-blank. The shotgun boomed, flinging the attacker back like a rag.

The sniper on the hill fired a second five-round group, but he must have heard the shotgun and for a split second forgot his discipline. He raised his head above the boulder for a peek. I had the SIG already aimed through a shattered window, and I emptied the thirty-round clip. He disappeared behind the boulder.

I shoved in another clip and jumped from the plane. The man Lily had shot lay on his back doing a frog kick in the gravel. The Kevlar vest he wore was shredded.

I dashed out from behind the plane in a crouch and dove behind a boulder. Waited for the shot. Nothing. I waved a hand to one side to draw the sniper's fire. He didn't shoot. I threw myself around the other side and scrambled uphill to another boulder. Still no shot. I dashed up the hill from boulder to boulder. By the time I got to his position, I was pretty sure he was dead, but he wasn't. The right side of his face had been chewed off when I fired the clip. He sat there with a worried look, opening and closing his mouth, an overweight guy in a dark blue fleece and brand-new Timberland boots. He wasn't Asian. He had long greasy hair and a stringy moustache. The rifle with the bipod lay nearby. He pawed at the air with an outstretched arm, as if to reach for the weapon. I squatted down in front of him, unzipped the fleece.

His shirt was soaked in blood. I put a finger against his neck. The pulse was thready. I pulled his jacket open. He had a pistol in a canvas rig. I took it out and removed the clip, jacked a round out of the chamber, and stuck the pistol in my belt.

I went through his pockets. No ID, but he had a plastic wallet that contained what looked like some kind of mission document. A map showed the detail of an inlet with a cove at the end; the coordinates put it in the Barrens. Tucked into a separate compartment were some photographs. I was just about to pull them out when I heard the faint crackle of a radio. Very close. I grabbed the MPX and flattened myself against a boulder. Then I heard it again. It came from just behind the gunman. When it crackled a third time, I located it—a bloodied earpiece wedged against a rock. The Caravan was trying to contact the sniper.

I grabbed the sniper rifle. Checked the magazine. Full. I sighted on the plane. I had no time to correct for wind, so I just guessed and squeezed off two rounds at the cockpit. Either I hit the plane, or the pilot had binoculars trained on the hill and spotted the muzzle flash. The Caravan pivoted into the wind. The engines roared as it began its takeoff. I squeezed off the rest of the magazine, but that's not what stopped the plane. What stopped it were the two black specks that dropped into view five miles in front of its nose and rapidly increased in size.

The F-18s flashed over the Caravan, the scream of their passage splitting the air. The pilot of the Caravan got the point and abandoned the takeoff.

The shooter opened his mouth again, but nothing came out, and the light faded from his eyes.

Lily had pulled away the tattered remains of the Kevlar vest and taped a compression bandage on the second shooter's wound. His skin was gray and waxy. His face and arms were a mess. Lily had put a morphine patch on his wrist. His eyes were closed, and his breath was raspy and shallow. I opened his jacket and went through the bloody pockets. Nothing.

A Jet Ranger from the mine arrived first. I watched it approach across the lake. The F-18s must have radioed. The helicopter came straight in and landed on the shore. As soon as the skids touched the stony beach, an EMT crew jumped out.

"Two in shock," I yelled over the roar of the engine. "This one, and one inside."

They knew what they were doing. They had Mitzi and the wounded guy stabilized and loaded into the chopper in five minutes flat. One of the guys jumped back out, dashed under the rotors, and made a quick inspection of the cut on Lily's face, cleaned and re-bandaged it, turned to Pete, and with three quick moves reset his shoulder.

"So, we're full," he shouted at me as the rotors turned faster and the pitch of the engine rose. "Mounties should be here in forty-five minutes. Those two"—he jerked his thumb at the chopper—"will be medivacked out to Yellowknife on the evening jet."

When the chopper disappeared back across the lake, a deeply peaceful silence fell on the scene, made even more profound by the thin whistle of the fighters as they flew a pattern high above, keeping watch on the Caravan.

We sat there in the sunshine, passing around a thermos of sweet tea the medics left us. The Caravan wallowed in the chop. A falcon drifted into view above a ridge. A ground squirrel leapt into the air and came down running, squealing warnings as it vanished among the rocks. I knew the police plane was close when the F-18s stopped circling and flew away.

The white Beaver with the RCMP logo landed near the Caravan. Three officers crossed in a rubber dinghy. Five minutes later two men in handcuffs were helped out of the Caravan, and a single Mountie started the engine and took them back to the Beaver. Pete was watching with binoculars. He handed them to me.

"Mountie flight crew on the Caravan," he said as the black plane started up and turned into the wind. I watched it take off, then took a look at the Beaver. As soon as the prisoners were aboard, three officers boarded the dinghy and headed for shore. I took out my phone and snapped a picture of the map with the marked locations and the two pages of Chinese text. I tucked them back in, remembered the compartment with the photographs, and pulled them out.

There were five. Each one high-gloss, full-color, five-by-seven format. I wasn't surprised to see Jimmy Angel, Mitzi, and Pete Parson. The other two: honestly, not expecting those. Shot with a long lens but still crisp. Getting out of a plane.

Yesterday.

Me and Lily.

10

We landed at the floatplane dock in Yellowknife not long after midnight.

"Morning, sir," said the constable. "Inspector Savard would like a word with you and Ms. Ostrokhova, if that's convenient."

"It's not convenient," Lily said, stabbing him with a glare she'd been sharpening for hours. "Convenient would be you taking us back to our hotel and dropping us off and then going away so we can sleep and change our clothes and fix our lipstick." She jerked her head at me as she said the word *lipstick*, as if I could use some makeup too. I'd been picking bits of Plexiglas from my forehead, but I was camera-ready compared to Lily. The bandage on the side of her face had slipped again. My efforts to fix it in place had opened the cut and soaked the bandage. After that, she wouldn't let me touch it. Now she looked ready to come over the side with a cutlass in her teeth.

You couldn't blame her for being mad. We'd been sitting on rocks in the hot sun all day while Mounties in hooded white overalls and booties crept over the crime scene inch by inch, mapping every bullet hole and shell casing. A staff sergeant with bloodshot eyes and a tendency to sweat took our statements in an agonizingly slow exercise, as if he had been sentenced to a term of penmanship and would only be released when it looked just right. Then we discovered that the cooler with our food had caught a bullet, and blue freezer-pack goo had saturated everything. We'd long since finished the thermos of sweetened tea. The staff sergeant listened carefully to Lily's terse request, then sent someone back to the Beaver for "provisions." These turned out to be three bottles of water and a family-size bag of Cheetos.

"They're made with real cheese," I said, reading from the bag. Lily gave me the same look she was giving the constable now.

"The inspector was very clear," the constable said stolidly, opening the door.

"Oh, piss off, you big lunk," she growled, storming past him and climbing into the back seat.

One of the crime-scene techs handed the constable a large sealed envelope. We drove up the hill and through the empty town and parked in an underground garage. The constable let us out and card-swiped us into the elevator.

We went down a carpeted gray corridor. All the doors were shut. The constable let us into a room furnished with a single metal desk, chairs, and a battered filing cabinet. He placed the sealed package on the desk, then left.

Coffee rings stained the cracked linoleum desktop. Last year's calendar hung on the wall beside a faded picture of Queen Elizabeth. She gazed serenely into the room, as if she'd seen worse and wasn't going to be troubled by the musk ox head that peered from an open game bag on the floor. Its tongue hung out, flecked with blood.

The door clicked open and Luc came in, followed by the constable.

"Jesus, Cedric," he muttered when he caught sight of the gory head.

"Sorry, sir," the constable said. "The fish-and-game people use this room. I'll get rid of it."

"Leave it. Just get some coffee." He snapped the seal on the bulging envelope and spread the contents on the desk.

The constable glanced at Lily. "Medic, sir?"

Luc ignored the question. The constable left. The door closed behind him with a loud click. Luc began to arrange the material from the envelope. No satanic grin this time. He had the harried look of a man up all night trying to answer questions from his boss, and failing.

He studied some photographs for a moment, then pushed them aside and frowned at the report. "Tell me how you knew you were going to be attacked," he said, keeping his eyes on the statement. He hadn't looked at me since he came in. I waited. He pretended to study the material on his desk, but he'd had it for hours. It would have been phone-scanned and sent to him the moment the staff sergeant had finished writing it.

"Because that was a lot of fire power you brought along," he said. "You and your friend." He picked up a page of the crime-scene report. "Submachine gun. Sawed-off twelve-gauge." He tossed the page back on the desk. "Not the kind of equipment people usually take on a flight to look for a missing person. Maybe where you come from. Not up here."

"Is that right, Luc?" I said. "It seems to be exactly what you need up here. Up here is where somebody tried to take me out on a cab ride in from the airport. So I'm glad I had it, which you already knew because you didn't confiscate it at the airport when your guy went to bring in my bag and took five minutes."

The constable returned with a tray and dealt out Styrofoam cups. The coffee had an oily film and tasted like acid. Lily sat there like a coiled rattler, her eyes drilling holes in Luc.

"You're an intelligence officer of an allied government, Alex," Luc said. He shoved the papers aside and put his elbows on the desk. "So I cut you some slack in the matter of undeclared firearms and generally trying to feed me bullshit about why you're here." He pointed a finger at Lily while keeping his eyes on me. "Your sidekick doesn't represent anybody but herself. She's a foreign national currently residing in Canada. Nobody's going to bat for her if I drop her in a hole until she provides some plausible explanation for why Chinese hoods are ready to go to war in my country, and why you two are in the middle of it."

I could see where Luc might think that was a good move—grab the small woman in the suede pixie boots and give her a good shake and see if anything falls out. But it was the wrong way to go with Lily. She was already in a rage. Also, Lily didn't scare. While still in her teens, she'd been raped and tortured by Russian gangsters trying to force her to reveal information, and she hadn't broken.

She leapt to her feet and slammed her hands on the desk. The bandage on her face came loose and flopped against her neck. She tore it off and flung it away. It landed on the musk ox. Blood started dribbling down her cheek.

"This is how you treat a legal Canadian resident and taxpayer attacked in your jurisdiction by foreign assassins armed with sophisticated military weapons you allowed them to bring into your country through your own appalling negligence?"

A bright thread of blood was just completing its journey from her neck into the remnants of her shirt. The Glock was concealed by the leather jacket, but not as well as Lily thought.

Some people can't string two words together when they're mad. Me, for example. Lily was the opposite. And just as good in English as in Russian. Her mother had taught English at the polytechnic in Mirny, the Siberian diamond-mining city where Lily had grown up. Lily could recite Hamlet's soliloquy and "The Rime of the Ancient Mariner" before she was old enough to go to school.

"A helpless woman in a remote place, injured and abused—and you threaten her with jail?" She slammed her hands on the desk again. "Go ahead! I can hardly wait to appear in court."

Luc watched her coldly. "Who said anything about court? You won't go to court. The first time you'll see a judge will be when we put you on a flight to Russia and he reads you the expulsion order under the terms of the Official Secrets Act."

So at least one thing was clear. Compassion for our personal suffering was not on the agenda.

"Sit down, Lily," I said. "Let's hear what's on the man's mind."

11

Luc opened a drawer, took out a file, and placed it on his desk. It had a scarlet cover and a tamper-proof seal—a strip of clear tape that fogs as soon as it's broken. Luc slid a thumbnail through it, opened the folder, and studied it for a moment.

"Let's put some basic facts on the table that we can all agree on," he said.

Luc had the rank of inspector in the RCMP. In my department, we had a working assumption that Luc's Mountie status was a cover. We thought he worked for CSIS.

Until 1984, the RCMP was Canada's spy agency as well as its national police force. A scandal involving illegal surveillance embarrassed the government. They created a separate agency—the Canadian Security Intelligence Service—to take over espionage. Illegal surveillance didn't stop, but the politicians in Ottawa hoped that CSIS would be better at it. Among the new agency's responsibilities was spying on foreign governments, with us at the top of the list. So if Luc was going to share information, there was something he wanted in exchange.

The Canadians had tracked Pete's Otter with one of the geostationary satellites on constant watch above their Arctic territories. They'd seen the Caravan take off from its camp on the North Arm of Great Slave Lake and tail us into the Barrens. Luc assumed their aim was to discover where Jimmy had been exploring, since that was where Mitzi would start. He realized something more dangerous was happening when they saw the Caravan approach so close to the Otter at a point where they knew both planes were in thick cloud.

"I didn't think satellites could see through that," I said.

"Microwave radar," he said.

"And that's when you scrambled the F-18s, when you saw the Caravan come up beside us."

"The mine picked up the first part of your mayday call. That's when we sent them off."

He shuffled through the crime-scene report and withdrew four black-and-white glossies found in the Caravan. They were the same pictures I'd found on the sniper: Pete, Mitzi, Lily, and me.

"We have the air crew on ice downstairs," he said. "They say they were forced to fly the mission." He waved a hand dismissively. "The thing is, there was never any chance you'd lose them in the cloud. They had advanced radar."

"Why didn't they just wait for us to crash? They had to be behind the contaminated fuel."

"That was the plan. With all the lakes, they knew the Otter would find water to land on. When it did, they would land too, and pick off Pete and Mitzi."

"But they changed that plan."

Luc shuffled the papers together and shoved them in the file. "Their spotter in Yellowknife saw you board. The kill team had your picture. Same as the two who tried to scrub you on the way in from the airport.

So they knew there was a pro on the Otter. Certainly armed. New plan: Don't wait for the contaminated fuel. Kill before you can land and mount a defense."

It was two A.M. Lily fumbled for my hand and gave it a weak squeeze. She looked drawn. Her tirade had worn her out. Luc caught the exchange. His harsh expression didn't waver.

"We're both trying to understand the same thing here," he said. "Motive. Let me put it plainly. What is so important that people like the twins buy into Jimmy Angel's company and then kill him? Because that's what we're both thinking."

"Is that what we're thinking, Luc?" I hadn't told him anything about Fan and Mei, and if he was making a guess, I wanted to know why.

"Don't fuck with me, Alex," he said, his lips tight with anger. "We know about the twins. A lawyer from Vancouver is filing writs for control of Jimmy Angel's company. He works for Fan. If they want to muscle their way in here, there's not much I can do to stop them." He stared hard at me. "The Chinese will retaliate if we don't release Mei, and they can hit us hard."

The Canadians knew China. They'd been selling wheat and timber and machinery to the Chinese for twenty years by the time Kissinger and Nixon bragged about opening China to the West.

Luc stood up and paced to the window and stared out at the sleeping city. "Xi Mei," he said. "Always a step behind her brother."

I was only really starting to smell the musk ox now, so it hadn't been there long. My guess, they'd put it there on purpose. Something for us to think about. This could be you.

"We think she's the one pulling the strings," Luc went on. "Fan is enraged about his sister's house arrest. Maybe it's fear, he's panicky. We don't know. What we do know is that the Chinese leaders the twins made into billionaires are taking a wrecking ball to some of our biggest trade deals. My job—and I'm reminded of it on an hourly basis by my superiors—is to not make things worse."

Luc went back to the desk and sat down, picked up the file and opened it. He glanced through a couple of pages, then put the folder down again. He didn't need to look at anything. He knew the contents cold.

"Here's what we're going to do. You and me are going to go down to Vancouver and have a sit-down with Mei." He jerked his thumb at Lily. "And she's coming." His eyes darted back and forth between us. "We're going to get on a plane and go down there and see if we can find out what they want. And if we can, we're going to give it to them."

He yanked open a drawer and glared inside, then slammed it shut. He was pretty mad. The only one in the room who was completely calm was Queen Elizabeth, but she was trained to it.

"And you're OK with that?" I said. "They commit murder and assault in your territory, so the response is to give them what they want?"

"How does it work in Washington, Alex? They make sure you're OK with it before they tell you what to do?"

"Why Lily?"

"Because she's the one Mei asked for."

12

The British Columbia supreme court was a modernist complex of concrete and glass on a plaza in the middle of Vancouver. The cruiser that led us in from the airport stopped at the entrance to the parking garage. We swept by and went down the ramp and drove to an elevator. A Mountie in a dark suit, wearing an earpiece, was waiting for us. He muttered something into the mike in his lapel, punched a code into the keypad, and the doors opened. He stepped in after us and hit the button for the second floor.

"Is she here?" said Luc.

"On her way, sir." He checked his watch. "Her hearing resumes in an hour."

When the door opened, he led us down a red-carpeted corridor, opened a door, and we entered a spacious conference room. It had a long, teak table with red leather chairs. A glass wall looked out on a strip of park. The benches were packed with a lunchtime crowd, chopsticks flashing in the sun as they devoured the contents of their bento boxes.

A man in an apron wheeled in a food cart, set up a coffee urn, and laid out a platter of croissants. Lily picked one up and tapped it experimentally on the table, where it left a heap of flakes. She poured a coffee, handed it to me, poured one for herself, and we sat down.

She was looking better. An RCMP medic had patched her up before we'd left the building. At the apartment, she'd taken a long hot shower. Her skin glowed pink when she came out. Her black hair clung to her head in coils. She roughed it dry with a thick white towel. The tips of her elvish ears poked out. The bandage had come loose in the shower. It hung from her cheek. I'd peeled it carefully away and put a fresh one in place.

"I'd almost forgotten I'd met Mei," she said.

"Oh, for Christ's sake, Lily."

She grabbed my arm and looked intently at me. "The twins were just starting out. They needed a quick way to make money. China was becoming a huge retail market for diamonds. I was handling all that rough from Mirny. It was natural we'd meet. I suppose she remembers me."

"That must be it."

Between Lily and me there was always calculation. How could it be otherwise? I'd forced her to make one that night at Brussels airport, when I turned her. I'd used her for my own ends. Now she'd do the same to me. So I picked the sliver of resentment from my heart and fixed her bandage.

My phone pinged with the message that Luc was waiting. "Finish the story another time," I said. "You can probably improve it." And we went downstairs.

If she was lying, the lie, like all really good ones, made sense. The twins could have created a profitable diamond business by taking advantage of the discount for stolen rough diamonds. Lily was handling millions of carats of top-grade Russian rough for the people who were stealing it.

But what about Luc? He hadn't asked Lily why Mei would ask for her. That suggested he already knew. If what Lily told me was true, that the twins had approached her about buying rough, that was exactly the kind of detail Luc could have learned. When the Chinese were looking for help to develop their own mineral assets, they turned to the Western country they'd been dating the longest—Canada. Canadian geologists and mining companies poured into China, hoping for a slice of the coming boom. It was a safe bet that some of those people weren't reporting only to head office.

The plainclothes Mountie on the door came in and spoke to Luc and went back out again. "Ten minutes," Luc said. He shot me a probing look. It was the same glance he'd given me when he'd dropped the bomb about Mei asking for Lily. He was wondering what I knew about Lily and Mei. I kept my face as blank as possible. In the circumstances, not hard to do.

Mei came rustling through the door in a burst of sapphire light. Her dress blazed, and her glasses flashed, and her heels clicked across the parquet floor. Her lips were curved in a slight smile. She seemed untroubled by either the security guards who trailed her or the court-ordered electronic monitor strapped to her ankle. She sat down and placed her large handbag on the table. Her eyes rested on Lily for a moment.

Her lawyer slid in beside her like an eel. His yellow eyes darted suspicious glances at us. "I am George Wu," he said in a frosty voice. "May I ask who is in charge of this irregular affair?" He looked around the table. "I have advised my client against this meeting. We really must wait for Mr. Xi Fan, her partner and closest adviser. He was in Ottawa, pleading his sister's case, and cut the meeting short the moment I informed him of your imminent arrival. We can all meet after today's hearing."

Mei watched him through her coke-bottle lenses while he spoke. Her lips were curved in the same half smile. She had a thick neck, narrow shoulders, and small, delicate ears. She had the posture of a drill sergeant—straight back and head erect. Her lustrous black hair was pulled back by the lapis lazuli clips. Her eyes looked like raisins behind the thick glass. She winked at Lily.

"I think your client's in charge, but I'm Inspector Savard," Luc said to Wu. "This is Ms. Liliana Ostrokhova, a private person whose attendance your client requested. The gentleman is my colleague from the US Treasury, Mr. Turner."

Wu looked bleakly at me. "I hope you are not contemplating another American government fishing expedition to fill in the blanks in your meritless extradition case against Ms. Xi," he said. "Perhaps it would be better if I just called the court clerk and put you on my witness list and deposed you under oath this afternoon."

A loud *meow* came from Mei's big purse. "Oh, dear," she said, leaning forward and unsnapping the catch and opening the bag. A tawny head with enormous ears, hazel eyes, and a snow-white chin popped out and blinked at us. *Meow*, it said again.

"Brutus," said Mei in a tone of mild reproach. She plucked him out of the purse and put him in her lap and stroked his head. "He's such a boy," she explained to Luc. "Very macho."

"We're here at your request," Luc said. He didn't look like a man who wanted to hear about a cat. In fact, he looked like hell. He had bags under his eyes and a two-day beard, and in his wrinkled suit he looked like what he was—a guy who'd been up for forty-eight hours, watching a disaster unspool before his eyes and knowing that his bosses would blame it on him. We all must have looked pathetic. Lily and I were tired, peppered with tiny cuts, and fighting to keep ourselves alert.

"I understand there's been some terrible calamity," Mei said smoothly. "I want to see if there's anything I can do. And maybe also," she said, glancing at me, "help people see that we're not monsters who need to be locked up, but businessmen who want to contribute."

Luc gave her a bleak look and pulled a folder from his briefcase.

"Whatever 'calamity' there may have been," Wu said to Mei, "it's nothing to do with us."

Mei tracked her lenses around to look at him directly. "Let's switch to listening mode for a moment, shall we, pumpkin?" she said in a hard voice.

Meow, said Brutus.

Wu reddened and sat back and folded his arms.

Luc opened the folder and took her quickly through the attack in the Barrens. He placed the events in the context of Jimmy Angel's disappearance and mentioned the flurry of legal activity to take control of Jimmy's company, Angel Minerals. I watched Mei closely as he did. A frown creased her forehead, and her lips tightened when Luc described the final assault. He closed the folder.

"You and your brother own the company that made the investment in Angel Minerals," Luc said. "Now you're trying to take control." He spread his hands. "Then the attack."

"Golly," Mei said. "That's horrible." She looked at Lily with real concern. "How terrifying."

Wu's phone pinged. "Ah," he said, picking it up and tapping the screen. "Fan's here. He's on his way in from the airport. He'll be here in twenty minutes. We must wait."

Mei stared at Wu's phone. For a moment she seemed stunned, as if a snake had suddenly slithered into view and coiled itself around Wu's hand. A strand of hair came loose and drifted in front of her face. She unfastened a clip and tucked the hair back into place and snapped the clip shut again. It made a sharp, clean sound, and it seemed to bring her back to the present. And here's what happened.

Mei looked pointedly at Lily. Lily met her eyes, then turned her head to glance at Luc. Luc shot a quick look at the plainclothes guy with the earpiece. It was like watching a pinball racket around inside its box, dropping into one hole and springing out of another. Earpiece stepped over to Wu and said, "Excuse me, sir. Her Honor has asked to see you."

Wu frowned and checked his watch. "In court?"

"In her chambers, sir."

Wu looked puzzled. "We'll have to go," he said to Mei.

"Did she ask for me?" Mei said to Earpiece.

"No, ma'am."

Wu stared around desperately. He couldn't ignore a summons from the judge. He scowled at Luc and me as he got to his feet. "Say nothing!" he told Mei.

The second he was out the door, Mei snatched up her bag and moved to the chair beside Lily. They began to mutter back and forth in what sounded like a mixture of Chinese and Russian in which I recognized only the words *diamond* and *Mitzi*.

"The judge thing," I said to Luc. "Bullshit, right?"

"Yes," he said.

"Do I get to find out what's going on?"

"You can always ask," he said tiredly. "You're the one who lives with her."

13

on't be such a bear," Lily said as she balanced a martini glass on the two-inch-wide railing. "I've already told you I knew her from when I was in Mirny. They were trying to fast-track into diamonds. I had a lot of product to sell. We met."

"But that was years ago. I've never heard you even mention her, and she's the most famous woman in Asia."

"Abused and railroaded by your government!"

"Don't try to change the subject. Suddenly we're all piled in a plane—you and me and Luc—rushing off to Vancouver. The second her lawyer gets tricked into leaving the room, you're into a secret huddle. What the hell is going on?"

"She needs advice from someone, Alex. Is it so strange she'd turn to me?"

I sure thought so. She handed me a beer and went inside. We'd checked out of the hotel and moved to an apartment in a building that rented furnished suites. The main room opened to a terrace that overlooked a little lake with rocky bluffs. Beyond the martini glass, a girl with blonde hair flashing in the setting sun paddled a kayak furiously up the lake.

Lily returned with a bottle of vodka straight from the freezer. She looked better. I'd taken her to the hospital when we got back from Vancouver. They'd tidied up her cheek. She'd gone to bed and slept for ten hours straight. As soon as she got up she phoned a spa and asked for someone to come over for a mani-pedi. "And hair," she'd added. The nails-and-hair guys made a big fuss over Lily's pointy ears—"perfect!"—and murmured their approval of the cosmetics she'd looted from the jet. So sure, she looked good. But she was roped together tight, and I wasn't fooled by the way she was trying to blow off her previous connection to Mei.

"Try to stay with me," she said, bombing a generous slug of vodka into the glass trembling on the railing. She plucked up a white linen napkin and drenched it in vermouth. Then she held it stretched taut above the martini glass and blew through it. Lily's life was governed by a set of certitudes. One was that God took care of people who expressed devotion to Him in the form of large cash donations to the Catholic Church; another, that blowing through a vermouth-soaked cloth deposited a layer of vermouth atoms onto a surface of super-chilled vodka, creating the perfect martini. She tossed the napkin aside, took a sip, and sat down beside me on the wicker sofa, where she crossed her rippling ballerina's legs.

"When I was still in Mirny," she said, "Fan and Mei were just starting out. The new Chinese middle class were crazy for diamonds. The Indian polishers were just opening their first factories in China. The twins thought they could muscle in. They persuaded the Chinese government to back them. By buying cheaper stolen goods directly from me, they thought they could beat the Indians on price and steal the Chinese market."

"And you cheated them."

Lily held out the glass to admire it. The vodka shimmered like liquid ice. "It's all ancient history. Now I'm in a position to help."

"Fan didn't seem to think it was ancient history. He called you a swindler."

We'd run into him in the hall when we were leaving and he was rushing in the door, a volcano of rage that erupted at his sister, at the shame-faced Wu, at us.

"He didn't have to hit the cat."

Fan had grabbed Mei's arm and shaken her and shouted into her face in Chinese. Her purse wasn't fully closed. The tiny animal had thrust out his head, flattened his ears, and hissed ferociously at Fan, who'd lashed out and struck him with the back of his hand.

Lily wasn't telling me much. She and Mei been ready for that meeting. Luc too, or it wouldn't have happened. I had no doubt the room had been wired to the max. I'd done the best I could with the mike I had inside my shirt. I'd sent the recording to Tommy but hadn't heard back yet.

"Here's the real question," I said. "What's in this for the twins? Just iDragon by itself is a $100 billion company. Even if the generals own most of it, the twins are very rich. Why this urgent interest in a diamond mine?"

Lily stared at her martini. Her face had a somber look. She took a sip and set the glass down carefully. "I made a fool of them. This is a chance for them to wipe that out. Those people are all about face."

"Thanks for that penetrating analysis of the Asian mind."

Maybe I sounded harsher than I meant to. She tried to smile, but it didn't work. Never mind the mani-pedi, she'd been roughed up. It was going to take more than good nails and a martini to make her a hundred percent again. But I had a problem. Someone was trying to kill me. Whoever it was had been trying to kill me since I'd set foot in Yellowknife. I didn't think the reason was going to turn out to be that China's generals wanted to help their boy feel better about being a chump.

"Come on, Lily. The bigger picture. What are the twins going to do with a diamond mine? They're going to use it as a wedge. They'll take out one competitor, and then the next, and in the end they'll control the whole Canadian Arctic diamond field."

She finished her martini and gave me a despairing look. I'd been raking her over the coals since we got back. Like an interrogator, asking the same questions over and over, ready to seize on any discrepancy.

"I can't go on, Alex," she said. "I know you're angry. I can't help that." She got up and seized my hand. "We have to get out of here."

We left the apartment and took the elevator down to the parking garage. Lily thumbed a button on the keys. The F350 beeped and flashed its lights, and the doors unlocked with a clunk. She sprang eagerly into the cab and waved a wand at the garage door. It rumbled open. We thundered out onto the street. She put the windows down, filling the cab with the rush of evening air.

She took a roundabout route that circled the lake and skirted the airport. We left the city behind and flew out along a narrow highway that wound through the forest. Lakes shivered through the trees. The sun was getting lower in the west, slashing the road with ragged shadows. The wind peeled Lily's skirt from her thighs. Her face relaxed as the massive truck devoured the road. A sign for a canoe launch appeared at the side of the road. Lily stabbed the brakes. The tires squealed and the truck slewed around, and we shot down the rough track in a storm of dirt. The rutted trail bent through the woods until it ended at the shore of a sparkling lake. She turned off the engine and gazed at the wrinkled surface twitching in the sun. The deep silence of the forest poured around us. It wrapped us in a soundlessness made more profound by the ticking of the engine as it cooled. She unbuckled her seat belt and let it snap away. She turned to me and yanked my T-shirt over my head, twisted out of her skirt, and flowed across the cab. She straddled me and pulled my face to her breasts.

Afterward she clung to me. She wound the fingers of one hand into my hair and with the other grasped my back. She gasped and began to shudder. I felt hot tears on my shoulder. She pressed her face into my neck to stifle her sobs, until a long, terrible cry wrenched itself from her body and she abandoned herself to fear and pain.

"I thought we would die out there in the plane," she sobbed, and after another tremor shook her, "Alex, I'm afraid."

We swam out into the icy lake. The coldness of the water calmed her. We sat on the rocks to dry. In the deep blue sky a single cloud caught fire, its top scalloped in orange flame. We inhaled the fragrant air.

"The forest smell reminds me of Siberia," she said. I thought she must be thinking of her childhood, until she said, "I met them at a dacha near Mirny."

It took me a moment to realize she was talking about the twins.

"Mei and Fan?"

"Yes." She laid her head against my chest. "I never did business at the dacha. It was a retreat. But when Mei made contact with me, they were already in the city."

"And you wanted to keep the contact secret."

"Until I knew how to proceed."

She meant until she figured out how to cheat the oligarchs out of a share.

"So you met them both."

"Yes, but only spoke to her. She could speak a little Russian, and I hadn't let them know I could speak English."

"To keep them at a disadvantage."

"Of course. It made Fan angry that only she and I were talking. He kept interrupting her for explanations. He was afraid of being cheated, even though they had an expert with them."

"He was afraid the expert would sell them out."

"Yes."

"And I guess he did."

"Of course. I gave him a cut."

"And the twins got a few hundred thousand carats of garbage."

She put her hand against my chest. "I wish we could be different with each other."

"You could always start by telling me the truth."

She pressed her lips against my chest and nestled her head again. "But then I would be the only one doing so."

"Maybe it would start a trend."

We dressed. She handed me the keys. I drove slowly out through the trees and onto the paved highway that led back to town. Lily opened her purse and took out a small bag of cosmetics and angled the rearview mirror. By the time we got back to Yellowknife, she didn't look like a woman who had cried. Or had anything to cry about. Lily often accused me of locking my emotions away with my past. I don't think she saw it in herself. She believed her tendency to erupt into the moment meant she was in touch with herself. But eruptions don't reveal the past. They bury it.

She applied the last touch of lipstick, smacked her lips at the mirror, and practiced shaping her mouth into a smile.

14

itzi waited for us on a bench at the end of a pier. She looked like a figure in a Hopper painting, alone and stark, separated from the rest of humankind by a force field of personal isolation. The marina was near the floatplane dock. As we walked out, a plane flashed past behind her with a roar and landed in the channel.

Her dark brown hair hung in a tangled mop. A shaved patch on her scalp was stained orange by surgical disinfectant. A neat row of black stitches closed the wound where a splinter had cut her head. Like us, she was peppered with tiny cuts. A bandage covered her most serious wound, the gash inside her thigh. She finished a can of root beer, crushed it in her hand, and tossed it in a garbage bin. She tried not to wince when she stood up.

"Hey, guys." She brushed the hair from her eyes. She looked even younger than she was. Lily grabbed her and gave her a fierce hug. Mitzi made an awkward move to disengage, and stumbled on the bad leg. "I know," she said. "Sorry. I mean, thanks." She turned away with a red face. Her shoulders heaved as she drew a deep breath. She rummaged around in her bin of disguises and managed to find a scrap of a grin. We got into her boat and motored out onto the dark water.

Mitzi lived on a houseboat in Yellowknife Bay. She went back and forth from the marina in a fiberglass inboard with a small wheelhouse and a freight deck that took up the back half of the boat. When we were underway she left the wheel for a moment and stepped from under the canopy. She swept the sky for incoming planes. Satisfied, she turned across the channel and increased power. A thin blue film of exhaust crawled behind us on the wake. Mitzi stood at the wheel, in the same cargo shorts and faded denim jacket with the sleeves rolled up. Her hair blew around in the breeze, the orange stripe of the scalp wound flaring into view. She gathered solitariness around her like a cloak.

As we crossed the bay, brightly painted houses appeared, their west-facing sides ignited by the sinking sun. The houses sat on platforms moored to rocky islands or anchored just offshore in the shelter of the land. A few were shacks, squatting on rafts and patched with sheets of corrugated tin. Most were in better shape—two- and even three-story houses surrounded by decks with planters full of flowers. Some had balconies on the upper floors. A fleet of watercraft bobbed against the platforms—aluminum fishing boats; wooden scows with huge outboards for ferrying building supplies and fuel; canoes and kayaks and sailboats rocking on the swell.

We pulled in beside a steel barge with a white clapboard house on top. A wooden landing stage was moored to the barge, and a flight of steps led up to a deck covered in Astroturf. Pete was scraping at the grill of a gas barbecue, an empty sling hanging from his neck. He clicked the starter button, and blue jets of gas sprang to life. He shoved his right arm back in the sling.

"Pete," Lily said. "You flew through an attack by trained assassins. Both your arms were injured. You managed to land on rocks without killing us." Her skirt was rippling in the breeze, and the tips of her ears were peeking from her dark curls. She unveiled the smile she'd been working on since we stepped aboard the boat. "*Plus*"—she tapped him on the chest—"you cook! Women have fantasies about men like you." She cocked her head at Mitzi. "Can I have him when you're done?"

"It seems kind of greedy," Mitzi said. "Haven't you got one already?"

"But he can't cook," Lily said sadly. "I'm not saying he isn't great, but just at the one thing."

Pete and I stared into space while the women finished batting practice. Finally the coals were ready, and the meat hissed onto the grill. The topic turned to why caribou backstrap was better than filet mignon and how the great herds that roamed the Arctic were vanishing.

"Except in Russia," Lily said. "One of the Siberian herds has more than half a million animals."

She put her knife and fork on the side of her plate and gazed across the water. "This reminds me of my home," she said. Her voice was somber now. "Mirny is on the same latitude as Yellowknife. If we traveled west in a straight line, we would come to my city." She smiled, but her face had taken on a tragic look. Lily hated Mirny. She had barely survived the torture she'd suffered there. But it wasn't really Mirny she was thinking of, or even Russia. She was thinking of the enchanted country of her childhood. The sun had set; the afterglow was fading from the sky. The little city glowed in the tea-colored light. "I've seen the sky turn just this color," Lily murmured.

No high spirits now. From anyone. The mood was sinking into the encroaching night. I could see the exhaustion taking over Mitzi's face. The EMT guys at the diamond mine had stabilized her and hooked up an IV saline drip so her blood pressure wouldn't crash. They'd medivacked her out to Yellowknife in a stupor. The ER docs at the hospital in town had put her under and spent three hours in the OR, untangling the hardened mess created by the blood-clotting spray and picking splinters and bits of cloth out of the wounds. Now the crooked smile had turned into a grimace, and her skin had a sheen of perspiration. She picked up some plates and headed for the house. I grabbed a few things and followed her in.

"This isn't going to stop," I said. "The people behind the attack—they're not done with you."

She rinsed the plates and put them on the counter, took a platter from me and rinsed that too. When she was done, she leaned against the counter and stared out the window.

"Where do we even start?" she said.

"We start with you telling me what Jimmy found."

15

We left the house and entered Jimmy Angel's diamond lab. Mitzi closed the heavy door behind us. It locked automatically, the bolt shooting home with a spring-driven *thunk*. The fluorescent bulbs flickered for a moment before flooding the room with a strong, harsh light. A bench with a microscope and diamond scales stood in a corner. Clear Ziploc bags with mineral samples sat on some cabinets. But the most striking feature of the room was on the walls—a fantastic composition of line and color that blazed around us.

Colored squares and lopsided rectangles swarmed over the surfaces. Bold black lines slashed through the strange design. The weird geometry of the shapes gave a mysterious order to the work. Only when my eyes adjusted did I see what was really there. A single map. The entire construction was a giant map of the Barrens.

It wrapped around three walls. The center panel showed the heart of the diamond field. The enormous swath included the middle part of Lac de Gras, with its huge north-reaching bays, and above them, the Ekati mine. Each diamond pipe was clearly marked, the mine buildings and the airstrip neatly drawn in. On the right side of the central map was the Diavik mine, depicted in the same detail. An *X* marked the location of the main pit, a massive structure protected by a coffer dam that allowed the mining of a pair of diamond pipes once covered by the lake. The panels on the walls to the left and right extended the mapped area to the west and east.

The scale of the map was stunning. A great diamond field, a thousand square miles, spread out in amazing detail—every wrinkle in a shoreline, every ridge and esker. And diamond pipes. At least a hundred. When I stepped closer, I saw that each pipe was described in immaculate hand-lettering. Which had diamonds and which had none. The specific minerals that had drawn explorers to each pipe were meticulously recorded: pyrope garnets, chrome diopsides, even microdiamonds—the tiny dots of pure diamond less than three one-hundredths of an inch in diameter, found in only the richest targets.

"The colored sections are claim blocks?"

Mitzi nodded. "They're color-coded by owner and date of exploration. Mostly the owners are the big mines."

I leaned in closer and examined some of the largest blocks. The exploration dates printed on them were long in the past. "I thought owners had to perform active work on a claim in order to keep the title."

"Normally that's what you have to do. You stake a claim, and you have to spend a stipulated sum every year to keep title to that claim. But if an owner discovers a deposit big enough to mine, they can apply some of the costs of the mine development on the discovery claims to the title requirements for the rest of the claims. They call it 'spreading.'"

"And those costs are enough to cover a very large area."

"Easily. Just think." She stepped closer to the map and spread her hand over the Diavik mine. "Build a coffer dam. Then dig the hole—tens of thousands of tons of rock to move." She tapped her finger on a black shape. "Build a processing mill to get the diamonds out of the ore." She swept her hand over the whole scene. "And all the construction equipment has to come in by air or on the winter road."

"Winter road?"

"The ice road. For six weeks in the coldest part of winter, the ice is thick enough to support heavy trucks. They plow a road from lake to lake, from Yellowknife to the diamond field."

"And all that money the mines spent allowed them to keep title to large areas," I said.

"Uh-huh. And once they have the ground for ten years, they can convert the claims to leases. A twenty-one-year lease on two thousand acres costs them two dollars. They have hundreds of square miles tied up for basically pennies. That's what all that red and blue territory is."

"If the mines hold all that ground, where did Jimmy explore?"

She hesitated. "This is proprietary information. It's what we own."

"Sure, and if the lawyers have anything to do with it, it's proprietary information that will soon belong to Xi Fan. This is a bad time to clam up on me, Mitzi. The people who tried to kill us will certainly try to kill Jimmy too, if they haven't killed him already."

She closed her eyes.

"I'm sorry," I said, "but I know it and you know it. So help me understand this before somebody comes in here with a court order—or a gun—and takes it."

She buried her face in her hands. Her hair fell forward and uncovered the incision on her scalp. The wound looked pitiful in the harsh fluorescent light. But when she took her hands away, her eyes were dry.

"The small white blocks," she said. "They're unstaked." There were dozens of them. "Most of them are here." She drew her finger over the central part of the map. "And the rest are over here at the eastern end of the lake."

"Why were those claims not already staked by other people or by the mines?"

"Lots of reasons. When the diamond rush happened in the early 1990s, it was just crazy. It was winter. They were dropping posts into the snow from helicopters. Claim jumpers were coming in and knocking out posts and putting in their own. Even small prospectors got claims. A lot of them didn't have financing. They couldn't afford to explore the claims, so they lost title."

"And Jimmy staked them for himself?"

"At first the big companies grabbed the claims as soon as they came open. Sometimes Dad did contract staking for them, flying in and restaking the claims for the mines. But they didn't always keep the paperwork on the claims up to date, because they had such large blocks already."

Or maybe it was Jimmy not keeping things up to date or creating filing errors that he could take advantage of later. Maybe it was Jimmy knocking out the posts.

"So the claims Jimmy owned, the claims he used to attract the twins—which ones were they?"

She kept her eyes on the map. "Dad was secretive," she said. "I don't know what he showed them to get their investment. He would have given them some good indicator minerals and let them test the minerals independently."

"But how would Fan and Mei know what claims they were buying into?"

"They were buying into Angel Minerals, and the company owned all Jimmy's property. He defined it all by map coordinates."

"And they wouldn't know exactly what location the minerals came from."

She shook her head. "He was always afraid of claim-jumpers. He knew he was onto a major discovery but wanted to keep it secret until he'd explored it thoroughly."

"But all these minerals," I looked around at the samples ranged on the shelves, "you must have helped collect them."

"I did. But Dad took the samples and arranged them according to his own system. There are minerals in this room that I collected. I tagged them and marked them according to where I collected them and when. Then I turned them over to him. When he was alone, he'd remove the tags and use his own identifier code."

"There must be a key to the code somewhere."

"I guess so, but I don't have it."

She was lying. She'd spent her life on those claims, sampling for Jimmy every summer.

"OK," I said, "but where were you planning on staking when we went out to look for Jimmy?"

She frowned. "You mean why did we have staking posts?"

"Yes."

"We never go into the Barrens without posts. There's still open ground, sometimes unstaked wedges close to the big mines. You never know."

I didn't believe that either, but a knock on the door interrupted us. "Boat coming," Pete said when Mitzi pulled it open. "It's Larry. There's a couple of Chinese guys with him."

Her features hardened. "Are you kidding me? Coming out to my *home*? In the *night*?" She yanked open a tall cabinet and grabbed a twelve-gauge Remington. She shoved in two slugs and was pumping one into the breech as she limped out the door and headed for the landing stage. I took a few quick snapshots of the map with my phone. I would check later, but I was sure I recognized a section in the middle. Take away the lavish detail and the colored blocks, and it was the same map the killer had in his wallet. I gave it one last look, pocketed three plastic Ziplocs full of garnets, and went outside.

16

Moonlight silvered the bay. A big Whaler with twin outboards was etching a dark line across the surface. Four men stood by the wheel in the center of the boat. Mitzi had the shotgun cradled in her right arm and was just handing a pair of binoculars back to Pete. The boat made a sweeping approach, slowed, and idled in to the landing stage.

The man at the wheel was the one who'd been waving papers in Mitzi's face at the plane dock. The beanpole in the good suit was George Wu, the Vancouver lawyer. Beside him was the muscle.

One was a stocky kid who wore a long-sleeved tee, tight so he could cross his arms and show off the build he'd got at the gym. His traps bulged like shoulder pads. He had a Mohawk, gold earrings, and tattoos that curled into view at his neckline and wrists.

The other guy was a mountain. Had to be six-four and pushing three-fifty. I made him for the heavy often standing behind Fan and Mei in the photos from the swanky watering holes, keeping his eye on the crowd. He had hands the size of frying pans, and his arms hung out from his body. His shaved head seemed to be placed directly on his shoulders without the inconvenience of a neck. His face was as unreadable as a block of stone.

"Hey, Larry," Mitzi said as the engine noise died, "if you step onto my property, I'll put a slug through your boat."

Possible that the big guy didn't understand English. Not possible he could fail to catch the drift. She had a make-my-day expression, and call it what it was, a face that could deliver it. A suture must have opened when she'd stomped across the deck: the bandage was red, and a trickle of blood ran down the inside of her leg. Twelve-gauge shotgun at her shoulder. Who thinks that's a bluff?

Him.

The mountain looked at Mitzi with icepick eyes, grabbed the coiled stern line, and sprang from the boat. The guy practically floated. Tinkerbell disguised as a nose tackle for the Chicago Bears. He landed on his feet as lightly as a cat and was bending down to tie the line to a cleat when Mitzi put a slug through the decking two inches from his hand.

The boom of the gun reverberated on the windless bay. A flock of panicked ducks flew up and tore away, their black shapes winging across the silver water. Very slowly, Tinkerbell stood up. He brushed wood chips from his shiny head. The eyes he fastened on Mitzi glittered like chips of coal. Mitzi racked another slug into the chamber. The spent casing flew through the air and rattled onto the landing stage. The barrel of the gun was as steady as a rock. And it wasn't pointing at the deck.

"I will kill this man, Larry," Mitzi said.

Wu uttered a sharp command in Chinese. The man on the dock didn't move. He was locked on Mitzi. Not a tremble in his massive body. His face was a mask. Wu barked at him again. He unpeeled his eyes from Mitzi.

"Jesus Christ, Mitzi," Larry said when Tinkerbell was back in the boat. "Do you know what's going to happen to you when I report this to the police?"

"Why don't we find out?" she said. "Call them." I don't think anyone missed the fact that the safety was still off. "These people tried to kill us."

"Mitzi," Larry started, but Wu put a hand on his arm and shook his head.

"Ms. Angel, I'm George Wu," he said smoothly. "I represent your father's company, Angel Minerals."

"News to me," she said.

"I understand it must be. I regret we weren't able to communicate with you earlier."

"I think you did communicate."

"Ms. Angel," he said calmly, "I've only just arrived in Yellowknife. The reason I came is that my colleague"—he nodded at Larry—"informed me he was having some difficulty enforcing the decisions of my client." His lips formed the shadow of a smile. "In the circumstances," he said, "it seemed to me that I should come up right away to secure the interests of the company, and that would include your interests too, as you are an officer of the company."

Everyone was watching her. "Come on," she muttered to me. "You're the big-time fed. Say something."

"What circumstances," I said to Wu.

Wu kept his eyes on Mitzi for a beat, then slid his glance to me. "I beg your pardon?"

"You said that in the circumstances you had to come up. What circumstances?"

"And what exactly is your involvement here?" he said.

"Jimmy has only been missing a week," I said, ignoring his question. "We're looking for him. What's the big rush to grab his company?"

The stocky kid was glaring rivets at me and shifting his weight from foot to foot in agitation. "I'll show you what the rush is, tough guy," he snarled, jabbing a thick finger at me. Tinkerbell placed a square foot of hand on the kid's shoulder to calm him down. The boat was starting to drift out from the dock.

"Nothing can be more urgent," Wu said evenly, "than protecting the interests of shareholders when a company's affairs have become"—he spread his hands—"uncertain. In that regard, I have some papers Miss Angel absolutely needs to see, because they document my right to take immediate control of the company's property until such time as James Angel is able to exercise that control himself."

By now the boat was a yard away and twisting in the current. Wu had to shift position to face us. The kid with the tats was squirming with suppressed rage. Tinkerbell's face was a blank slab.

"Refusal to receive and acknowledge these documents," Wu said, trying not to look ridiculous as the strip of water between the boat and the dock widened, "will constitute a breach of Ms. Angel's fiduciary duty as an officer of Angel Minerals. The sanction for such misfeasance would be immediate dismissal from office, a substantial financial penalty, and such other punitive measures as the court may deem appropriate."

He was running on empty. If he had any right to take over the company, he was still waiting for a judge to agree. Otherwise he wouldn't be standing here gassing on the bay. He'd be coming out with cops. By this time the boat was so far out Wu realized he was in danger of looking foolish. He made a signal to Larry, and the engines rumbled into life.

"I'm sorry you choose this path, Ms. Angel," he said. But it was me he was looking at.

17

T hese are amazing," Lily said. She already had her loupe out. One of the garnets shone in her tweezers like a drop of frozen blood. She brought it to the lens and rotated it slowly in the daylight.

I shoved the coffee cups aside and emptied the rest of the Ziploc onto the white balcony table. The cascade of stones rattled onto the painted metal. I sat down and stirred them with my finger. The light rippled through them like liquid. Lily dropped the stone she was looking at the pile and plucked up a darker one.

"Like a grape," she said, holding the mineral directly between the sunlight and her lens. "Very purple." Her face flushed with excitement. She took a deep breath. I could smell her mint toothpaste when she exhaled. When I didn't reply, she slid a glance at me. "Very unusual, Alex."

"Yes."

She tightened her lips impatiently and sorted through the garnets with her tweezers, pushing some of the darker, more deeply purple stones to the side. They burned against the white surface.

"I hate it when you do this. You go monosyllabic. These are not gem-stone minerals," she said in the tone of someone prompting a dull child for an easy answer. "There is only one reason to collect them."

"I know what you're getting at, Lily."

"Well then, say it. These are amazing diamond indicators." She plucked up a stone and let it drop. It plinked onto the table. She tossed the tweezers impatiently into the garnets. She positioned a chair in front of her, stretched out her perfect legs and crossed her ankles on the seat. She clasped her hands demurely in her lap. Lily had unshakeable confidence in her ability to gain an edge in any confrontation with a male by simply letting them see how good-looking she was. Diamond trading is a male business, so it sometimes worked. If it failed, she could switch to yelling. I had seen it happen on the street in Antwerp. In the diamond quarter, the people she was yelling at were Hasidic Jews and Indian diamond traders. I doubted the shouting had much effect, but everyone enjoyed it. With me she took a different tack.

"You have strong feelings against your father, Alex. It poisons you." She fixed me with a grave expression.

He poisoned more than me while he was at it, but I didn't think my scarred psyche was the theme Lily really wanted to develop. I took the tweezers and Lily's loupe and picked up a garnet.

"He made one of the greatest mineral discoveries of the modern age," she said. "It shattered the old diamond cartel."

The stone was the color of dark red wine. I rotated it in front of the lens. A deep purple shadow flashed through it. The shadow vanished and then appeared again as I moved the garnet in the light. In the depths of the stone, I saw a flicker of black.

"Your father invented a new science," Lily went on. "Diamond indi-cator minerals. If you found these minerals, you found diamonds. That's what you always told me."

I put the loupe and tweezers on the table. A thermos of coffee was shoved to one side with the coffee cups. I poured a cup, took a hit, sat back, and watched the girl with the flashing blonde hair. She was back in her kayak, windmilling up the lake as she followed a line of yellow markers. A bike path paralleled the shore, and a man was pedaling along it with a stopwatch in his hand, bellowing out the time as she passed each marker.

I glanced at the heap of stones. "If you're asking me to say what these garnets mean, the truth is I don't know. I'm not a mineral chemist."

My father was. He discovered a way to help geologists pick diamond exploration targets. Diamonds are formed in the mantle at depths of a hundred miles. They come to the surface in small volcanoes called pipes. The lava they ride up in is called kimberlite, but not all kimberlite has diamonds in it. He figured out that if you found a certain kind of garnet in a pipe, that meant the pipe would contain diamonds.

I picked up another stone and let it catch the light.

"These garnets," I said, "we don't even know where they came from."

Lily tilted her head at me. "Darling, you stole this bag and two others. So you think they have something to do with something. We both know that diamond indicator minerals help geologists find diamond mines. Jimmy Angel is a geologist. He's been looking for diamonds. Conclusion: these minerals have something to do with that."

I got up and leaned on the iron railing that ran around the terrace. The girl in the kayak had finished the course, and the guy on the bike was yelling something to her from the shore. A pair of tundra swans coasted in and landed by a rocky point.

Why was Lily here? It had been her idea to come with me. At one point she'd said we needed to work on "learning to be a couple." Not surprising in a relationship in which calculation and betrayal traded places with passion according to the demands of the moment—a condition

Lily called "interpersonal challenges." She could master any jargon and deploy it in service of her story. But what exactly was that story? It had something to do with Mei and Fan.

It wasn't just a case of Mei remembering Lily from long ago. They'd been in touch more recently. I was sure of it. In Vancouver, they'd fallen straight into an intense dialogue the second Wu was out the door. It was clear they knew what ground to cover. In the record I'd got back from Tommy, our translators had managed to extract only a few words and phrases from the poor recording. "Pipes" had been one. "Diamond indicators" another. "Garnets" came up twice.

Those two had been in touch. Luc knew it too. He'd said that Mei asked for Lily, but he sure hadn't looked surprised.

And where did Mitzi fit in? Lily had known about her before we got to Yellowknife. How? Lily had no mining background. She was an industrial-scale diamond thief. And suddenly she's all about pyrope garnets?

"I'm trying to remember where you picked up your interest in exploration geology."

She took me by the shoulders and turned me to face her, so I could look into her eyes and see her deep sincerity. The breeze ran its fingers through her hair, and the tips of her elvish ears peeped into view. I smelled her toothpaste again. Her lips were slightly parted, and the easiest thing in the world would have been to lean forward and kiss them. Instead, I reminded myself that before she was twenty, Lily had devised a scheme of rounding off diamond weights that allowed her to steal millions of dollars' worth of rough from the Russian state diamond sorting facility in Mirny. More than one male had been given a chance to stare deeply into those gray eyes and find sincerity. When I kept my distance, a twitch of annoyance wrinkled her forehead. She drew back and tilted her chin at me.

"Sue me for taking an interest, Alex. For trying to move closer. Believe it or not, I'm still trying to untie at least a few of the knots tangled up inside you. You grew up with these minerals. It's too bad your father was a bastard. He made a discovery that changed the world. When I knew we were coming here, I read up on his work. It seemed obvious that a prospector who'd disappeared in a diamond field might have been looking for diamonds, and those"—she pointed at the garnets on the table—"are how you look." She put her hands on her hips. "If they weren't important, you wouldn't have stolen them."

She wanted me to tell her that the garnets pointed to a diamond discovery, so she could advance whatever scheme she had. How could it be any other way between us? We were shaped to fit matching holes inside each other's hearts. That wasn't the same as trust.

"There's something valuable up there," I said. "Otherwise people wouldn't be trying to kill us. Maybe it's a diamond mine. We can't tell that from a bag of garnets. There were dozens of targets on the big wall map Jimmy Angel had. But the mineral samples are coded. Mitzi said she didn't know the code."

"Do you believe her?"

"No. But that's not proof of anything. Prospectors always think they're on the trail of a big find, and they're always secretive about it. That doesn't mean they've got a discovery. They get it wrong more than they get it right."

The girl in the kayak heard it first. I saw her turn and stare at the sky. The guy with the stopwatch got off his bike and looked in the same direction. A low, hoarse whisper slid into the sky. The sound advanced through the air like a warning of approaching doom. The lake seemed to shudder as the noise grew into a thunder. A giant aircraft with its landing gear down went booming past and sank below the trees. The squeal of its tires as it landed and the roar of air brakes tore the day to shreds.

Two silver shapes flashed by, followed by the scream of their jets. The Canadian F-18s. They flicked across the sun and flew above the airport, almost grazing the soaring tail fin of the landed plane. The F-18s cut into a hard turn and slipped away. The roar of the massive aircraft's engines died to a whine as it trundled onto a taxiway.

A Lockheed C-5 Galaxy. The US Air Force's main strategic heavy lifter. It can carry a battalion with all its war-fighting equipment. It can carry helicopters and Bradley fighting vehicles. I wondered what it could be carrying that anybody in Yellowknife would want, and I wasn't the only one asking the question. Three quarters of a mile away, on the main road from the city, a line of vehicles with flashing roof lights sped toward the airport.

Then my cellphone pinged. A bush pilot had found Jimmy's plane.

18

A flat gray sky sat on the Barrens like an iron lid. The lakes glowed like dull metal. We droned northeast below the cloud. The bleak landscape rippled with flashes of white as the caribou fled in panic from the low-flying plane. The pewter sheet of Lac de Gras slid into view.

No one spoke in the cabin. Mitzi sat with Pete in the first row behind the cockpit. She already occupied the lonely space of someone isolated by a death. No one expected to find Jimmy alive. The pilot who'd spotted the plane had reported a wrecked camp and no sign of life. Mitzi's face was the same carved mask it had been since she'd arrived at the dock and boarded the police flight.

I sat with Luc. In the row behind us were a sergeant; Luc's sidekick, Cedric; and another officer. Two crime-scene techs and a photographer sat in the back. Everyone stared fixedly out the window or quietly inspected their equipment. A sense of shame suffused the cabin, as if we were the ones bringing death to Mitzi.

We reached the far shore of the lake and crossed a ridge. The plane bumped hard on an updraft. Beyond the ridge was the big, ragged bay that extended north from the main body of the lake. One of the exploration targets marked on the wall map had been at the foot of an inlet of the huge bay. I took out my phone and scrolled through the map until I found it. I looked out the window to match the shoreline with the tiny image, and compared it to the one I'd taken from the dead sniper. They were the same.

The inlet ended in an unusually shaped cove—a half-circle so geometrically perfect it looked as if it had been cut from the shore with a sharp knife. Clip Bay. We splashed down and taxied in.

A burly figure in greasy overalls waited on the beach beside his plane. Wisps of his thin gray hair lifted in the breeze. He stood behind the flare he'd planted in the gravel to show the pilot the best place to come in. His hands were shoved in his pockets, and he blinked back tears when Mitzi came ashore.

"Mitz," he said, but his mouth started to quiver, and he clamped it shut.

She stopped in front of him and put a hand on his broad chest. "It's OK, Billy," she said to the old pilot. They stood silently together for a moment. It struck me what a small society they were, who made their lives up here. And how diminished by a single death.

An esker loomed behind the wreckage of the camp. A land breeze stirred the tattered shreds of canvas. Jimmy's Beaver creaked against a mooring line. The camouflage drooped forlornly. The second mooring line had come loose, and the plane lay sideways to the narrow beach. It shuddered as successive waves pushed it against the shore.

"Is he here, Billy?" Mitzi said.

"I think he might be," he said hoarsely. He took a breath before he gestured at a scattering of something a hundred feet away, at the base of a granite bluff.

Fragments of bone were strewn around on the rocky soil. A body had been devoured by animals. A jaw studded with teeth, partially hidden by rags. Boots with the leather gnawed. A steel-cased watch with the khaki nylon strap intact. Mitzi knelt down and picked it up, held it to her ear, then slipped it in a pocket. One of the crime-scene techs started to object, but the sergeant, a ramrod with a moustache like a clump of steel wool, shot him a look and shook his head.

"Can I have a minute?" Mitzi said. Her voice was low but steady. She had already come to this place in her mind.

"She knew he was dead," Luc said. We were standing beside a patch of scraped ground between the tent and the shore. Mitzi and Pete had made their way around the site and were now sitting on boulders on the little ridge to the right of the camp.

"We all knew," I said.

He nodded. "One of the techs says there's a bear skull by the camp, with what looks like a bullet hole." He stared around. "Where the human remains are, not much to go on. The animals don't leave much. Wolves will eat the bones. The tech's going to comb the site for scat."

"We can figure out what ate him," I said. "The question is what killed him."

I could see a garnet on the ground. I thought that Jimmy must have sampled the scene, because the ground was scraped bare, and I saw a stake and a length of twine nearby. It seemed strange that he'd have missed a garnet, so obvious that I could see it still there, two weeks after his disappearance.

The forensic techs had put on white nylon suits and split the scene. One was picking his way carefully through the remains while the other busied himself with the devastated tent.

Cedric crunched across the gravel. "Sir," he said to Luc when he reached us. "I think you should see what we found on the plane."

Luc strode off after him. I stepped over to the clear space near the scattered stakes, scooped up the garnet and a handful of loose dirt, and followed.

The sergeant indicated a hole in the metal rung of the ladder. He'd marked it for the techs with a strip of flagging tape. The metal was peeled away at the edge of the hole, as if it had been blown apart.

"High-impact bullet?" Luc said.

"Looks like it, sir. And the angle, the way the metal is torn—if it was a bullet, it hit the top of the step."

"OK."

"Well, sir, that would mean it was a high-angle shot."

We all swung around at the same time, scanning the esker first and panning around to the granite ridge. And there, standing now, was Pete. When he saw us looking, he waved.

Five minutes later, the sergeant and I, Luc and Cedric were all gasping for breath on the ridge while Pete pointed out two pale marks on the top of a boulder, where the lichen had been scraped away.

"Bipod," I said.

He nodded. "Sniper. And right here is where he made a place to kneel." The shooter had shoved some gravel aside and placed a smooth stone behind the boulder. I looked around at the ground, but Pete shook his head. "No casings. I checked."

The crime-scene techs were finishing up at the campsite when I joined Mitzi on the ridge. The pilot who'd discovered Jimmy's plane had flown out. He'd offered Mitzi a lift, but she'd wanted to stay.

"It's OK," she said when I sat down. She took a deep breath, as if to steady herself. "You know, this is where he'd want to die. He loved this more than he loved anything." Her gaze roamed the lakes and the distant ridges. "He kept everyone away," she said. "He didn't even like me calling him Dad. He said we were all the same, just matter born of matter. The elements that make up the rock are what made us. The elements came from the furnace of the stars." She gave me a sad smile. "That's how he talked. He made it seem like you were watching creation happen. I didn't really have a mom. She died when I was a kid. I don't remember her. Dad said the earth was my mother." Suddenly a look of the purest hatred swarmed into her face. She turned away to hide it.

The wind picked up. It stirred the water and tore holes in the cloud. Where the sun broke through, it paved the water with a silver light. From the ridge you could see how perfect the shoreline below us was—the neat arc at the end of the inlet.

"You know it's a pipe, don't you," she said.

"I guessed. How did it go undiscovered for so long? It's in the heart of the main discovery zone."

"Look where it is. The first pipe discovered in the Arctic was under a small, round lake. Prospectors learned to look for targets like that and drill them through the ice in winter. This doesn't look like a round target. Only when you look at the shore from above can you see the circle continue under the water."

"Where the water's black."

"Uh-huh. Perfect shape for a pipe."

"And the black lines on the wall map." I'd been thinking about them, remembering what my father had told me about the Canadian discovery. "Those lines marked the flow of the glaciers."

Her expression changed. Some of the loneliness left her face. She got up, walked a few paces, knelt down on the rock, and traced her fingers along a straight, even depression. It was one of a series of parallel grooves that creased the granite surface of the ridge.

"These are the lines," she said. "You can find these marks all over the Barrens. They show the exact direction that the glaciers advanced ten thousand years ago." She looked up at the forbidding landscape, the miles of gray rock broken by frigid, gunmetal lakes. "The land was scraped and scoured by the passage of the glaciers. It's the glaciers that revealed the diamond pipes."

It wasn't only geology she was talking about. It was her childhood.

The last of the cloud had blown away. The inlet shone and the huge bay beyond it. A dozen miles away, the wrinkled sheet of Lac de Gras glittered in the sun.

"In the last ice age, glaciers formed and came south across the Barrens. Hundreds of thousands of tons of ice pressed down on the rock." She stroked the clean, concave depression that ran downhill beside her. "When the ice slid over the softer rock of the diamond pipes, it gouged out that softer rock and smeared it over the granite in trains. Ten thousand years later, when the ice age ended and the glaciers melted away, the water filled the depressions left by the gouged-out pipes. Instead of pipes, all we saw were lakes."

And Jimmy Angel figured it out. In 1991 he tracked a smear of minerals to the edge of a small round lake. In the winter he came back. He hauled a drill rig up the ice road and dragged it onto the lake. He drilled through the ice and through the mud. He hit boulders. He bent the drill and hauled it up, replaced the shaft and sent it down again. And he hit a diamond pipe.

"By that time he was so far in debt that other people owned the discovery," Mitzi said. "He spent his lifetime trying to find another."

The wind picked up. It moaned across the immensity of rock where Jimmy Angel had spent his life, and where it ended. The cold wind carried the first message of the coming winter. Of the planet tilting its northern face to the darkness. Of the brevity and hopelessness of life.

Grief took over Mitzi's face in a swift assault that drew down her mouth and made her lips tremble. A bitter sob escaped her. She buried her face in her hands and wept as only orphans weep, with the certainty that nothing can ever console them.

On the flight back she became stern and unapproachable again. She'd passed through the dark valley and wanted to show she'd come out the other side. Except she hadn't. Waiting on the dock was Wu. This time he'd come with the police, and he explained to Mitzi exactly how much of her father's property she could call her own.

None.

19

Those Chinese bastards are up to something with the Canadians," Tommy yelled as we pulled out of Teterboro airport and got on the I-80 for New York City. "I'm telling you, they're dating our girl, and the way we're starting to see it, she's ready to two-time us if the price is right."

He had to shout because he had the top down, and the noise of the traffic heading into the city and the rush of night air as we merged onto the freeway at eighty made normal conversation impossible. Also, Tommy liked to shout.

"That Chinese shyster rolled over Mitzi Angel, and the Canadians didn't do a thing to stop him. She's an American citizen," Tommy bellowed, stabbing a thick finger in my direction. "An American citizen blatantly stripped of her inheritance rights by the people who murdered her father." He was really booming now, sucking in oratorical power from the rushing air and painting his picture of a helpless American preyed upon by foreigners. In his head, Tommy was always addressing a jury. What he really thought was anybody's guess. It would come out when he was ready.

The seizure of Jimmy Angel's company and assets went down with stunning speed. A stack of writs with red court seals was handed to Mitzi when she got off the plane. By the time she got home there was nothing left. The map was gone. The garnets, gone. She was instructed that the house, office, and the barge itself were the property of a company she did not control.

"But I'm a member of the board," she'd said.

"At a special meeting duly held today in the law offices of the company's counsel," Wu told her, "a quorum of directors voted to replace you. Thank you for your past services."

Nothing put Tommy in a better mood than the prospect of a fight. He fell on the legal case with savage pleasure, as if it had been a runner trying to get by him on the field. But he'd have been in a good mood anyway. His car guru had finally located a 1957 Cadillac Eldorado Biarritz to replace the one he'd wrecked last year. The real reason Tommy had come out to Teterboro to pick me up was to show off the car.

The massive tail fins and restored coachwork gleamed under a fresh coat of Dakota Red. The Caddy carved a hole in the traffic. We cannoned through the E-ZPass tollbooth and onto the George Washington Bridge. Tommy wore a vintage lilac bowling shirt with the name "Dream Boy" stitched on the pocket in flowing script. The shirt rippled in the wind as he waved his catcher's-mitt hand at the dash and listed the car's attributes. I'd already heard about the Hydra-Matic transmission and the 364-cubic-inch engine when he had the last one, but pointing that out would accomplish nothing.

"Horsepower: three hundred and twenty-five," he bawled. "That's the kind of power plant you want for a vehicle with a curb weight of two and a half tons."

I gazed downriver at the blazing slash of light. The nighttime view of Manhattan gave me a kick of pleasure. Its brashness and optimism and bravado. The city that never says "I'm sorry," even when it should. Especially then.

We took the ramp that curled down to the Henry Hudson Parkway. The Caddy rose and fell on its springs like a ship on a gentle swell. The lights on the New Jersey side sparkled on the river. I was grateful for the cocoon of wind and traffic as we joined the stream flowing south to the city.

Yellowknife had gone cold fast, and I don't just mean temperature. Two days ago Lily and I had been called to a meeting at the RCMP building. We'd arrived on the dot. The desk sergeant in the lobby made a big show of leafing through his logbook. Asked us to wait. Half an hour later Cedric appeared.

"Inspector Savard is in Ottawa for consultations," he told us. No preamble. No apology. He wore a neutral expression. Only his eyes showed any feeling: curiosity. He was interested to see how we'd react. Like a pair of lab rats whose maze just had a new twist installed.

"We had an appointment," I said.

"Did you, sir? I'll be sure to mention it to the inspector."

"Who's in Ottawa," I reminded him.

Cedric spread his hands. "If he calls."

"We might as well go for lunch," Lily said as we climbed back into the F350. "There's a place on the water that sells buffalo burgers."

"They're turning over our apartment," I said. "That's why they called us here."

"Of course they are, darling. Let's give them plenty of time. Otherwise it will just be embarrassing for everyone."

"The garnets are in the room safe."

She shook her head. Her big purse was sitting on the console. She lifted it and let it drop. The minerals clicked like a bag of marbles.

"What's inside the safe, then?" I'd checked it before we left.

"Low-value garnets from that hobby shop at the mall. I mixed in some gravel from the parking lot. I put it all into Ziploc bags exactly like the ones Jimmy Angel used, and labelled them with GPS coordinates from three different places in the Barrens."

Lily had a Russian's native distrust of officialdom. She always assumed the worst, and prepared for it. It would take whoever ended up with the minerals months to figure out they'd been had.

We had a great lunch. When we got back, sure enough the place had been done. It was a neat job, but the searchers hadn't taken pains to conceal their intrusion. Lily's clothes were put back perfectly folded, but in a different order than she'd left them. Hangers were shoved to the end of the rod. Someone had fanned through Lily's fashion magazines and left them on a different table. There were no lock-picking scratches on the door, so they'd had a key. The safe was empty. They hadn't even bothered closing it.

We packed, went downstairs, and paid the bill. I'd already got the message to report back to New York. Lily had decided to move to a Catholic retreat center on a nearby lake. "Excellent security," she'd explained, and since her private cabin had been arranged by the priest who'd provided the sawed-off twelve-gauge, I didn't doubt it.

I knew who'd brought me to New York, and it wasn't Tommy. I'd flown on the secretary's Gulfstream again. The only authority that could yank a plane from someone with cabinet rank was the White House.

"By the way," Tommy said as he turned off the West Side Highway at Fourteenth Street, "maybe I should give you a heads-up, in case you want to check your makeup and try not to look too stunned. Tabitha's waiting for us."

"So I guess it's her meeting?"

"See, that's just the kind of boner I'm trying to save you from. If you can get through the meeting without sounding like an intern, everything will go smoother."

We turned onto Hudson Street and drove into Greenwich Village. The summer night had packed the sidewalks. People poured in and out of bars and restaurants like schooling fish. We turned right onto Leroy Street. Ancient plane trees spread their branches above the narrow road. Old-fashioned streetlamps splashed the dark foliage with a yellow light. Couples sat on the steps of a redbrick townhouse, talking in low voices and passing a joint. A red dot glowed briefly to life. I heard the sound of a tab being pulled on a can of beer.

"It's called inter-functionality," Tommy explained. "People like Tabitha go where they're needed. I needed her, so here she is."

The idea that Tabitha would go a quarter of an inch out of her way because Tommy needed her was the flat-earth theory of the day. Tabitha worked directly for the president. She prepared the intelligence bulletin known as the President's Daily Brief. Her security clearance was higher than mine. It would be Tabitha's meeting, and that was irritating Tommy. She was half his age.

We turned onto Washington Street and took the first left onto Clarkson. Tommy eased the Eldorado into the restricted space in front of a row of eighteenth-century redbrick townhouses. Most of the property in that part of the Village belonged to the young millionaires with bonus packages who worked on Wall Street, a fifteen-minute ride away on their electric scooters. They'd be surprised to know that behind the black-shuttered row, a team of accountants and code-breakers on the payroll of the US Treasury was tapping their phones, bugging their clients, and reading their email.

The place was deserted. We made our way along the hall and upstairs to Tommy's top-floor office. Tabitha looked just as she had when we still shared a pair of crummy offices in the basement. The same mass of untamable auburn hair floating around her head, the same tendency to blush. Terrific clothes that looked as if she'd just hauled them out of a footlocker. The combination of untidy appearance and expensive clothes made people suspect she was the product of an old, eccentric New England family holed up in a mansion somewhere. But Tabitha's last name was Kowalski. Her dad raised pigs in Minnesota. She'd gone to Vassar on a scholarship. She was an intelligence officer who'd been through Camp Peary, the CIA training base in Virginia that spies call The Farm.

"Wow, Alex," she said. "It's been so long."

She stretched out her arm and clasped my hand in a cool, dry grip. A flush bloomed briefly on her throat. The top three buttons of her shirt were undone, so the throat had extra room to run. I wouldn't call Tabitha sexy. She was more dangerous than that. I didn't mind. Whatever she was spreading, I had the antibodies.

We liked each other. I didn't hold it against her that she'd concealed her real assignment from me. I'd always suspected it. She'd been too qualified to be an assistant to a Treasury spook. She'd done what she'd been paid to do.

But feeling OK with it is one thing. It's wise to keep in mind the thing about deceit, and I'm speaking from experience—it gets easier with practice.

20

You could cut the rancor with a chainsaw. Tommy practiced scowling at the ceiling. Tabitha blew the hair out of her eyes and gave him her warmest smile. That office had been made for warfare.

Tommy hadn't changed a thing. It was as if my former boss, Chuck, had just stepped out for a minute to screw up somebody's life but would be right back to finish with mine. He wouldn't, though. Chuck had transferred to Washington, where someone shot him in the head.

Chuck had smashed out walls to create the huge office, and filled it with a custom-made steel desk and a conference table made of what looked like bleached railway ties. On the walls he'd hung a series of monochrome oil paintings, alternately black and white. Whenever he felt cornered at a meeting, Chuck would leap up and stride around the room, pausing at a painting to cock his head and utter a little chuckle so everyone would know how perfectly he understood it.

Chuck had tried to take the furniture with him to Washington. He'd hired a truck and moving crew to come around on a Sunday, when nobody would be there. But Tommy, like all lawyers, thought of his fellow human beings as fundamentally dishonest. Let's face it—it's the safe bet. So he'd already canceled Chuck's pass, and ordered his iris scan and fingerprints deleted from the entry system, as Chuck discovered when he got there with the movers. When he tried to sweet-talk the security detail into letting him pick up his "personal effects," they checked with Tommy. Tommy instructed them to call the police immediately and report that an unauthorized individual was unlawfully trying to remove material from a top-secret federal agency. It had taken Chuck a day to get out of the precinct holding cell.

Tommy kept the furniture. Not that he thought it looked good. He didn't care. Vintage bowling shirts and cars from the 1950s were as far down the road of aesthetic appreciation as Tommy was prepared to go. But the pieces suited his immense bulk, and the pictures gave him something to sneer at. Two for two.

He dropped his massive frame into the black leather executive chair. It didn't make him look any more in charge, and the problem wasn't the lilac bowling shirt. Tommy had wangled the rank of deputy assistant secretary when he took over the department, but the dominant scent in the room was the one you pick up in the Rose Garden.

Tommy stabbed a button on his desk. The lights dimmed, the windows tuned opaque, and a deadbolt in the door shot home with a loud *chunk*. In the hall outside, a winking red light would be warning that a secure meeting was underway. A slot in the ceiling opened, and a sheet of glass slid down. The glass was imprinted with circuitry. The software that ran it connected us to the supercomputers at Fort Meade.

"It's your show, sister," Tommy said.

A film started running on the screen. The view was a high aerial shot of a busy sea lane through a group of islands.

"The Haro Strait," Tabitha said. "On the right are the San Juan Islands off Seattle. The large land mass to the left is Vancouver Island. This is the main sea approach to the city of Vancouver." The camera zoomed in on a single vessel, a large container ship. "Left the port of Tianjin two weeks ago and offloaded in Vancouver."

The picture switched to a nighttime shot of a dock. Huge cranes trundled into the floodlights and hoisted steel containers from a ship directly onto flatbed trucks and railcars.

"Vancouver container port. We know where these containers are going and what they're supposed to contain. Canada logs them into a database. We can access it. The trade patterns are well established. Usually, no surprises. The same people order the same stuff one month as they did the month before. Like us, Canada imports billions of dollars' worth of Chinese goods. Impossible to check it all, but we can watch the patterns and see if anything jumps out. This time it did."

She pursed her lips for a moment as she studied the screen.

"That ship was a medium-size container vessel. It carried 6,400 standard forty-foot containers. Most of them fit neatly into the distribution patterns. But eighteen didn't. And we couldn't find them."

The image changed to a map that showed a section of western Canada. Three bright red squiggles ran from west to east.

"Those are the highway routes through the Rocky Mountains between British Columbia and Alberta. When we lost the containers, we threw it over to the NSA. We knew the containers had left the city by truck at night. They weren't headed south to the border, or we'd have known about it from US customs pre-clearance data. So we knew what to ask the satellite to look for—a night convoy through the mountains. We found them in the Rockies. Eighteen semis in a line at night. We followed them to Edmonton, where they refueled and headed north."

The film switched to a high aerial shot again. The picture quality was razor-sharp. The long line of semis wound their way along a highway through bush.

"The satellite we'd used before was tasked to a military mission, so we asked the air force for help. They put up a U-2 from Beale Air Force Base near Sacramento. This is from seventy thousand feet. As you can see, we could read the registration numbers on the containers."

The forest was thin spruce and pine. Patches of gray rock showed through. Here and there, the shoreline of a large lake came into view to the right. I knew it was Great Slave Lake. The film was edited, so we didn't have long to wait to watch the trucks arrive in Yellowknife and park in a large depot on the far side of the city. Night was falling by that time. The editors put in a few seconds of black for realism, and when daylight returned, the timecode showed that it was the next day. The trucks were gone.

21

The lights in the room came up as the sheet of glass slid back into the ceiling. We sat in silence for a minute. Tommy and Tabitha waited for my reaction.

"And this just happened."

"You saw the time code," Tommy said. "Two days ago."

"You already know it has to be Fan," I said. "This was an operation that took a high level of industrial expertise and planning. It involved originating a large cargo in northern China, because that's where Tianjin is. The cargo wasn't checked in Vancouver, so the Canadians pre-cleared it, even though it didn't fit the usual pattern of trade traffic. You ran the container numbers?"

"The manifests just gave a general description," Tabitha said. "Scientific mineral-exploration equipment. The shipper was a company with a long history of trade with Canada."

"And the ownership?"

"Mining supply company in Beijing," she said. "But that's a front. The computers practically blew themselves out trying to figure out who ultimately owns it. The title goes back and forth through a web of trading companies all over China."

"Will you guys cut to the chase," Tommy snarled. "We all know who it is."

"The twins wear a lot of hats," I said. "We need to figure out which one they're wearing now. If we know which of their companies is the true originator of the cargo, we are closer to knowing what they're up to. We've managed to get Mei held for extradition by cooking up fraud charges against her. We said she was concealing one of their company's connections to Iran from an American bank. But it's not financial crime that's making Washington wake up screaming in the middle of the night, is it, Tab."

Tabitha crossed her legs and smoothed her skirt. "We consider iDragon's 5G phone technology a threat to national security," she said. "We oppose any ally of the United States allowing it in. The Chinese government is the main owner, and they will use iDragon's position to back-door into our secure networks. Most of our allies in Five Eyes have agreed to exclude them. Canada is the only holdout."

Five Eyes was the intelligence-sharing cartel of the United States, Canada, Britain, Australia, and New Zealand. Washington had threatened to withhold the most sensitive intelligence from Canada if they greenlit iDragon. I doubted anybody was getting the most sensitive intelligence anyway. Otherwise we wouldn't all be spying on each other.

"The short story is that the Canadians don't trust us," Tabitha said. "They believe we're not a reliable partner and don't honor our obligations."

"I wonder where they got that idea."

"Maybe we can skip the dirty laundry of the Western world," Tommy growled. He gave me his take-charge look. "We have to know what that shipment is. If it's part of some 5G scheme, how does it further their aims? If it's a take-over-the-diamond-field game, then OK, how does that work?"

Tommy got up and paced around behind the desk. The machine that was Tommy's body couldn't sit on idle for long. He had to take it for a maintenance spin, a task he managed by suddenly performing some macho demonstration, such as lifting the end of his steel desk with his fingertips. This time he settled for a few squats, placing his hands on his hips and blowing out noisily to underline the exertion. The performance didn't work as well as he'd hoped. He grunted loudly as he wobbled up from the last squat and collapsed into his chair.

"And another thing," he said brusquely, "I thought you were supposed to be an American agent. You're spending a lot of time with the Canadians."

I'll give Tommy credit. If he could have swallowed that remark, he would have. Because, dumb thing number one: Who else would I be spending my time with? And dumb thing number two: He'd just confirmed he had somebody watching me.

Tabitha ran her hands through her hair, lifted her arms, and released the hair in a wild cascade. She watched Tommy with the cool expression of a butterfly collector who has netted a rare specimen and is wondering whether to let it go or kill it for the collection.

"Maybe whoever you have spying on Alex is the one who sprang a leak, Tommy. I mean, your operational security hasn't been watertight, has it? Or Jimmy Angel might still be with us."

Tommy actually smiled. He was only really happy when a fight moved into the open.

"Nice try," he said. "I'm not the one in the room who can pull the secretary of the treasury's Gulfstream and tell it where to go and when. You laid on the jet for Alex. How did the people waiting for him in Yellowknife know when it was coming?" He leaned back in the big chair and laced his fingers behind his head. "We all know somebody's reading our plays. So let's try to steal theirs. Take us back to first principles,

Alex. Even if the twins are spearheading some kind of operation against America, they still need a credible reason to be in the Arctic. We can't just say the Canadians are patsies and China's pushing them around. Investing in Jimmy Angel's company has to make sense on its face."

I gave them diamond investment 101. For a fund like China Hard Asset, the million dollars they'd paid Jimmy Angel was peanuts. They wouldn't miss the money if the exploration failed. On the other hand, if Jimmy discovered a diamond mine, the upside was in the billions.

Tabitha propped an elbow on the desk and looked at me, her head tilted into the palm of her hand. "And from a single discovery, they could expand, right?"

"Sure," I said. "Stake more claims. Look for other targets."

"And they could introduce iDragon's 5G on their own property."

"That's what you've been thinking all along," I said.

"Makes sense, though," Tommy said. "They say it's for internal communications. Link up with their other industrial properties in Canada."

I nodded. "And they'd have an operating telecommunications system inside North America."

I got the idea that's what they wanted me to say. They were nodding like proud parents whose dullard child has finally worked out two plus two.

"All we really need to know now," Tommy said, leaning back in his chair, "is how close they are to nailing a mine." He clasped his hands behind his head, and arched his back. The name "Dream Boy" bulged out prominently on his massive chest. "Noodle that for me, Alex."

For me, the question was a simpler one: who was feeding me to the Chinese? Because one of them was.

I reached across and stabbed a button on his desk. The windows cleared and the door unlocked with a loud snap. I shoved back my chair and got up.

"Noodle it yourself, Dream Boy."

22

I could hear her heels clacking along the sidewalk behind me. She caught up and slipped her arm through mine. Her hair floated out in the warm night air and brushed against my face. She gave my arm a squeeze.

"You can't run away from this, Alex. The department is leaking like a sieve."

"And you're going to pin it on Tommy."

"He's running the place."

We turned right onto Bleecker Street. The sidewalk was packed with the usual mix of New Yorkers heading for the bars and tourists searching for Pete Seeger.

Tabitha's default Village eatery was Via Carota, where a diner's main responsibility was to ignore the movie star perched at the marble counter and concentrate on the food. But we walked past Grove Street and waded into the mass of people crossing Seventh Avenue.

"Can I drop you somewhere, Tab?"

She laughed and shot an elbow into my ribs. It was taking me a while to get used to the new Tabitha. She towed me into Murray's Cheese.

A guide had a crowd of foodie pilgrims gathered around him. He was explaining how the cheese shop that had occupied the same address for eighty years had morphed into a hallowed New York destination. The locals stamped around them in exasperation. Tabitha knifed her way through to the deli counter and shouted for two Pastraminators—a sandwich that had transformed pastrami, sauerkraut, jack cheese, jalapeño, and chipotle aioli into a cult.

She led the way to a narrow sliver of park at the corner of Bleecker and Sixth Avenue. We sat on a bench and unwrapped the sandwiches. A river of yellow taxis streamed uptown. To the south, One World Trade Center cut a silver gash in the glowing sky. Tabitha popped the beer and handed me a can.

As we ate, the city cocooned us in its noise. We finished the sandwiches and rolled up the foil wrappers and tossed them in the trash at the end of the bench. Tabitha swigged down the last of her beer and crunched the can. Her eyes took on a predatory look. She'd been a power forward at Vassar. She cocked her arm and sailed a two-pointer across the little park and into the bin on the other side.

"You didn't know about Jimmy Angel," she said.

"That Tommy was running him? No."

"How does that strike you?"

"Stop trying to make me a witness for the prosecution. How does it strike me? It strikes me as par for the course. When do we ever tell each other anything until we have to?"

"But the operational reason. He gave you a reason before he sent you up."

"A reason for recruiting Jimmy? FinCEN picked up a transfer from China Hard Asset."

"How?"

"Routine surveillance."

"Come on, Alex. Since when would surveillance of a target like China Hard Asset be routine?"

I finished my beer and waited for Tabitha to get to the point.

"There's another China Hard Asset connection. The twins put them into a company called Shanghai Specialty Fabrics. They make expensive, short-run materials for the women's fashion industry. When top designers want an exclusive fabric, something no competitor can ever get, that's one of the places they go for it."

And right on cue, the green Bentley came slowly up the crowded street. Minnie Ho at the wheel and Tommy riding shotgun. They stopped a dozen yards away, deep in conversation, waiting for the light to change on Sixth.

"You're telling me Minnie Ho gets her fabrics from a company owned by the twins and the Chinese brass?"

"Alex, they own her business."

"I thought Minnie's financing came from her father." Ho Wang Wei was a Chinatown tycoon who ran a private banking operation.

"That's right," Tabitha said. The light changed, and the Bentley glided across the street. She gave me time to connect the dots.

"And China Hard Asset owns him too," I said.

"Lock, stock, and barrel."

I felt a little sick. You'd think I'd be used to it. The business I'm in—it locates the soft tissue of your heart and surrounds it with a hard shell. Lately that shell had been flaking off in bits. But it wasn't warmth or human tenderness that seeped in. It was despair. I watched the Bentley turn down a narrow lane and disappear.

"Must be in a hurry," I said. "They didn't even stop for a Pastraminator."

"As if," Tabitha said. "She has a guy holding a parking spot outside Minetta Tavern. Tommy will have the thirty-three-dollar burger."

"And he always gets the same booth, so you probably have it wired."

"Minnie will have her usual. Island Creek oysters, grilled, and a half bottle of the Meursault," she said, confirming the table was miked.

"Uh-huh, but correct me if I'm wrong. You haven't caught Tommy feeding secrets to Minnie. If you had, he'd be tied to a board with a wet cloth on his face in one of those black sites we're not supposed to know about."

We left the park and made our way back to Clarkson Street. I opened the window to let in the night air. My office was in the basement. The window opened onto an alley. Only the rats would hear the rest of what we had to say.

"So you ran a wire, got nothing, and now you want me to help set up Tommy."

She watched me closely for a moment, letting that ice-green gaze chill its way across my face.

"I wouldn't need any help with that," she said, and let the statement lie there like a cocked gun. If the business of the night was to show me who was going to be in charge, she wasn't wasting time.

"Let's put Tommy and his Chinese-asset girlfriend aside for the moment," she said. "This diamond action in the Arctic—it's now a top priority. We have to understand it. I don't know everything the Joint Chiefs of Staff tell the president in those meetings in the Situation Room she's being called to every day. But I write the Daily Brief, so I know the headlines. Right now we have two aircraft-carrier battle groups from the Seventh Fleet steaming through the South China Sea. They're there to give the Chinese something to think about, because at the moment they are giving us plenty, and frankly, we don't know what's up."

She had a slim folder with her. It was stamped with the seal of the president of the United States. She flipped it open and ran her eyes down a page.

"Know anything about NORAD?" she said, closing the folder and getting up.

"Only that it's our military air defense alliance with Canada."

"We have a flight from Teterboro tomorrow. We're visiting the Colorado headquarters. Departure nine P.M. That should give you enough time."

"For what?" I said.

She gave me a level look. "Let's not fence, Alex. You're going to see your father tomorrow. No one knows more about how to judge the prospects of a diamond discovery than he does. We have a puzzle to solve, and he has some of the pieces. But he doesn't have all of them. I think we're all agreed that the twins' diamond play is about more than money. We're going to meet some people who think so too."

"And now I report to you, is that it, Tab?"

We were both standing now. She seemed very close. Her hair drifted around her face, and she flung it away with an exasperated gesture. "Why the hell don't you just kiss me."

And I grabbed her and ran my hands into her hair and kissed her beautiful, soft mouth. Maybe it was anger at Lily, or at Tab herself, or maybe I just didn't have the antibodies anymore. I kissed her again, and then I tore myself away. The green gaze had lost a little ice.

"Alex," she murmured.

And I took her wrist and pulled her through the door, and we went outside into the night.

23

The street was quiet when we came out. A lone figure leaned against the fender of a red sports car, scrolling through her phone. "Don't tell me that's Annie," Tabitha said.

At seventeen, my daughter looked more like twenty. Something I wasn't happy about. Not that there weren't other things that bothered me more at the moment. Such as the fact she worked for Minnie Ho.

"Wow," Tabitha said when they shook hands. "Is that raw silk?"

"A special rayon. We have an exclusive on it," Annie said, plucking at her T-shirt while she ran her eyes over Tabitha's outfit. "That's the latest Co, isn't it?" she said, eyeing the shirt. "It really slays."

We said good night. Tabitha picked an imaginary piece of lint from my lapel, smiled at Annie, and clacked off into the warm night. I got into the passenger seat as Annie started the car, revved the engine, and picked her way swiftly out of the Village and onto the West Side Highway. She drove fast and well, showing off how quickly she could run up through the gears and daring me to complain when she blew through amber lights. At Seventy-Second Street she got off the expressway and took Riverside

Drive. We were passing the Soldiers and Sailors monument before she said what was on her mind.

"Dad, you're still with Lily, aren't you? I mean, don't you go to Montreal to explore the viability of a shared life?" I knew where phrases like that came from. My ex, Pierrette, could make a relationship sound like elective surgery. "Because, Dad, I just don't know how aware you are. That woman—Tabitha?—she could eat you alive."

We got off Riverside Drive and took West End Avenue to Ninety-Fourth Street. Annie slid the Miata into a spot a few doors down from the apartment.

"She wasn't even wearing a bra."

Think about all the available responses from an adult male to a remark like that from his daughter, and if you get a number higher than zero, you're ahead of me.

I had a shock of recognition as soon as we walked in. The Andy Warhol print of David Bowie that Pierrette had hung at the end of the hall was back in place. She'd taken it with her when our marriage broke up. Against her objections, Annie had insisted on moving into the apartment when I started spending time in Montreal. She'd spent a lot of her childhood here. Pierrette loathed the idea, but at least it gave her the chance to hang the Warhol in my face.

The place had been repainted. The pale gray of the living room made a perfect background for the huge blowups of fashion shoots Annie had pinned to the walls. My old sofa blazed in a tiger-stripe velvet. Ditto the easy chair. Annie made me sit, and disappeared to the kitchen to return with a frosted pitcher and a single long-stemmed glass with three small round onions skewered on a toothpick. She handed me the glass, filled it, and returned the pitcher to the fridge.

I took a sniff. "Martini."

"Gibson," Annie said. "It's where you put in onions instead of olives. It's more chic." She sat down and watched me take a sip. "You notice I'm not drinking," she said, "even though I think the rules are totally brain-dead. I mean, twenty-one? Hello? You can die for your country, but you can't have a drink in New York state?"

"Were you planning to die for your country?"

"They call that sophistry, Dad," she said, giving me what she thought of as her withering look. "It's where you're just trying to look smart."

"And good luck with that, right?"

Annie was a serious kid. She'd spent most of her life in the company of adults, even more when Pierrette and I split up and they'd moved full-time to Tuxedo Park. Pierrette had inherited the property—a four-thousand-square-foot house on a lake. Tuxedo Park was a private village with controlled access and its own police force. Not exactly teeming with teenagers.

She'd also suffered things that set her apart from other kids. An assault by Russian gangsters. Capture by a psychotic killer who'd held her and Pierrette hostage at the house to lure me to a showdown. It ended in the killer's death, but it's not like that made everything OK. Nothing would make everything OK. What made it better, though, was Minnie Ho.

Minnie had given her a job and enrolled her in the design program at Cooper Union. Using her muscle as a top designer, she'd worked out a deal where Annie got credit for the work she did at Minnie's studio.

I was grateful to Minnie for what she'd done for Annie. And Tommy was the closest person I had to a friend. Now I was going to spy on them.

Later that night I logged onto the secure server. I typed in the code Tab had given me. It transferred me out of the FinCEN domain to a temporary file at the NSA. If the data posted to the file had stayed in the FinCEN domain, Tommy could have found it and discovered what Tabitha didn't want him to discover. That he was now officially a target.

I doubted it would have surprised him. Tabitha was smart, but you could see her coming. She was too excited by her power not to use it. I would bet real money that Tommy was sitting at home that night looking at a code-protected NSA file of his own. That one would reveal a target too.

Me.

It wasn't personal. Intelligence is a game of check and double-check. It's governed by foundational assumptions. One of them is that nothing is coincidence. No one just happens to be somewhere, with someone, at a certain time. So in a business where duplicity is just the common cold, you pay attention to who's sneezing.

24

I got up before dawn and put on my shorts and ran the block to Central Park. At that hour there were only dedicated runners on the Bridle Path. I picked a guy who looked my age and tried to stay with him. Maybe he could hear me pounding along behind him on the dirt, because as we passed the Guggenheim, he put the pedal down and went up the hill fast, leaving me behind.

I'd had little to do with my father since I moved out of his last diamond camp in Africa. As soon as I was old enough. We'd met once when I was investigating his role in a stock-market fraud around a diamond called the Russian Pink. Just the prospect of seeing him again filled my mouth with a bitter taste.

I settled into a steady run and did a couple of laps of the reservoir—three miles. I managed to blow most of the anger out of my head and into the cool morning air. How could one old man create so much havoc.

But he would know what to make of the stone. No mineral could keep a secret from him, and for sure not a garnet.

We left at six A.M. to beat the traffic. We drove up to Ninety-Sixth and took the traverse through Central Park and kept on straight to the FDR. Annie had the top down. Her tawny hair flailed in the wind. We went down the East River to Thirty-Fourth Street and took the Queens-Midtown Tunnel under the river and onto the Long Island Expressway.

On the way we covered a lot of territory. Annie confided that her pronouns were *she* and *her*; that Pierrette's new boyfriend, an orthodontist named Glenn, "with two *n*'s," had an eighty-two-foot ketch he kept at Newport; and that the fashion industry produced 150 billion pieces of new clothing every year, almost all of which ended up in landfills.

"Dad, it can't go on!"

"No."

"The fashion industry *must* accept responsibility for what it does to the planet."

"Absolutely."

Annie launched into a passionate speech that included the horrors of microfibers and, on the plus side, a new way of making silk from orange peels being pioneered in Italy.

"Dad, seven hundred thousand tons of orange peels that would have ended up in a Sicilian landfill are now a *fabric!*"

Two hours later we crossed the causeway at the end of Long Island. Orient Harbor sparkled to our right. In front of the yacht club, kids were rigging their dinghies and tacking out to catch the morning breeze. We drove into the village of Orient. Massive shade trees spread their leaves above the old white church. Past the town, we turned onto a sandy lane that wound through a pine grove and came out at a gray-shingled house with white trim. The parking area blazed with a fresh load of bleached clamshells. A bank of wild roses filled the air with scent. The brass lantern mounted by the door glowed from a recent polish.

Annie leapt from the car and charged through the door. By the time I got inside, she was giving Mrs. Cutler a hug and telling her not to bother. But I doubted anything short of chaining her in the basement could keep Dad's housekeeper from whatever the moment called for. In this case, breakfast, and we were sitting at the gleaming table spooning scrambled eggs out of a china serving dish before we'd been inside five minutes. Dad inspired that kind of service. If you wanted to know why, you'd have to ask someone other than me.

He looked older, more sunken in on himself. But his white hair was still thick and his eyes bright with watchfulness, and he still had that way of setting his jaw that reminded me what a ruthless bastard he was. He kept darting his eyes from Annie to me and back again. I wasn't supposed to know about the regular trips Annie made out here. She wanted a relationship with him. She had a hunger for family. I was an only child, and so was Pierrette. With all that had happened to her, Annie felt adrift. She knew how I felt about my father, although I'd never said a word about it to her.

"I know you guys have things to discuss," she said when she'd finished helping Mrs. Cutler clear away the breakfast dishes. She put down a silver carafe freshly filled with coffee. A few minutes later I saw her dash across the lawn in a bathing suit. She ran onto the dock, dropped into a Laser, and went knifing out into the shining bay.

Now we were alone. Most of my bitterness had been blown out in the run around the reservoir, but even the dregs had an acid taste.

Lane Turner was a hard man. He'd made a discovery so important it broke the grip of the old diamond cartel. Before the discovery, it was the cartel that had a lock on how to look for diamonds. After, it was Dad. They tried to buy the secret from him. He'd refused.

He sold his knowledge one mineral grain at a time. Prospectors could send their exploration samples to him, and he'd tell you what they said. Some secrets he kept for himself. He'd have been a wealthy man if he'd sold the cartel what he knew, but that wasn't what he wanted. He wanted his own discovery. He dragged my mother and me out into the African bush to find it. He failed. The man who helped others find diamond mines couldn't find his own. It turned him into an embittered man.

I remembered a tent at night in the Kalahari. A lion padding around the camp. We'd heard the cough. We could smell it—the rank, animal odor. My father hissed for his rifle. But it wasn't in the tent. It was in the truck.

In the morning, he couldn't let it go, blaming my mother. Sneering at her. Useless, he called her. When she brought him his eggs, he grabbed the plate and dumped the contents on her dress. She started to cry. He jeered at her in front of the camp helpers. I was six, and the shame stung me like a lash.

"Why didn't *you* bring the gun?" I shouted. The camp fell silent.

His eyes snapped to me. "Eh?"

My mother grabbed my arm to pull me away, but I yanked free. My eyes were brimming with hot tears. "Why didn't *you* bring the gun!"

His hand snaked out faster than a striking snake. My face had the mark for days.

"You don't approve of Annie coming here," he said. His eyes glittered with malice. Men are always what they used to be. The old lumber lies piled in a corner. The right spark will kindle it again. I was that spark. He couldn't conceal his antagonism. It twisted his mouth.

"I think you know the kind of man I am, Dad," I said. "You should keep it in mind."

"You're vengeful," he spat.

I kept my eyes fixed on his. "She's young," I said.

"You think I can't be trusted." His spite was like a physical ailment for which there was no cure. "Then suddenly you need me. So I have a use after all. Until you get what you want. Then I'm garbage."

"Jimmy Angel," I prompted.

"Did you bring them?"

I took out the garnets and placed them on the table. Even through the dull plastic of the Ziploc bag they glowed with a dark intensity. At the sight of them, the venom drained from his face. The hunger that replaced it was the driving force of his whole life, from the time he was a young chemist with the ink just dry on his PhD. He'd got a postdoc at Harvard and started looking for a way to make his name. And found it.

He took the Ziploc and pushed back his chair and led the way to the little lab. A workbench faced the bay through a wall of windows. A large microscope, a digital scale, and other instruments stood in an orderly array. He placed the bag of garnets beside a pad of bright white paper. He pulled out a stool, sat, and opened the bag. With tweezers, he plucked out a single garnet and placed it on the paper.

He sat as if hypnotized by the stone. It surged with color, deep purple and crimson. He moved it with the tweezers, and the garnet throbbed in the light. Finally he placed it on a glass plate beneath the microscope. He flicked a switch, and a thin beam of light lanced out. A purple flame shivered under the lens. He leaned forward and placed his eye to the instrument. He stared at it for what seemed like minutes. When he sat back, he fished a handkerchief from his back pocket, wiped his eye, and replaced the garnet with another.

"I've only seen garnets like these once before," he said harshly. "Until now, the best ever." He gave me a stern look. "But these are just as good. Classic G10s. Pyrope garnets, very high in chrome. And as you know, because you had to listen to it as a boy," he said, trying on a rueful smile and then letting it go, "high chrome points to diamonds."

"Who sent them?"

He tightened his lips and exhaled through his nose. "You know I can't tell you that," he said. "My clients expect privacy. You know perfectly well how vital that is." He switched off the microscope with an irritated flick.

"Can you say when the client sent them?"

He stared out at the water. "Brought them in person. About a month ago. I shouldn't even tell you that." Far out in the bay, the Laser flashed yellow in the sun. "Let's say I'm doing it for her." He plucked the garnet from the microscope and dropped it with the others. "Maybe we could actually be civil to each other."

I unfolded a copy I'd made of Jimmy's map and spread it out on the bench. He bent over the familiar diamond field. His face recorded anger, and then despair, as he took in the ragged coast of Lac de Gras. He knew the geology well. He'd never set foot in the Arctic, but his work on indicator minerals had helped Jimmy Angel find the first pipe—the discovery that launched the staking rush and uncovered the fabulously rich new diamond zone. After that, other diamond explorers sent him their minerals too.

"You've analyzed garnets from all through here," I said. "If I leave you one, can you tell me where it came from?"

He took in a deep breath and let it out slowly. He raked the garnets together in a tight group, like raking the embers of a fire. The stones flickered darkly. "Maybe. I don't know. I'll have to go through my old records. The problem is, to say for certain where a mineral comes from, you have to have a good sample of minerals from the same place. Then you have a big enough data set to identify shared characteristics."

I pulled out the small parcel with the garnet I'd taken at Clip Bay. It contained a handful of dirt and loose stones. "This one has surrounding soil. Is it enough?"

"I'll try to do something with it." He gazed at the glowing stones. "If these G10s are all from the same pipe," he said, his voice cracking with bitterness, "it will be the richest diamond pipe on the planet."

He did his best to look cheerful for Annie when we left, but his posture betrayed him. He sagged with defeat.

"Do you hate him, Dad?" she said when we were going through Mattituck. "I'm not a child. I know he was mean to you when you were a kid."

"I don't hate him, Annie."

She let it go at that. There was a lot of other material to cover, including an engrossing account of how grape skin can be turned into a material that feels like leather. "I need you to promise me, Dad, you will never wear a garment made from the skin of a real animal."

She dropped me off at Teterboro airport and gave me a bone-crushing hug and drove off in her red sports car.

You have to be happy when that happens.

That's what I kept telling myself.

25

A light drizzle was falling as Tabitha and I left Peterson Air Force Base and skirted Colorado Springs. The big, long-haul rigs that own the night boomed overhead as we went under the I-25. Tabitha drove.

We took Colorado Route 115 south for a couple of miles, exited right onto NORAD Road and began the crawl uphill through the switchback turns that ended at the floodlit entrance to the Cheyenne Mountain Complex.

The air was cool when we got out and heavy with the sweet perfume of ponderosa pines. Two young women in gray air-force fatigues waited at the guard post, one of them with a sidearm in a white canvas holster. The other wore the single bar of a first lieutenant. She watched carefully as we showed our IDs to the gate staff, then led the way through a series of concrete obstacles and into the mountain.

"Been here before, sir, ma'am?" the lieutenant asked as we turned right down a second tunnel. We said no, and the officer gave a brief description of the command headquarters of the joint US-Canada North American Air Defense Command.

In the 1960s, miners took five years to excavate 693,000 tons of rock from the granite mountain. That left 2,500 feet of granite to protect the spring-mounted surveillance and battle-fighting center inside from a direct missile strike. Two twenty-five-ton blast doors would dead-bolt into the rock in the event of an attack, and while the rest of the world faced nuclear holocaust, less than two hundred people would sit inside the rock and fight World War III.

"There's six million gallons of water and 510,000 gallons of diesel fuel in reservoirs cut out of the rock, and a 10.5-megawatt power plant."

At the end of a maze of passageways, the lieutenant opened a door to a dim room where two young men, one with a sergeant's stripes, sat at a console watching a strip of desert scroll by on a screen.

"This is what you wanted to see, ma'am," the lieutenant said to Tabitha. She left and closed the door behind her, and Tabitha and I sat down.

"This crew is flying a drone in Syria," Tabitha said. "You know how it works. Troops on the ground laser-paint the target, and these guys manage the kill. I wanted to see how this new warhead works. This is a simulation." She leaned forward. "Go ahead," she said.

"One minute to target acquisition," the sergeant said. "We are flying a Reaper armed with a Hellfire variant, the R9X." He turned to Tabitha and grinned. "We call it the Ninja."

An open truck appeared in the distance. The camera on the Reaper zoomed in to reveal a group of figures seated in the back. Cloth dummies. A red dot appeared in the middle of the group. "Target acquired," said the sergeant. "Fire." The missile scratched a line of vapor into the air, and a moment later two of the figures on the truck exploded into shreds. The sergeant turned to Tabitha.

"Almost zero collateral damage, ma'am."

"And those are, like, swords?"

"We call it a kinetic warhead," he said. "No explosive. Six blades snap out into position. Excellent on soft targets."

A sharp knock sounded on the door, and the lieutenant stuck her head in. "They're ready, ma'am. The event is underway."

"They're expecting you, Alex," Tabitha said. "I have another meeting. I'll see you after."

The Global Strategic Warning and Space Surveillance Center was a cavernous hall awash in dim green light. At a curved console, servicemen in headsets monitored the satellite feeds. An outline of North America glowed on the enormous central screen. The map included the surrounding oceans and the encroaching landmass of eastern Russia.

"Our target arrived a little earlier than we-all thought," the three-star general said in a southern drawl. He nodded to an officer at the console. "Switch it, Corky." The map of North America vanished, and the big screen changed to a solid, murky green.

"This is underwater real-time surveillance of a passage through the Bering Strait. It's not a camera picture. This here's an image constructed by software from sensors and data collectors tethered to the seabed. We don't operate the system, but our navy friends patch it through when we ask." He glanced at the console. "Corky?"

"A thousand yards, sir. Sixteen knots."

"Chinese boomer," the general said. "Coming up pretty fast. We've been tracking her since she left Yulin two days ago."

"Five hundred yards."

"Here she comes," the general said.

A hush fell on the immense space. The quiet chatter at the console stopped entirely. All eyes were fixed on the central screen. It was hard to see at first. Just a blurry patch of darker green that formed in the center of the screen. As the submarine advanced, the image swiftly changed. It darkened, then hardened into a black onrushing shape with stubby dive planes and a conning tower. The screen snapped to a side view. It was like watching a train go by. No one moved. A clock peeped out the seconds until the image slid away and the map jumped into view again. A winking red light appeared in the middle of the Bering Strait.

"Jin class nuclear submarine," the general said. "Carries twelve JL-2 ballistic missiles, each with a range of 4,600 miles. Just to put that in terms we can all understand," he said, making it clear he meant me, "a missile fired from that sub right now would arrive in Houston in twenty minutes. Every city in Canada and the United States is within range." He turned to a Canadian brigadier standing beside him. "General, I think you have some observations?"

"Thank you, sir. Here's the situation," he said to me. "The polar region is rich in resources such as oil and minerals. Climate change has lengthened the shipping season in the Arctic. Those resources are therefore increasingly easy to get at. The Chinese are a resource-starved nation. They want a share of the Arctic. They now describe themselves as a 'near-Arctic power.' Chinese submarines and surveillance ships have increased their presence in the Arctic Ocean."

He was a stocky sparkplug of a soldier, as straight as a pipe. His fatigues crackled with starch, and he spoke in the clipped monotone of a military briefing. But now his eyes took on a sharper look.

"Of the keenest interest now," he said, "would be any Chinese industrial activity in the Canadian north. Any industrial activity capable of retasking—we would consider that to be strategic." You could have heard a pin drop. He looked carefully at me to satisfy himself that I understood. Then he snapped his eyes to his superior. "I believe I have articulated the view of the command, sir."

"Y'all nailed it, General," the three-star said, patting him on the shoulder. The brigadier kept a stony face. He didn't look like the kind of man to pat, even if you had three stars, as the one who did have them now seemed to realize. He dropped his hand and nodded stiffly at the officers around him. "I'll show you out," he said to me, and led the way to an exit. The first lieutenant was waiting for me.

"Y'all understand what he meant by 'strategic'?" the three-star said.

"Time to stop talking."

"There you go."

I thought he was going to pat me on the shoulder too, but the central screen went to green again, and in the quiet of the vast room, the low voices died away. The countdown clock began to peep.

"Five thousand yards," a voice intoned. "Seventeen knots." The three-star walked away and joined his officers. Another Chinese boomer was coming through the strait.

26

The morning sun was flicking darts of green light through the pines when we came out of the mountain. A fall of snow glistened on the nearby peaks. We turned our passes in at the gate and went snaking down the mountainside. A pair of red-tailed hawks rode the thermals, waiting for the sun to coax a cottontail from its hiding place.

When we got back to Peterson, an escort car met us at the gate and led us to a distant corner of the base, where a wooden house nestled in a thick grove of pines. The house was painted dark brown. It had a balcony that made it look like a Swiss chalet. A crewcut man with a master sergeant's insignia on his sleeve hopped out of the escort car's front seat and opened Tabitha's door.

"Your car will be here at fourteen hundred hours, ma'am," he said to her. "Yours, sir, a little later. We'll have an exact time as soon as your flight is confirmed." He delivered a sharp salute, hopped back in the car, and we were alone.

We'd hardly spoken on the flight from New York. Tabitha had been tied up in a back-and-forth with White House staff. The plane she'd be catching later would take her to San Diego, where the president was delivering a major speech about American naval power, with the home port of the Pacific fleet as her backdrop.

This was a Tabitha I hadn't seen before. The cog in the gearwheel of world power. A hard package, but immaculately wrapped. Her mass of hair was pulled back from her face into a knot speared with an ivory pin. She wore a dark gray jacket with a white silk T-shirt. The shirt didn't look as if it had been made from orange peels. The black pencil skirt emphasized her slender hips and long, bare legs. The stiletto heels made a sharper click than her usual slingbacks as she led the way up a flagstone path and into the house.

The main room had a pair of sofas in front of a stone fireplace. An open kitchen took up one side of the room. She tossed her briefcase on a sofa, strode across the white broadloom, and made her way behind the granite counter. Shoving her phone in a pocket, she yanked open the huge Sub-Zero fridge and grabbed a carton of apple juice. She opened it and took a gulp straight from the carton. A thin dribble of juice glistened on her chin. She wiped it away and stared at me across the room. The phone in her pocket made an urgent buzz. She grabbed it and glanced at the screen.

"Fuck," she muttered, and took the call. "Kowalski."

She listened, her lips tightening.

"No," she said sharply. "The Chinese don't have as many boomers as we do. They have *half* as many boomers. Jesus Christ, Todd. It's not the darkest secret in the world. You can look it up on Wikipedia. The point the president will make is that they have six more under construction. She'll say that their intention is to surpass us, and that's why they are a clear and present danger."

She ended the call without another word, put the phone down on the counter, and kicked off the stilettos. They banged against a lamp and landed on the carpet. She took another swig of apple juice.

"Did you bring it?" I said.

She padded around from behind the counter, opened her briefcase, and handed me a palm-sized, plastic device. It was surprisingly light for what it would do—suck the data from a nearby cell phone in less than twenty seconds. You can buy a Universal Forensic Extraction Device online for two hundred dollars. But you won't get one of these.

"This is the new one?"

"Uh-huh."

"And it can unscramble coded data?"

"It can get past any security Lily has."

"Who said anything about Lily?"

She shook her head and laughed. "C'mere, bruiser," she said. She grabbed my hand and headed up the stairs.

The broadloom continued on the second floor. I followed her through a large bedroom and out onto the balcony. Snow-covered peaks blazed in the clear sky. A pair of B-1B bombers sat gleaming in front of an enormous hangar. A C-130 transport had just landed on the main runway. The roar of its four powerful engines reverberated across the airfield.

"After 9/11," she said, "the military created a new Unified Command Plan. This base is the headquarters of Northern Command. In the event of an attack on the homeland, this is where we run the defense of the United States."

She leaned on the railing. A few strands of hair slipped loose in the light breeze and caressed her cheek.

"That's what I look at all day long—attack scenarios. Who's got the latest weapons? Where are they putting them? Did they move missiles in the night? Are they retargeting? State actors. Non-state actors. Ships and submarines. It never stops. The nightmare is we'll miss something. Some play will get past us. That's what we're afraid of now. The thing we'll miss."

She went back inside and shrugged off her jacket. She dropped it on the carpet and sat on the bed.

"And that's what you're afraid of too. You don't trust Lily. Why would you?" She spoke the words matter-of-factly. "We don't trust, Alex. They pay us not to." She reached back and pulled the pin from her hair. It cascaded onto her shoulders. "You've got alarms on every one of her accounts, waiting to see if she'll move money and where she'll move it to."

She stood up, unzipped her skirt, and let it slip to the floor. She tugged off the silk T-shirt and dropped it on the skirt. She moved against me and took my face in her hands and kissed me softly on the mouth. "You know she'll betray you," she murmured.

"But so will you."

She pulled the covers back and slid into bed and lay there with her hair spilling across the pillows. She unsnapped her bra and dropped it on the floor. "I'm not asking for anything, Alex."

I'd never seen her look so desolate.

I still had the UFED in my hand. I dropped it in my pocket and went downstairs and walked to the passenger terminal.

27

I was alone in the cabin. The digital map on the bulkhead showed that we would soon be over Great Slave Lake when the cockpit door opened and the captain came back.

"Just a heads-up," he said. "Going to be a bumpy approach. There's a big system that's moved in. Turned into a full blizzard."

"And they didn't close the airport?"

"They did, but this is a NORAD flight. We don't need civilian air-traffic control. Canadian military ATC will bring us in. Somebody wants you down there."

Instead of closing the cockpit door behind him, he latched it open. We'd already started our descent. The plane hit a downdraft, bounced hard, and climbed back to its approach path. The whine of the engines rose and fell as the pilots struggled to keep the plane on an orderly descent. I watched the approach on the bulkhead display. The plane shuddered and thumped as we crossed the lake and reached the far shore and flew up the bay toward the city. The snow streaming past the window obliterated the wingtip navigation lights. The big landing lights switched on and drilled a hole in the storm.

I caught a brief glimpse of the city to the left before it was wiped from view again. We continued to descend. Then a powerful gust buffeted the plane. It slewed with a sickening lurch, then hit another downdraft. The gray water of the bay appeared through the snow. The gale lashed the waves into a froth. We were dropping fast. The pilots grasped the throttle, the co-pilot's hand on top of the pilot's. In a fluid movement they brought the engines to full power. We climbed back into the driving snow.

I thought we were going to circle and make another approach. Instead, I found myself pressed against the window as the jet tilted sharply to the left in a tight turn. Patches of light flashed by below. The plane leveled and then came down fast. A road appeared with streetlights, the airport fence, then the broad slashes of white that marked the beginning of the runway. The wheels must have been almost on the ground when a savage crosswind punched us sideways. An alarm went *whoop whoop* in the cockpit, followed by a stern mechanical voice that said "Pull up." We didn't. I caught sight of a fire engine starting onto the field with its strobes flashing. The airframe moaned, and slowly, by inches, the nose came around to face down the runway and the pilot slammed the jet down hard. The cabin lights went out, and a coffee urn broke loose from the galley and shot across the plane, bursting against the main door and spraying the cabin with scalding drops.

Outside, the fire engine appeared out of the snow and paralleled us on the runway. A fireman had a nozzle trained on the plane in case the landing had ruptured a fuel line. I saw the pilot give the fire crew a thumbs-up from the cockpit. Five minutes later we were parked on an apron beside a huge shape that loomed from the snowstorm like the phantom of a giant. The US Air Force Galaxy.

❖

A young two-star in rumpled gray fatigues. The name Mackenzie stitched in black letters on the pocket. We'd met before, but if he wasn't going to mention it, that was fine. We sat in his small office in the belly of the plane. Instead of the usual load of tanks and helicopters, the cargo deck held a mobile command center. Radar screens displayed the information collected by a pair of Boeing 707s fitted with airborne warning and control systems. The AWACS planes were circling high above the Arctic. The stream of data they supplied helped refine the information pouring in from satellites and from a pair of American hunter-killer submarines shadowing the Chinese boomers. A young lieutenant with a clump of red hair stood with his hands clasped behind his back.

"It's not a real alert," Mackenzie said. "It's just a shit-show with lots of expensive units in play so the Chinese will know we can afford the gas." He lit a cigarette, dragged deeply, and blew the smoke into an induction fan that carried it outside. "The Canadians know bullshit when they see it. They think it's a cat's paw in the guise of a joint NORAD exercise so we can spy on them and interfere in their domestic affairs."

"After all we've done for them," I said.

The lieutenant with the red hair stifled a laugh. The general shot him a hard glance and stubbed out his cigarette. I heard an irritated snuffle from beneath his desk. He pushed back his chair and stepped over to a wall map. A dilapidated bulldog tottered to its feet and followed him. When it reached where he was standing, it slumped to the floor, gasping for breath. "Who's a good boy," Mackenzie said absently. He peered at a line that straggled northeast from Yellowknife through the wilderness.

"That's the winter road," he said, stabbing a finger at the line. "It runs pretty close to this place here," he indicated Clip Bay. "The place where they found the remains of the American prospector."

"Jimmy Angel," I said.

"Sure."

He studied the map and the photographs pinned to the map. They had that quality of hyperrealism that makes a satellite shot look like the surface of another planet. Time codes ran across the top and exact latitude and longitude. Surveillance targets were pinpointed with circles and crosshairs. One showed the landing strip at the Ekati mine. Another, Jimmy Angel's campsite.

"What I need to know is this," he said. "Is that Chinese guy going to build a mine there?"

"The Xi twins," the red-haired lieutenant interjected.

Mackenzie shrugged. "Let's stick with who's calling the shots."

The lieutenant was going to say something else, but the general clenched his jaw, and he shut up.

"Whether he greenlights a mine," I said, "would depend on what he learns about the target. I don't know the exact state of his knowledge. Normally, if he thinks it's promising, the first thing he'd do is dig a big enough hole to take out what they call a bulk sample. Then he counts all the diamonds in it and extrapolates the richness of the deposit."

"That first hole, the one for the sample—would that involve a lot of machinery and steel?"

"Yes."

"And that would all have to come up the winter road?"

I waited until he turned away from the map and looked at me.

"Help me out," I said. "I thought the army had engineers on the payroll who could answer questions like this."

His face and hands were crisscrossed with tiny scars. Something in his military past had torn him up, and the surgeons who'd repaired him had been in a hurry. A smooth strip on his forehead and another on his chin showed where they'd grafted on skin harvested from elsewhere on his body. The face that looked out from that past was without bitterness, but it had been emptied of illusion.

"I remember you, Turner," he said. "You killed that psycho colonel. You and I exchanged information."

"Yes," I said.

"Well, not this time. I guess your people tell you what they think you need to know. I'm not here to fill in the blanks. There's a whole shitload of Chinese hardware milling around up here, and that's my problem. This"—he slapped his hand against the map—"this is yours. I use the assets they give me. At the moment, you are one of those. So if you don't mind."

Picking up on his master's tone, the bulldog growled and struggled to his feet. He looked around with bleary eyes and snuffled through his mashed-up face. "For Christ's sake, Carstairs," the general snapped, "the dog needs a piss."

"Yes, sir," the lieutenant said. He snapped a leash on the bulldog and led it outside.

"The ice road is the cheapest way to move heavy equipment into the Barrens," I said, "but they don't have to wait for it. If they don't care about the cost, they can fly in what they need."

"The big mines can," Mackenzie said. "They've got landing strips."

"Fan could build his own."

"In the middle of what's basically a slab of rock with no roads?"

"Easier than you think. There's a big supply of gravel out there. Dumped by melting glaciers in the last ice age. It sits all over the Barrens in neat piles called eskers. In fact"—I went to the map and pointed to the red circle that marked Jimmy's camp—"there's a big one right behind this site."

It didn't take long for the general to understand what that meant.

"They chopper in a couple of backhoes," he said.

I nodded. "I'd be surprised if it took them longer than two weeks."

"Well," he said, staring at one of the drone shots, "now we know they weren't just enjoying the view."

This one was time coded yesterday. Before the blizzard. Late in the day. Long shadows extended from the small group standing on the esker at Clip Bay. The satellite's enhancing software had worked like a charm. In the crosshairs, Fan—hair shaved close at the sides with the shock of black hair on top combed straight back. Pale skin and coal-black eyes. Even the people outside the crosshairs were in sharp focus. Tinkerbell bulging placidly beside the boss. And on the other side, hands shoved into the pockets of her cargo pants and an unreadable expression on her crooked face, Mitzi Angel.

28

By the time I left the Galaxy, the blizzard had blown itself out. A biting north wind took its place. It howled around the aircraft and across the field. A black Chevy Tahoe with a two-star license plate waited on the tarmac with the engine running. Nobody offered me a lift.

Carstairs stood with his hands thrust into the pockets of a parka. The bulldog shivered in the cold. It whimpered and pawed at Carstairs, who hunched more deeply into his parka. "This cold front's supposed to pass through," he said. He'd been waiting for me.

"You wanted to make some point about the twins?"

But he'd changed his mind. He shook his head. "Not a big deal."

I turned up my collar and set off into the wind.

My eyes watered, and the tears turned to ice. A white gauze of snow slithered along the concrete. I passed a Canadian army Humvee bristling with antennas parked on a taxiway. A soldier in the front seat had a pair of binoculars trained on the Galaxy. The only other airplane in sight was a large business jet parked at the terminal. On its tail fin, the yellow iDragon spread its claws and spewed a tongue of flame.

Luc was waiting for me when I came through the doors into the terminal. His face was twisted into the fiendish grin that no one would mistake for a smile.

"I thought you were toast on that landing," he said, not sounding as if it had bothered him much.

The white SUV was waiting outside with Cedric at the wheel. Luc got into the back with me. A Plexiglas panel separated the front seat from the back. Luc slid it shut with a bang, and we drove out of the airport and along the highway into town. The back seat still smelled of vomit, but at least I wasn't the only one who had to breathe it.

Luc scrolled through his phone for a minute, but he wasn't reading anything. He was mad and trying to control it.

"You know," he said, shoving the phone in his pocket and staring straight ahead, "you're the most powerful nation in the history of the world, and the richest. Yet also—and here's what the rest of us struggle with—the most paranoid. What's it going to be today? That's the question every country has to ask. Who's showing up today, the paranoid asshole or the washout who screws his allies? We just never know."

He was wound up tight, clenching his fists until the knuckles were white. It was clear that the joint NORAD exercise was a long way from being as joint as the Canadians would have liked. But I wasn't his therapist.

"Tell you what, Luc. Next time somebody flies a couple of planeloads of your citizens into a building in Toronto, give me a shout and we'll have a chat about paranoia. Until then, what do you want?"

The window had frosted over. Luc didn't answer. He rubbed a clear patch in the frost with his hand and stared out glumly. We drove through the small downtown and turned left at the bay. We crossed the causeway and drove up a hill to a restaurant at the top.

Cedric went straight to the bar and ordered a coffee. Luc led the way to a table by the windows with a view of the bay. A waiter wearing Ugg boots and a fur hat with dangling ear flaps gave us each a menu. Then she bent down with her hands on her knees so she could gaze into our eyes. "You will never forgive yourself if you don't try the northern buffalo poutine," she said.

"What's that?" I asked her.

"It's a variation on the classic Quebec poutine, but instead of just curds and gravy, it has buffalo meat too." She flashed her white teeth. "We're famous for it."

"Burger," Luc said. "Medium. The works."

"Make that two," I said, handing back the menu. There was a long list of things I'd never forgive myself for. One more wouldn't matter.

Luc waited until she'd left before he spoke. "Who's fighting who here, Alex? A week ago I get a notice that you're on your way to investigate a missing American. Your paperwork says something about protecting the interests of American shareholders. Fine. Turns out we're interested in what's going on too, so I think, let's see what he finds out. OK so far?"

Luc was making it sound like a collaboration. But the two times we'd sat down for a chat—when I first arrived, and later, after the attack in the Barrens—Luc was the only one calling the shots.

"Now there's a two-star general parked in his plane at Yellowknife airport, AWACS in our airspace, and Canadian officers slamming doors in our face when we try to find out what's going on."

"They're not briefing you?"

"They say it's a joint NORAD exercise, but they don't seem too happy."

We finished eating. The waiter with the Ugg boots cleared the table and brought us coffee. She pitched the Saskatoon berry pie.

"Will I forgive myself if I take a pass?" I said.

She winked. "*I* won't forgive you."

"Two," I told her, "plus one for the guy at the bar."

Luc stared out the window. A Canadian army helicopter clattered past in the direction of the airport. "It's not just this wargames charade that's hard to figure out, Alex. It's Fan. You saw his plane out there. How does it make sense for him to fly to Yellowknife? He must know he's a suspect for the attack on the Otter and for Jimmy Angel's death. Why come here and rub our faces in it?"

"Too big to take down. He's got our countries at each other's throats over his sister. He's betting there's no way you'll detain him. And you won't."

He shook his head. "I still have the same problem. It's not like he's taking over Apple. He could run this from his phone. It's a diamond play. You drill the target. Find diamonds: dig a mine. Don't find diamonds: go home."

"He's not going home, Luc. He's got eighteen tractor-trailer loads of some kind of mining equipment that he went to a lot of trouble to bring up here."

Luc nodded. "You were counting too."

The pie was great. We ate in silence, washed it down with coffee, and watched the F-18s make low passes over the airport.

"Your girlfriend spent a lot of time with Mitzi Angel when you were away," Luc said when we'd settled up with Ugg boots and were putting on our coats. "Why is that, do you think?"

"You know," I said. "Girl stuff. Nails, hair. What's your favorite color."

We walked outside. Cedric got in the driver's side and started the SUV. Luc climbed in and sat looking out the windshield.

"I knew it had to be something simple," he said.

That night I ordered a trace on Mitzi. FinCEN would locate her bank accounts and log every movement in and out. I wanted to see if anything connected her to Lily.

Outside, the sky was closing like a steel lid. A slate-gray slab coasted in and crushed the frail day. No message from Lily since I got back.

I went out on the terrace and did some stretches and shadow-boxed, punching through a series of rapid combinations. Like Bruce Willis would do if he'd discovered his girlfriend was playing him. I punched and threw in a few kicks and breathed in the cold, pure air to drive out the confused thoughts and focus my mind into a hard, calculating instrument. Like Bruce. Then I went inside and lay in bed and stared at the digital clock while it counted down the night.

She got home late. I didn't hear her key. I didn't hear her steps because she was part cat. A puff of air told me the bedroom door had opened. Her clothes rustled to the floor. She slipped beneath the covers like a blade and pressed her cold body against me. She twined her fingers in my hair and whispered a Russian phrase. It sounded romantic, but I don't speak Russian. It could have been, "Hey, Dumbo, you'll never guess what I was doing." She fell asleep like a stone dropped into a well, the way she always did. I lay there the rest of the night listening to the noises of the building and wondering what Bruce would do.

29

At five A.M. I got out of bed and grabbed some clothes and went quietly out of the bedroom. I left the door ajar. In the living room I dressed in the dark, then stepped back to the bedroom door and listened. Nothing. I found her purse, took out her phone, and placed it flat on the counter. I pressed the little switch on the UFED and rested it on top of her phone. Twenty seconds later a tiny light flashed green. I pocketed the UFED and slipped the phone back in her purse. The keys to the F350 were on the coffee table. Lifting them carefully so they didn't make a noise, I left the apartment and took the elevator down to the parking garage. I drove to the McDonald's on Old Airport Road and had a bacon, egg, and cheese biscuit with a side of hash browns and a large black coffee. Have that for breakfast and try feeling bad. Not possible.

When I was through, I got two large coffees and a baked apple pie to go and drove out of town. The highway wound through the forest until it left the last of the houses behind and snaked its way out into the lakes and the granite hills. A silver light came off the snow and shone into the spiky branches of the spruce trees. The turnoff to the Dogrib village of Dettah came up on the right, and then the Chinese depot. The parking lot was empty. The guard in the gatehouse was watching TV, the flicker of blue light splashing on his face.

I drove past and kept on through the forest until I came to the end of the road. I left the truck in a lot carved out of the forest and walked down to the shore of Tibbitt Lake, where I sipped my coffee and stared out at the dark water. The winter road would start right here when the ice was thick enough. Teams of huge plows would head out onto the lake and clear away the snow. It would take them six weeks to complete the road. When they were done, a four-hundred-mile-long highway would twist its way across the lakes and over land portages into the heart of the diamond field. When everything was ready, four trucks at a time, each with a forty-ton load, would head out onto the ice at thirty-minute intervals to begin the annual resupply of the diamond mines.

I got out of the truck, walked to the edge of the lake, and knelt down to inspect the thin plate of ice forming at the shore. The ice extended no more than a couple of feet. It would be months before the plows arrived and construction of the winter road began.

A blush of pink light was seeping into the eastern sky. The fringe of ice around the lake took on a rosy glow. I went back to the truck and ate the apple pie. I opened the second coffee and placed it in the cup holder on the console, settled back in the big leather seat, and dumped the contents of the UFED into my phone. The pink glow faded, and dawn broke on the forest. I tapped in my password and opened Lily's email.

Lily was an orderly person. Files and emails spic and span. Every-thing neatly placed in clearly labeled folders. However, she was also deceitful, so the labels didn't mean a thing to anyone but her. Lily wasn't about transparency. You don't run a long-term theft operation against a state mining company and its gangster bosses by leaving a trail through your data. I had the advantage of knowing a fair amount about her finances already, just from tracking the millions she was trying to hide from me. The problem was that Lily had been a large-scale diamond thief long before I met her. For sure she had money in places I didn't know about.

What did I really suspect? I asked myself. Start there. I suspected that she had a plan, formed before we got here, and was now executing it under my nose. I'd never find it by rummaging haphazardly through her documents. I needed a system. As I sat there in the truck, I tried to put myself in Lily's mind. An organized and tidy mind. What would she need before engaging in an enterprise that would certainly have a large sum of money at its heart? What did she need before she could move that money? One thing for sure. A lawyer.

Lily was obsessed with the minutiae of the law. She wanted to keep what she had, and that meant scrupulous observance of the rules. She broke the rules to get the money, obeyed them to keep it. That meant she would want advice. When a banker or a lawyer gives advice, there are two people they need to protect. The client and themselves. That doesn't happen with a phone call. So now I knew what to look for. An attachment.

I searched her emails for files with a PDF identifier and soon had a list of about twenty. I clicked on the latest, and there it was.

Leclerc, Goldberg, and MacTavish
Lawyers, Notaries

1 Place Ville Marie
Montréal, Québec H3B 2B6, Canada

June 29, 2020

Dear Lily,

In reply to your query of June 21, the numbered company 86043 Compagnie Limitée is a duly incorporated private company under the laws of the Province of Québec and domiciled at this office. As I confirmed when we spoke, you may buy, sell, trade, and dispose of investments in any Canadian property or properties at your sole discretion as provided in the articles of incorporation. There are no restrictions on such activities.

Please find enclosed as directed by you a certified cheque drawn on the company's account and payable to you in the amount of $2.5 million (two million five hundred thousand dollars).

Please do not hesitate to call if I can assist you in any other way.

I remain as always,

Yours sincerely,

(Auguste Leclerc)

Managing Partner

He'd signed the letter *Gus* and added the scribbled line: *Adrienne sends her best.*

The letter told me several things. For one, Lily had a company I hadn't known about. For another, she'd had it long enough that she was on a first-name basis with the top dog at a high-end law firm. Adrienne must be Leclerc's wife, so they were on close enough terms that Lily had met her. My guess was that she'd had the company from her first days in Antwerp, before I'd turned her.

Most people know Canada as a first-world country with free health care and a reputation as one of the world's good guys. That's not the Canada everybody knows. People who don't need the free health care like another thing about it—its 24/7 money laundry. The dirty cash moves through discreet law firms with toney offices in Toronto, Vancouver, and Montreal. And it moves quietly. I'd lived in Montreal with Lily for six months and never met Leclerc. Not to mention Adrienne.

The certified check meant that Lily was walking around with a two-and-a-half-million-dollar piece of paper she could turn into cash with a signature. And whatever it was she had in mind, she had the jump on me. The letter with the check was dated before I'd even learned about Jimmy Angel.

What explained it? Lily must have known about an investment opportunity, or she wouldn't have even come to Yellowknife. Had Jimmy approached her himself, then changed his mind and done a deal with the twins instead? Or had she developed a relationship with Mitzi? A deal with either of them would account for Lily's obsession with the garnets, because the garnets were the evidence of what they had to sell—a diamond pipe.

But where did Mei come in? That sudden rush to Vancouver. I didn't for a second believe Lily's nonsense about Mei needing a sisterly chat about diamonds. Mei didn't need that, and certainly not from Lily. She and Fan had their own experts. But Mei had needed something—something she either couldn't get from Fan or was afraid to ask for—and Lily had brought it to her.

I forwarded the letter to Tommy. He would give Leclerc's bank accounts a shake, and see what fell out. Then I drove back to Yellowknife. There was another job to do. An urgent one. And a lot more dangerous than rifling Lily's mail.

30

I t's a cinch, darling," she said, turning to me with sparkling eyes. "We'll come back tonight."

Lily loved a crime.

We were sitting in the F350 on a dirt road that squiggled through the bush and came out on a rocky hill behind the Chinese depot. On that side, the forest ran right up to the fence. Even in the flat gray light I could see the coiled razor wire glinting along the top. Between the fence and a rear fire door lay an open strip of ten or twelve feet. I had my binoculars aimed at the corner of the building.

"Mark," I said when the guard appeared. Lily tapped her phone to stop the timer. "How long this time?"

"Thirty minutes," she said. "Same as last time. Like clockwork. They make the circuit every half hour."

We timed him as he made his way along the back of the building, stopped to check the fire door, and disappeared around the next corner. Two minutes. We'd have twenty-eight minutes to breach the fence, disarm the fire-door alarm, find out what kind of machinery, or even electronics, was inside, and get back through the fence before he appeared again.

I turned around and drove slowly back down the narrow track. Lily was aglow with anticipation. In her excitement she looked so fresh and alive—I don't know, so open—that I had a sudden urge to stop the truck right there in the trees, tell her what I knew, and ask her straight out what she was up to. But then I remembered who we were.

Father Louis was waiting in his car when we got back. He followed us into the garage and parked beside us. He hauled a bulging hockey bag from his trunk, and we rode upstairs. Lily made him a double espresso and put it beside him while he laid out the contents of the bag.

"Where do you get all this stuff?" I said.

He tossed back the espresso, put the cup back down, and turned his bright blue eyes to me. "People hear the word of God. They change," he said, picking up a sawed-off Beretta twelve-gauge and examining it. He racked the pump and hefted the gun. "In their new lives, they don't need these. I help them understand that."

I didn't doubt it. I'd run him through the computer. Yellowknife had been struggling with a wave of drug crime, and some kids had got hurt. That had stopped when Father Louis arrived to take up his new duties as the parish priest. He had a skill set over and above what you'd pick up in the seminary.

He was what Catholics call a "late vocation," the term for someone who comes to the priesthood after trying some other line of work. In his case, bedlam. He'd been an enforcer for a Quebec City biker gang. One afternoon, in an RV park on the St. Lawrence River, the gang had torched a motor home owned by the head of a rival outfit. As it turned out, the target wasn't there. But his six-year-old daughter was.

When the priest heard what happened, he got on his bike, rode to the clubhouse, went inside without a word and blew the leader's head off with a shotgun. I don't know what make. It wasn't in the file. He took a few bullets but got away. The bikers hunted him until, a few days later, a thumb drive arrived in the mail at the Sûreté du Québec gang unit in Montreal. The cops rolled up the club in a week.

The Mounties had taken our weapons as part of their investigation of the attack in the Barrens. It didn't seem like a good idea to ask for them back. Canadian law doesn't take the same broad-minded view about the possession of assault rifles and submachine guns as we do.

I put the Beretta back but kept a really nice Heckler & Koch submachine pistol with a suppressor. I loaded it with dum-dums. With the silencer, it would make no more sound than a light cough, and the dum-dums would turn whatever they hit into mush. He had some flash-bang grenades too, so I took a couple. He'd also got hold of some Fiocchi Extrema, Lily's favorite ammunition. She still had her little Glock.

Last, I grabbed the wire snips. He'd brought those too.

Lily and I left the garage at midnight. I drove around Yellowknife for twenty minutes checking for a tail. Then I took the highway that led out of town. The streetlights ended and the last house slipped by and the highway wound into the forest. Five minutes later, a bloom of light appeared in the trees. We rounded a bend, passed the Dettah road, and the main gate to the Chinese depot came into view. Banks of floodlights on steel pylons poured an intense illumination onto the sprawling installation. A steel barrier with a red stop sign blocked the entry lane. A quarter mile past the gate, I turned off the headlights and slipped onto the track that led through the woods.

The trees slashed the moonlight into patterns on the snow. We got out where the road ended on the rocky hill and picked our way down through the pine and spruce until we came to the fence. Fifteen minutes later we heard the crackle of the foot patrol's radio. He came around the corner of the warehouse and trudged along the fence until he reached the fire door. He checked it, turned his key in the security box, continued along the back of the warehouse, and disappeared around the far corner.

"When we're in," I whispered, "you take the right. I'll go left. Maximum time inside: ten minutes."

I cut through the fence, and we ran across the open strip to the fire door. We stood in the shadows and listened. I disarmed the alarm. The lock took two minutes to pick. I opened the door, and we stepped in.

The smell was overpowering. Dense and damp. It stung my eyes. My nose filled with the odor. It wasn't what I'd expected. Mining equipment would have smelled of oil and steel and the strong smell of huge rubber tires. There was none of that. The pungent odor—it was wood. The warehouse was filled with the almost dizzying smell of sawn wood.

I peered into the huge interior. Pitch black. A warning went off inside my head. Too dark. I tried to think of a single industrial building I'd ever been inside that didn't have night-lights. I was going to signal Lily to go back, but she'd already melted into the darkness.

As my eyes adjusted I could just distinguish massive black shapes. They towered to the ceiling. Narrow aisles separated one immense cube from the next. The smell was so thick it was choking.

I touched the side of a block and felt the coarse texture. At the end of a stack, I stepped into the narrow space that separated it from the next. As I eased into the slot I felt a sharp stab against my chest. I froze, then very slowly raised my hand and examined the spear-like tip. That's when I realized what they were. Staking posts. The whole warehouse was filled with staking posts. I was about to step from the crevice when I heard a muffled sound from the other side of the room, followed by the squeak of shoes on concrete. The sounds of a silent struggle. Someone had caught Lily. They'd been waiting.

I eased the HK from my jacket and screwed on the silencer. Then I heard another sound, this one closer. I listened and heard it again. The careful, slow intake of a man controlling his breath. He was approaching along the side of the posts.

I reached into my pocket and drew out one of the flash-bangs. I stood stock-still. He breathed again. I couldn't hear him move, but he was closer. He must be waiting too, not sure where I was. When he took another breath, I ripped off the detonator and flipped the grenade into the aisle. In the confined space it made a deafening boom and emitted a blinding flash of light. I stepped from cover with the HK ready, and a hand like a steel glove clamped onto my wrist and twisted hard. The pistol clattered to the floor. I looked up to see a beatific smile and a cocked fist the size of an anvil.

"Tinkerbell," I said, and the world went black.

31

A freight train went charging through my head, slammed into my skull, and headed around for another run. Needles of hard white light pierced my eyes. The left side of my face felt caved in. My chin rested on my collarbone. I heard a light drumming sound, like rain pattering on metal. I struggled to lift my head, and opened my eyes enough to see a face glowering across a desk. The light from a desk lamp stabbed through my eyes into my brain. I let my head fall forward.

The drumming resumed. A huge hand covered my head, grasped my hair, and yanked my face up. The man staring at me across the desk trembled with malevolence. His breath came in white puffs in the cold air. My teeth chattered. I realized I was naked and handcuffed to the chair. The man opened his rosebud lips as his eyes strayed over me.

A languid waif with blonde hair and enormous glassy eyes sat on the edge of the desk and goggled at me. She sniffed loudly. She had rosebud lips too, like the man's, and the same shade of lipstick.

"Fan," I croaked. The left side of my mouth was swollen shut.

"You are in some total shit, guy," he said. "Some very big total shit."

That didn't call for a reply, so I gave in to the shadows swarming in my head. I felt my chin hit my chest and blacked out.

I came to with ice-cold water dripping from my face. I tried to bite down to stop my teeth from chattering. My mouth felt stuffed with bloody pulp.

Where was Lily? I tried to turn my head. My skull exploded in pain as the locomotive hurtled down its track and crashed into my skull.

"He's looking for the Russian whore," Fan said. "Help him." The huge hand clamped down hard again and swiveled my head. I almost blacked out again but settled for throwing up in my lap.

Lily stood pushed against a wall. The cut on her cheek had opened again. A smear of blood extended to her chin. The gym rat with the tats had a grip on her arm. He grinned at me and stuck his free hand under Lily's sweater and grabbed her breast hard enough to make her cry out. She wrenched her head around and spat in his face. The kid yanked his hand out of her sweater and slapped her hard enough to make her head snap.

Fan's fingers played among an array of instruments in front of him. He wore a long black scarf looped around his neck. It trailed onto the desk, and he flung it aside with a growl as his fingers clattered through the tray. I could see a scalpel and stainless steel pliers. The pliers looked like something you might see on a dentist's tray. With his eyes still fixed on me, he picked these up and handed them to the waif. She received the instrument with both hands, reverently.

She moved her legs. Her bony hips poked at the material of her skirt. She had a model's starveling body and a washed-out expression, as if she'd been put through the rinse cycle too many times. She stared raptly at my crotch.

Fan put his hand under the waif's skirt. She uncrossed her legs to accommodate him. "She likes dick," he said. "Maybe not exactly the way you hope. So let's hear your story, guy, before she adjusts your equipment."

"I'm police," I said thickly.

"Asshole," he hissed. "My men saw you on that Angel cunt's houseboat. You're the Treasury agent. You and your fucking country are trying to railroad my sister and steal my property." He was trying to control his face, but his anger was spilling through the cracks. He snatched up one of the knives and flung it at me. It nicked my shoulder. "What did you say to my sister! Why were you at the courthouse! Time to start talking, guy!"

He jerked his head at the waif. She slid off the desk and crouched in front of me.

"You loser," Lily snarled.

Fan's face went red. He tried to ignore her.

"The tough man," she said in her guttural voice. The tat kid shook her. The blood was streaming from her face. "The tough guy who abuses women and rides on his sister's brains."

"Shut that cunt up!" Fan screamed, and tat kid clapped a hand on her mouth.

The waif sniffed and wiped her nose with a finger. With one hand she cupped my testicles. She stared up at me with her glassy eyes and parted her rosebud lips. A fleck of lipstick gleamed on a tooth. Very slowly, she drew the pliers along my penis. And again. She watched intently, then bent down and breathed, bathing the skin with warm, moist air.

When the inevitable happened, she squatted back on her heels and gazed in satisfaction. She picked the scalpel from the floor where it had fallen. She plucked with the pliers and drew out a tag of skin. Above the blonde head, Fan watched with bugging eyes. A strand of lipstick-stained saliva glistened on his chin. The waif slowly pulled the skin out taut, twisting with the pliers. I put my head back and roared at the high ceiling.

But instead of a cut, the scalpel clattered to the floor. So did the pliers. And I saw what she had seen. The flicker of red light.

It danced among the dark web of steel framing that supported the roof, and when I looked down, it glimmered along a door frame and flashed at the edges of the drawn window blinds. I heard a door slam outside. Fan screamed an order in Chinese. Tinkerbell hurried across the room and disappeared briefly through a door. When he returned, he muttered in Fan's ear. Fan seized his hair and shrieked with rage.

He jumped up and strode across to Lily, the long black scarf twitching behind him like the tail of a predatory animal. He grabbed her chin in one hand and twisted her face and clawed her wounded cheek. "Russian slut!" he screamed, and disappeared through the door. The waif looked longingly at me, then followed.

Lily was gasping for breath in big, ragged gulps and searching for the key to the handcuffs when Cedric came in with Larry on his heels. Larry was delivering a stream of verbiage that included phrases like criminal trespass and armed assault, until Cedric saw me, and my condition, and Lily with her blood-smeared face, scrabbling for the keys. Larry noticed at the same time, gaped in horror, and retreated through the doorway Fan and the others had used. The sound of car doors slamming shut and engines starting came from outside.

"Get that gate closed," Cedric shouted to an officer who'd followed him in. But they were gone by the time he got outside.

On the way to the hospital I cradled Lily in my arms. She was shaking like a leaf. We pulled up to the ER entrance, and I carried her inside. I sat in the empty waiting room while Cedric went to find someone. He came back with the triage nurse, a tiny woman with gray hair. She started snapping orders, and they bundled Lily into an open bay. A minute later the nurse came back. She peered at me and shook her head and led me into an empty bay. "Who started it?" she said, swishing shut the curtain. "You or the moose?"

32

Fractured zygomatic arch," the young doctor said. "Translation: busted cheek bone." She gave me a radiant smile. "Lucky for you, the hospital board finally decided to hire a plastic surgeon." She looked at Lily. "Are you going to hold him down for me?"

"If I take my clothes off and lie on top of him," Lily said, "he'll behave."

They smiled companionably at each other. She'd already taken care of Lily's cheek. I thought there was more to treat, but Lily would take care of that herself.

"OK, now," the doctor said, "here's what we're going to do." She scooted her stool close to the examination table and angled a strong light at the side of my face. "I'm going to do what's called an open reduction of the zygomatic arch." She snapped on a pair of blue surgical gloves and ran a finger along my hairline. "I'll incise the scalp right here," she said, "and then insert a long instrument called an elevator down under the skin to the fracture site. It's pretty bashed in there, but the fix is straightforward. I work the elevator under the bone and basically just pop things back into place."

"Will you have to put in something to hold it all together?" Lily said.

"Nope. No wires, no plate. Because I don't open the cheek, not even much of a dressing. A few stitches here." She touched my head again. "Precautions post-op, he should try to keep his head upright to reduce swelling and bruising. No nose-blowing. Stick to a soft diet." She slapped her hands on her knees. "All set?" She jumped to her feet. "See you in the OR."

Three hours later I signed myself out of the hospital against the doctor's advice and made Lily drive me to the restaurant on the hill. She wavered between fury at me and some inner darkness. Powerful men had done violence to her before. She had never bent or yielded. She'd always fought. Men got to the bedrock of Lily and found defiance. There's a price to make that happen, and Lily was still paying it.

"Remember—soft diet," she said as I got out, "and if you're not home in an hour, so help me God, Alex, I'm coming back here and dragging you out." Then she stamped on the gas, fishtailed out of the snow-covered parking lot, and went roaring down the hill into town.

Luc was waiting at the same table by the windows. Yellowknife Bay was a steely smudge through the blowing snow. The warm spell had been replaced by a blast of Arctic air. "Wow," said the waiter in the Ugg boots as she filled my cup with coffee and checked out my face. "Maybe you should've had the poutine."

Luc glowered at my face. When she left with our order, he said, "They could have killed you in there, and I doubt they'd even have been charged. You're lucky Cedric spotted your truck on that road and saw where you'd cut the fence."

"I'm not in the mood, Luc. I did you a favor. You wanted to know what was in there as much as I did, but your bosses in Ottawa wouldn't

OK the break-in. They don't want China any angrier than it is. Fine, but don't give me that crap about how lucky I was. Cedric didn't *find* the truck. You had somebody watching while I did your job for you. When we didn't come back out by the time the guard made another patrol, you knew they had us inside."

A burger arrived for Luc, and my plate of scrambled eggs. I was starving. I managed to get a forkful into the right side of my mouth without too much of it falling back on the plate. The waiter pretended not to notice when she came around for refills. Luc was scowling out the window at the snow.

"Nobody in Washington ever looked the other way for billionaire investors?" He was mad, but not at me. "It's always dirty. You and I get paid to make sure the bad guys don't actually get the whole country when they buy the politicians." He took another swig of coffee. A gust buffeted the windows. The snow was thicker now. "Fan's got a drill rig up there now." He put the mug down hard enough for coffee to slop onto the table. "He flew in an entire camp."

I watched the snow. "A whole camp? You mean, including staff? Please don't tell me from China."

"It's not a goddam crime," he said angrily. "The man owns rights to a mineral property. He's allowed to explore it."

I was stunned. "We're not talking about some guy with a pickaxe and a mule. He's the investment arm of the Chinese military leadership." The pain in the side of my face made it hard to concentrate. I tried to picture the scale of what Luc was saying. Dozens of men and huge pieces of machinery suddenly transported into the Barrens. "How could they get an entire camp in there in the first place?" I said. "Why didn't you know it was happening?"

But the answer to that was obvious. He did know it was happening.

Luc shoved his plate away and planted his elbows on the table. He bent his head and grabbed his hair in his hands and made a growl of pure frustration. "They let me know yesterday afternoon, when it was almost here. What happened was Fan's lawyers showed up in Ottawa. The Chinese ambassador was with them. They had a report that showed the Clip Bay pipe was one of the richest diamond deposits in history. They asked for temporary visas so they could bring in their own crew and get an immediate start. The pitch was that staffing would be one hundred percent local people if the discovery panned out as expected."

"I'm missing something here. How they got this done so fast. It's not like we don't have eyes at the airport."

"They flew their team directly into the Barrens. They made a deal with the Ekati mine to use the strip. They have choppers at Clip Bay to bring the cargo into camp." He turned in his chair and waved at Cedric to come over. When he was seated, Luc said to him, "Tell Alex."

"The word is out that Clip Bay is a diamond strike," he said. "It's all over town. That means there's going to be an immediate rush to stake any available claims within a hundred miles. It's called an 'area play.' Investors bet that where one rich pipe was found, maybe others will be too."

"How long before that starts?" I said.

"It's started. We've heard about staking teams trying to book planes and order posts."

"So Fan's got all the posts he needs," I said. "What's he waiting for?"

"He's almost ready," Luc said. "He's already locked up every chopper and bush plane in Yellowknife. That's why these other stakers Cedric mentioned can't find aircraft."

The front door slammed, and Lily blew into the room on a blast of snow. She stomped across the floor and glowered at Luc. "You can't see that the man has a severe injury? Would you try to use your head for *one* second? Two hours ago he was under general anesthetic. Are you completely out of your minds?" She slopped some of her icy glare onto Cedric too. "Get up, Alex. You heard the doctor. You are putting your eyesight at risk if you don't get rest. You could have a brain clot."

"But a great black eye," Luc said. "For his collection."

"Fuck off," Lily snapped, and I followed her out to the truck.

But we didn't head for the apartment.

33

She drove down the hill, turned right in town, and took the road that passed the airport.

"Where are we going?"

"For heaven's sake, Alex, we can't sit around in Yellowknife when Fan is launching some major action in the Barrens. We're meeting Pete and Mitzi and flying up to see what's happening."

"What about the brain clots?"

"Don't be such a hypochondriac." She opened the console and handed me a bottle of small blue pills. I read the label. Dilaudid. The side of my face felt as if someone had driven in nails and hung an anchor on it. I swallowed a couple of pills.

The highway ran along the North Arm of Great Slave Lake. I could see the water glint into view whenever we crested a rise, but mostly it was hidden by the forest.

"Isn't Mitzi part of whatever Fan is doing?" I said. "He and Mei control the company, but she has Jimmy's shares. Also some of her own. Or maybe you knew that."

"Alex," Lily exclaimed. "Quit trying to trick me into revealing my evil mastermind plan to take over the diamond field." She twisted the rearview mirror toward her and checked her lipstick, then angled it back. "You're so paranoid."

Not exactly a denial. "And it's Clip Bay we're checking out?"

"Yes. Mitzi wants to make sure Fan's not cheating her."

The sky was clear. A loose skin of snow slid and curled along the surface of the highway. A couple of miles ahead a small, tight cloud of snow appeared above the forest. It looked like a white tornado, boiling along above the treetops. At last a heavy rig hurtled into view around a bend, its powerful draft sucking snow from the woods into a maelstrom of white that seethed toward us along the highway. Lily slowed, and the truck roared by in a blinding whirl of snow.

"Remind me again of what your exact interest is in whether the twins swindle Mitzi," I said.

"Don't cross-examine me, darling. You're too battered. Not everything has to be a conspiracy."

Think about it, though. A Galaxy with a United States military command center parked at Yellowknife airport because of Chinese activity in the Arctic. Tycoons with close ties to the Beijing leadership drilling a diamond target. Mitzi, technically their partner, going up to spy on them. Lily wants me to come along, possibly because she has some scheme with Mitzi but doesn't trust her. Somewhere in there you could probably find a place for the word *conspiracy*.

My phone pinged for incoming mail. Dad.

The report was composed in his exacting style, the methodology explained and the lab work meticulously described. What it boiled down to was two clear statements. One—the diamond I'd picked up at Clip Bay didn't come from there; and two—it was identical to the garnets I'd taken from Jimmy's lab.

The conclusion was obvious. Jimmy had found a fabulously rich diamond target, probably richer than the original discovery that established the diamond field. And it wasn't Clip Bay.

An hour after leaving Yellowknife, we turned off the highway and drove through the village of Behchoko. We passed the Dogrib government office and St. Michael's Catholic Church and crossed onto a little island. We pulled into a gravel lot beside a stubby dock. A banged-up yellow Beaver with black pontoons was moored at the end. Pete had just finished checking the engine and was screwing the cowling shut. Mitzi looked as she had the first time I'd seen her—hair scrunched up in a topknot, strong legs planted on the dock, lofting bulky canvas bags into the plane. Even the cargo shorts were the same. Her only concession to the freezing wind that was slapping waves against the dock was a thermal vest.

She fired the two bags in her hands through the door and turned to stare at us. A purple zigzag ran down the inside of her thigh. Scabs had formed on the splinter cuts on her forehead and the side of her neck. Other than that, the same Mitzi—tiger's eyes and crooked grin and a stance that said: try me. She was what she always was. A loaded cannon. And she didn't like what she saw.

"Jesus," she said when I got out. "Who drove a truck into you?" And to Lily, "I didn't get that Alex was coming."

"In case we need someone to get punched," Lily said, and tousled my hair.

Mitzi shrugged, not bothering to hide her irritation. "The more the merrier. Let's get going. Alex, why don't you sit up front."

Pete clambered into the cockpit, and I followed. Mitzi cast off and jumped in after Lily. We taxied away from the dock and turned into the wind. The cockpit was smaller than the one in the Twin Otter, with the yoke on one side only. Pete grasped the throttle, pushing it forward as the big radial engine roared up to full power. We banged across the whitecaps, climbed away, and turned to the northeast.

The village drifted away beneath the wing. A snow squall swept out of the sky. The plane slipped and bounced in the turbulence. When we came out the other side, the vista of the boreal forest stretched to the horizon. Ragged clouds sped through the sky beneath a high ceiling of pearly stratus. Here and there the wind tore holes in the overcast, and sunlight flashed on a lake. I put the headset on, and Pete filled me in on where we were going.

Jimmy Angel had explored many targets, and one was only four miles from the Clip Bay pipe. Jimmy had brought a steel container up on the winter road. The container had built-in living quarters and a generator. Although he'd shifted his focus to Clip Bay, Jimmy had left the container camp in place. That's where we were headed.

"Four miles from Clip Bay," I said. "Won't the people there see us coming in?"

"There's a ridge between Clip Bay and the old camp. It will mask our approach."

I glanced back into the cabin. Lily was scrolling through something on her phone. Mitzi sat with her arms crossed and her lips pressed tight, glaring out the window.

By the time we reached the gray expanse of Lac de Gras, a black bruise was spreading through the sky. The cockpit darkened and the instrument lights glowed. The wind came out of the north like a boxer—jab, jab, punch. The airframe shook with the blows. My headset clicked. Pete's voice was terse. "Bad one coming."

34

We flew east along the southern shore of the lake. A fringe of ice lined the granite coast. The twin pits of the Diavik diamond mine came into view offshore, gaping holes that vanished into the depths. A coffer dam protected the pits from the waters of the lake. Waves with fifty miles to build broke against the dam, exploding into sheets of spray.

We left the mine behind, dropped to a thousand feet, and began a long, slow turn to the left across an archipelago of snow-covered islands. On the mainland, a straggling herd of caribou came into view. At the sound of the plane, they broke into a run. Their white rumps thrashed into the twilight. Ahead of us, a long white smudge stretched inland from the shore of Lac de Gras—the ridge. We began a steep descent.

In the gloom the altimeter needle moved swiftly around the phosphorescent dial, peeling off the feet as we scraped across a jumble of hills. Ahead, the wall of the ridge towered into the sky. Stripes of ice on the rock face gleamed in the fading light. The cliffside rushed toward us until the black water of a bay suddenly appeared. The right wingtip dipped as Pete cranked the plane into a tight turn. We flew up the narrowing inlet for a mile and landed in a gusting crosswind near the shore.

A draft of frigid air blew into the cabin as Mitzi opened the door. She clambered onto a pontoon. Waves lapped at her as she inched carefully forward with an axe. Grasping a strut with one hand, she reached out and smashed a path through the shelf of ice along the beach. We were pegging the mooring lines into fissures when the blizzard struck.

We sat in the harsh fluorescent light drinking tea while the storm howled and shrieked around the container. The generator hammered away outside, and the heater blew warm air. Pete doled out energy bars while Mitzi unrolled a topo map and pinned it to the table. We clustered around while she adjusted the angle of a light.

"So this is us right here." She tapped the paper. "And Clip Bay is over here. We'll hike inland about a half mile"—she traced a route—"to a low saddle. That's where we'll cross the ridge. From there it's an easy couple of hours to a hill that will give us a good view of the Chinese camp."

"And what exactly will you be looking for?" I said.

Mitzi kept her elbows on the table and her eyes fixed on the map. Lily inspected her fingernails. Pete folded up the wrapper of his energy bar into a neat rectangle and put it in his pocket. When another three seconds ticked by without Mitzi answering, he stepped away to fiddle with the heater. Finally Mitzi turned her head to look at me.

"That's a strange question, isn't it? Aren't you here to spy on Fan?"

"I'm here to spy on everybody. The real question is, what's your excuse? Fan's got operational control of your target. He's got your garnets.

Presumably he's checked them out. Now he knows they're very good diamond indicators. So what does he do? He has a diamond pipe, and he has minerals that came from the pipe that say it's rich in diamonds. What's the next step? The next step is he flies in a bunch of stuff and drills the target. Stop me when I say something that doesn't make perfect sense."

I left out that I knew the garnets the twins were relying on hadn't come from Clip Bay. I suspected Mitzi knew that.

She put her fists on the table and jerked her chin at the map. "Nobody has ever ramped up exploration at a remote site as fast as he has. Wouldn't you like to know why?"

"Sure, but I don't have the right to fly in and ask. You do. You own more of that pipe than he does. I understand he has the right to run the project, but that doesn't mean you can't ask how he's doing it. So I'm wondering why you have to camp out in a blizzard and wait for a chance to trek across the hills instead of landing at Clip Bay and making them show you around."

Mitzi gazed at the map and ran her finger along the route to the Chinese camp. Her face was tight. "I don't know what they're up to." The wind had stopped shrieking around the container. The only sound was the generator. Mitzi wouldn't look at me, and it struck me how hard she was trying to conceal herself. She wiped a tear from her cheek with a white knuckle. "They killed my dad. I want to see what they're doing. They're not going to get our diamonds."

Pete opened the door and stepped outside. The blizzard had moved on, and the sky was clear. He was about to come back in when a wavering sound rose into the night. It started low and rose to a high pitch, when another howl began. We all stared out at the wintry scene: the plane tethered to the shore, snow on the wings, the black water spangled with stars. We listened as other animals joined in.

"Wolves," he said. "Six or seven. They're on the next hill." He came inside and shut the door and took a Winchester 30.30 lever-action out of his pack. He clipped on a shoulder strap. "You guys have guns?"

In reply, Lily kicked one of the bags she'd brought. It made a loud clank.

"Are they going to be a problem?" I said.

"Don't think so." He rummaged in his pack until he found a box of ammunition. He loaded five rounds, pumped one into the breech, and pushed in one more cartridge. "Usually they avoid people. But they're starving. The big caribou herds are disappearing, so they're hungry, and they're wolves. They'll check us out."

Fifteen minutes later, we were heading up a defile with the ridge on our left. The clouds blew away, and the stars seemed close enough to touch. We slogged through the snow. The wolves were silent. No howling now. I looked around to see if I could spot them, but all I ever saw were shadows flowing through the snow.

35

In half an hour we reached the low saddle that made a passage through the ridge. As soon as we topped the rise, we could see a glow beyond the next hill—the Chinese camp. The first, faint sounds of machinery drifted on the cold night air. Pete stopped and checked his GPS. He put it away and slipped off his rifle and swept the scope in a slow arc across the way we'd come. When he didn't see any wolves, he slung the rifle and we dropped into a shallow valley.

The snow was hip-deep in the hollow. We floundered through it slowly, stumbling and sometimes falling. Pete led, then Mitzi, then me, and Lily at the back. She was the shortest and would benefit most from having the path broken. But the drifts were soft and dry, and the snow slipped back behind us we struggled through. I checked on Lily once. The snow was up to her hips. She made a motion that she was fine, and I turned back and wallowed after Mitzi.

As we climbed the last hill before the camp, we could hear the rattle of tracked vehicles. The air shook to the thrum of generators. Ahead, the top of the hill was outlined sharply by the lights of the camp beyond. The hill rose steeply for the last hundred yards. There was less snow cover on the slope. In spite of the steepness, we could move more easily.

Jimmy Angel's ruined tent camp had been wiped from the face of the earth. Arc lights mounted on steel pylons spilled a harsh light onto the bustling site. Men in hard hats filed out of a dormitory complex of steel ATCO units. They headed for the shore, where three massive drills were belching smoke.

Closer to the esker, a group with greasy overalls pulled on over their parkas swarmed around an open shed. A heavy machine trundled out and began to clank slowly down to the bay. A steel hydraulic arm on top of the vehicle held what looked like a thick rod mounted at an angle.

"So he has three drills going already on the shore, and here comes a fourth," Mitzi said. She leaned on a rock and slowly swept the site with binoculars. "Take a look at that rig they're moving down," she said, handing me the glasses.

I fiddled with the focus until I could make out the details of the rig. "Large diameter drill?" I said.

"Very." She took back the glasses and watched the contraption teeter across the uneven ground. "A bigger diameter than I've ever seen." She put the glasses away and stared down at the site. "I make it at least eight inches. When the drills break through into the pipe, they hit kimberlite. Kimberlite's softer than the surrounding granite. They can get through it pretty quick. I'm just guessing, but say that drill pulls six feet of eight-inch core an hour. Got to weigh about a ton, right?"

But she wasn't guessing. She knew it cold.

"Four drills, each pulling a ton of rock an hour. Four tons times twenty-four hours: ninety-six tons of rock a day. In a week, 672 tons. He's not exploring that target," she said. "He's taking out a bulk sample."

We lay there for another fifteen minutes, watching the feverish activity. Drills pulled rock from the target. A fleet of small trucks carried it away and piled it in a separate area. Men poured around the site like a busy colony of ants.

On the way back to camp, Mitzi and Lily walked together. I could hear the rustle of their voices as they whispered. The sounds of the Chinese camp faded away as we went through the saddle and turned downhill to the container. Nothing else moved in the silvery light except the starving wolves.

36

I recognized Tabitha from the air. She stood on the dock with her hands in the pockets of a stylish coat, her hair flying around her head in the gusting wind. A gleaming black SUV idled behind her, exhaust trailing from the pipe like a long blue snake crawling on the snow. We splashed down and taxied in.

"Who's the fashion plate?" said Mitzi, peering from the window.

"Alex's boss," Lily sneered. "I'm not supposed to know." She zipped her jacket up furiously. "She used to be his secretary."

I didn't know what part of that was supposed to be a secret. Mitzi darted an evil grin at me, heaved open the door, and the two of them hopped onto the dock and fastened the mooring lines. Lily stomped off to the Ford. Mitzi went over and stuck out her hand.

"Mitzi Angel," she said. "You probably know that."

"A pleasure," Tabitha said.

"You're another fed poking her nose in our business."

"Well," Tabitha said, "not just another fed. I'm the fed they send up to ask the tough questions once we've got you tied up in the basement with the electrodes in place."

Mitzi stared at her.

"Fed humor," Tabitha said.

"Ha-ha," Mitzi replied with a stony face.

Lily slammed the door of the F350, drove up beside me, and rolled down the window. "I won't be back tonight," she said. She didn't even glance at Tabitha. "I have business to take care of, and apparently so do you." She rolled up the window and gunned away.

Tabitha's SUV was the Tahoe with Mackenzie's two-star plate. She tossed her coat in the back seat and climbed in behind the wheel. She wore a gray wool skirt and a black cashmere sweater with the sleeves pushed up. She tugged the skirt up above her knees.

We drove off the island and through the village. Neither of us spoke for a few minutes, until Tabitha sighed and said, "Are we going to talk about exactly what business Lily has to take care of?"

"What makes you think I would know?"

We reached the junction with the main highway and turned left for Yellowknife. Veils of snow slid back and forth across the surface of the road. Three large ravens hopped off some roadkill and waited on the shoulder until we passed. I glanced in the side mirror as they hopped back out, indifferent to the storm of snow sucked up in our wake.

"We are not going to go there, Alex. This isn't the time to shadowbox. You've known from the moment Lily got on the plane to Yellowknife that she'd put herself in the middle of things if she saw a way to profit. That's why you asked for the UFED, so you could find out what she was up to. I'm not sure that little scrap about the Montreal lawyer you sent Tommy is going to tell us much."

Tabitha and Lily were like two panthers. When their scent trails crossed, they would always have to stop and snarl. Tabitha checked her watch. I could read her like a book. There was some topic she wanted to broach. She took a breath and plunged.

"Could the twins have another motive, do you think?"

"Other than what?"

"Other than finding a diamond mine?"

"You mean the dark plan to reduce America to bondage by using all this to sneak in their cell phone network, against which we have no defense but the most powerful military in the world and a currency weaponized by us to browbeat other countries?"

Tabitha drove in silence for a minute, cooling her temper. Finally she blew a clump of hair from her face and nicked my chin with the blade of an irritated glance.

"Yes, I mean that plan, or maybe a much worse one. So let's agree that you've got the peevishness out of your system and can now direct your attention to subjects where you actually know what you're talking about."

She let me chew on that for a moment before she continued.

"There's a meeting in the Galaxy. That's where we're going. We're having a crisis with our ally. We need you to help us make a case, so let me tell you what that case is."

The sun was out. The snow shone with a blinding whiteness. Tabitha slipped on a pair of Ray-Bans and brushed her hair back with an impatient swipe. She liked to drive fast. The heavy vehicle flew over frost bumps in the road and came down hard on its springs. I glanced at the side mirror again and watched the plume of dry snow spiraling out behind us.

"China's our biggest threat this century. Strong economy, rapidly-growing navy—you don't have to get the president's daily intelligence briefing to know this. We challenge them in the South China Sea. Those coral reefs they transformed into military outposts to claim sovereignty over the whole area—we sail by them just to get up China's nose. Now they threaten Taiwan. We sent those battle groups through the Taiwan Strait to show that we will defend our ally."

"Except we won't."

"They can't be sure. If we have a fleet in the strait and things get hot, one of our ships could catch a missile. If American sailors die, there has to be payback, and we would make it hurt. They know that."

"And this involves Canada how?"

"Because the Chinese want to show us two can play at that game. Boomers in the Arctic. We don't need some Chinese military cat's paw any closer than that."

"Diamond mining would be a way for them to get closer; is that the pitch I'm supposed to make?" I hadn't taken any painkillers since the day before. The pain was making me angry.

"This is the military, Alex. They're not going to ask you to assess a threat. They can do that just fine. But in strategic terms, we think of our northern border as the Arctic coast, including Canada's. We defend that border together, with NORAD. We've always seen eye to eye. Now we're not so sure."

"Surely you don't mean they have strategic ideas of their own? What a surprise. We pay zero attention to Canada, although we trade more with them than with China, share a five-thousand-mile border, and play the same sports. Their reward: illegal tariffs and punitive trade actions whenever the president needs a poll bump in the Rust Belt. And Canadians don't love and trust us? Go figure."

We'd just passed the Stagg River. Tabitha put on her blinker. She eased off the highway at a boat launch and parked in the snow. She unbuckled her belt so she could turn to face me, and put her fingers tenderly against my face. It melted me.

If I could have gone back right then to that bedroom on the airbase, I'd have crawled in beside her and taken her in my arms and crushed her long, beautiful body against me.

I came to know Tabitha in the year we'd spent in the basement offices on Clarkson Street. She was the smart kid seconded from the CIA so she could learn about financial crime. I'd never believed that cover. She was too well trained, too bright for a placement in an obscure little black-ops corner of the Treasury. And when I discovered that the person she'd been sent to keep an eye on was me, it didn't poison my affection.

Affection can survive betrayal, or there'd be no love anywhere. For me she'd always be the spirited young woman coming into the office in the morning in a pencil skirt and a plaid shirt she'd got on sale at Saks, clacking through the door in her slingbacks with a venti from Starbucks and the latest gossip from the top floor. We'd be howling in minutes. Or I'd come in from some blown operation, my face stippled with cuts, and she'd clack off to get the first aid kit and tidy me up for the showdown upstairs, then make me take her to Via Carota.

Now she let the air out of me with those green eyes and kept her fingers gently on my face.

"I'm sorry, Alex, but if you've got something for the pain, please take it now. Because this is serious. China means us harm. Fan is a Chinese government actor in all but name. They fund him and they control him. So frankly, fuck Canada. They let him in."

"They also put his sister in jail because we asked them to, Tab, so I'm not sure we have the high ground here."

She buckled the seat belt back on, checked the mirror, and gunned the big Chevy back onto the highway.

"I'm fine with the low ground, Alex."

37

They'd started before we got there. Facing each other at a small conference table in the Galaxy—Mackenzie and the Canadian brigadier. The brigadier wore battle ribbons from Bosnia and Afghanistan, and instead of insignia stitched on his collar, he wore shoulder boards. He was a rank lower than Mackenzie, but the glittering maple leaf with the crossed sword and baton surmounted by a scarlet crown made him look like the one in charge.

Carstairs sat beside Mackenzie. A Canadian major and an American half colonel were there for ballast. Tabitha and I pulled over metal chairs and wedged ourselves in.

"I'm just not getting the problem, Kev," Mackenzie said, continuing an argument. "It's an exercise. We bring in another Galaxy from Alaska with a small battle group. Chopper some guys into the Barrens and fire off a bunch of ordnance. Make some noise. Send the Chinese a message: allies present and alert."

"My superiors don't see the need for it, sir," the Canadian said. "If they did see the need for the kind of display you describe, we have the rapid deployment capabilities to meet that need ourselves. There would be no need for an American force."

Mackenzie was just managing to keep a lid on his temper. He shifted his position abruptly in a display of annoyance. A yelp sounded under the table, followed by a furious snuffling. "Damn it, Carstairs," he said, "let him out for a breath of air, will you? And don't just leave him out there like you did before. He's not a goddam malamute." He glanced at Tabitha. "Excuse the language, ma'am."

This gave everyone present—except Carstairs, who was dragging the bulldog out of the room—the chance to stare openly at Tabitha. She'd brought into the room more than the smell of shampoo and body soap and the lethal chic of her appearance. She'd brought the whiff of power that came from the person at the other end of her phone.

"Let's not worry about my lily-white ears," she said briskly. "We have a situation on our hands, and we'd all like to make sure it doesn't do any damage to such an important alliance." The brigadier arched an eyebrow and adjusted a paper in front of him. Tabitha went on, "Why don't we hear what Alex Turner has to say. Alex works for the Treasury," she said to the brigadier. "He knows a lot about the diamond business."

All eyes turned to me. They didn't need to be told who I was. They'd probably watched the flight to the container camp on an AWACS feed and, for all I knew, had thermal imaging of the trek through the snow to the Chinese camp. They studied the side of my face with the professional detachment of men whose job involved sending soldiers into places from which, if they came back looking like me, they had nothing to complain about.

"You took a look at the Clip Bay camp," Mackenzie said. "Would you call that a larger camp than normal?"

"That depends on the target," I said. "If Fan thought it was particularly rich, he might have wanted to get a big diamond sample out fast to see exactly how rich and be able to exploit it quickly. That could explain the size of the camp and the type of drilling."

"What do you mean by 'type of drilling'?" the brigadier asked.

"He has four drills, and they're all wide-diameter. Wide-diameter drills are used to extract a sample of the ore so he can count and evaluate the diamonds. But that's skipping a step. You have to know two things to decide if a target is rich enough to support a mine. The number and value of diamonds in each ton of ore is just one of those things. The other is—how big is the deposit? Xi doesn't know the size of the target because he hasn't done the exploration drilling to define it, and that's the usual first step."

"So he's brought in all this equipment," Mackenzie said, "ostensibly to prove the value of the target, but because of his methodology, he can't actually learn the value of the target." He shot a look at the Canadian. "What he does have is a site that he can claim is a valid exploration target but in fact is nothing but a pretext."

The brigadier drummed his fingers impatiently on the table. He wasn't hearing this opinion for the first time.

"With respect, that's not what he's saying. He's saying that Fan hasn't taken the usual first step. Presumably"—he looked at me—"if he finds a bunch of diamonds in the ore he's extracting with these bigger drills, he could then drill down to define the extent of the deposit."

"Sure, but I don't think he's going to."

"Why not?"

"Because he isn't going to find any diamonds."

38

That got everyone's attention. The generals stared, exchanged a quick glance, then looked at Tabitha. She splashed an icy green glare at me and then frowned hard at the table. She didn't like surprises any more than they did.

"Spit it out," Mackenzie said. "Are you saying this is all a hoax? Because if there's no discovery, the Chinese have no reason to be there. Am I right, Kev?" he said, sensing that things were turning his way.

"I'm waiting to hear Mr. Turner elaborate on his assertion, sir."

I shoved back my chair, got up, and went to the big map of the diamond field tacked across the wall. Close-up satellite photos were pinned to the map around Clip Bay. The drills surrounding the target looked like giant predatory insects, each with its long proboscis sunk into the rock. Another shot showed a crew hauling up the drill casing to extract the thick core. I pulled out the tacks and dumped the photos on a table so the map was clear.

"What makes the Chinese think there's anything here in the first place?" I tapped the round bay. "What did Jimmy Angel have to sell that they bought? This entire area, all around Lac de Gras, was surveyed and explored during the diamond rush in the 1990s. Jimmy had some of those old aerial surveys. One showed a strong magnetic signature right here at Clip Bay. A nice round target that stood out like a bull's eye from the surrounding rock. The thing is—there were hundreds of targets exactly like that. Dozens of planes were crisscrossing the Barrens towing sensors behind them, and every time they flew across an anomaly that stood out from the granite and had a round surface shape, it got marked as a possible diamond pipe."

"Too many targets," Mackenzie said, immediately seeing the problem. "Not enough resources." He'd confronted the same dilemma in war, where deciding which enemy formation to strike was a matter of life and death. "How did they decide this particular pipe was worth a closer look?"

"They sampled the surrounding ground for certain minerals called diamond indicators, such as garnets. Indicators are mineral grains found around diamond deposits. There are far more of them than actual diamonds, and they're easier to find. If the samplers found indicators, the target was worth drilling."

"I don't get it," the brigadier said. "If there were these indicators, these garnets, why didn't somebody find them years ago?"

"Because there weren't any. Until Jimmy put them there."

"And how do you know that?"

I explained how I'd found a garnet at the scene when Jimmy's body was discovered and how Dad had ruled out that it came from Clip Bay. Jimmy had to be the one who put it there, and if he had, he'd have put others too.

"And the Chinese knew where to look," Tabitha said, seeing it now, "because they tracked him to the site and killed him."

Mackenzie nodded distantly. Neither general seemed surprised by the murder. In the calculus they were used to, the death of a single man was an economy.

"He salted the target," Mackenzie said. He turned to the brigadier. "That's what they call it when you introduce minerals to a mine to make it look better than it is."

"I know what salting means," the brigadier snapped, dropping the "sir" in his annoyance. "What I don't understand is how it could happen to people like Fan and his sister. Wouldn't they check the information, demand some kind of proof that the target was what Angel was telling them?"

"Jimmy didn't reveal specific targets," I said. "They bought an interest in his property as a whole, defined by map coordinates. Anything in that defined area, they had a piece of. Of course they'd want to see where the garnets came from, and that's what Jimmy was preparing for them when Fan killed him."

Mackenzie pursed his lips and looked at the map. "So assuming Fan hasn't already figured out the target was salted, how long before he discovers the pipe's a dud?"

"He's got a crusher and a lab up there. He's processing the ore as it comes out. From the quality of the garnets, he's probably expecting five carats for every ton of ore. He's probably pulled about two hundred tons out of the pipe by now. So he'd be looking for about a thousand carats."

"Instead of zero," Mackenzie said to the brigadier. "So what's he going to do now, Kev? He's got a dud mine that was supposed to furnish him with a pretext for a massive staking campaign. If we're right, that's what his masters want—dozens of sites to bring in machinery, so many we can't monitor them all. If this one's a dud, then he's in an even bigger hurry."

The brigadier scowled at the map. "It's not going to be another Galaxy, sir. That's not how this is going to go."

39

The airman guarding the Tahoe snapped off a salute and opened the door for Tabitha. In his other hand he held a leash. The dog sat on the tarmac with a look of despair. Carstairs was nowhere in sight.

We drove across the airfield and out the main gate and took the road that led to town. The sun struck a blinding white light from the snow. The trees and the gleaming outcrops of pink rock took on a hyper-realistic quality, as if they'd been etched on crystal by the light.

We took the back road that looped through the forest. I recognized the building with the sign that advertised tours to see the northern lights. We were passing the place where I shot up the Harley when I decided to say what was on my mind. I'll try anything once.

"If you feel like sharing, Tab, start with what Mackenzie meant about Fan digging out the pipe for some purpose we don't fully understand."

"Oh, man," she said, running her hand through her hair. "They're afraid that if he gets a discovery, he'll use it as a pretext to stake every inch of free ground between here and the Arctic coast."

"I think we've all ticked that box."

"Sure, but then he starts digging out pipes, just like he's digging out the one at Clip Bay."

"OK. And?"

She blew out a long breath. "What shape is a diamond pipe, Alex?"

"Well, they're old volcanoes. Like a cone shape. In Canada they're mostly narrow."

"So basically, when they excavate, what's left is a deep, round hole in the ground. See if you can think of anything shaped like a deep round hole in the ground that the Pentagon would tend to worry about."

A missile silo. They thought the Chinese could use the pretext of exploration to dig out enough of the rock to accommodate a missile silo. They would bring up what they needed piece by piece, concealed with other machinery. The sheer amount of hardware that went up the winter road every year would make it hard to check. Once they had a landing strip of their own, heavy cargo planes could land.

"It's on the paranoid end of the spectrum, Tab."

"We're talking about the joint chiefs. That's the end of the spectrum they're supposed to be on."

I'd never seen her look so tired. For that moment her face had a bleak look, and I thought of the last time I'd seen her like that. Her hands gripped the wheel while some hole inside her got bigger. But she'd signed up for it. Be careful who you feel sorry for. She was still a spy. And had a surprise for me waiting down the road.

Tommy had his arms spread when we drove into the restaurant parking lot. A mob of kids clustered around him. His lavender bowling shirt with the chocolate piping fluttered in the Arctic breeze. The kids all wore woolen hats and rapt expressions.

"The runner comes right at you," he was telling them when I got out. "He wants to make you open right or left, and he will deke the other way and leave you there like a dope. But are you a dope?" The kids all yelled: they weren't a dope! "OK, then," Tommy said. "So at the snap, he comes at you fast, but you stay low." He went into a crouch and backpedaled as nimbly as an out-of-shape, overweight guy with a wrecked knee could manage. "The runner makes his fake, and you start to turn that way. He thinks he's hung you out to dry, and he dekes the other way. But you are low and balanced, and you just keep turning all the way around in a single, unbroken move." He stumbled in the gravel, but they got the picture. "By the time he gets the ball, you are all the way around and you are *on* that guy, and who's the dope?"

"The runner is!" they yelled.

Tommy dug in his pocket, pulled out a wad, and peeled off a fifty. He handed it to the smallest kid. "Take the gang to Burger King," he said. He scribbled his autograph on a beat-up football, and the kids went away with their eyes bugged out. You want to know what satellite TV has done for the NFL, that's what.

We went inside and took a table by the window. Yellowknife Bay sparkled at the bottom of the hill. An Otter roared overhead, banked hard, and splashed down by the floatplane dock. A Jet Ranger clattered by a half mile away and landed out of sight. There was only one place in that direction for a chopper to put down. The Chinese depot.

"How many does that make?" Tommy said to the waiter in the Ugg boots when she came over with the coffee.

"That's the third today," she said. "When I drove by last night, there were four already there."

"People must be getting suspicious."

"Suspicious—that's history," she said. "The whole town knows the warehouse is full of staking posts. The Chinese have started to move loads up to the Barrens. Guys at the Ekati mine spotted the activity at Clip Bay too.

There's a staking rush warming up. A couple of pilots were in for breakfast yesterday. They'd been hired from Calgary, and not by the Chinese."

She gave me a smile, and I don't mean an embarrassed one.

"You secret agents," I said. "You'll do anything to sell poutine."

She bent down and winked. "Doll, it could have changed your life."

"Stop flirting with the help," Tommy told her. "Did you get a fix on Lily?"

"Afternoon flight to Calgary," the waiter said. "Onward connection to Vancouver."

"And somebody's waiting in Vancouver to tail her?"

"I tipped the Canadians, like you said." Ugg boots padded off to take care of other customers. Who knows, maybe they were working for us too. It's not like anybody would feel they had to tell me.

Tabitha's phone made an urgent, high-pitched sound. She pushed back her chair and walked to the far end of the room. "Dollars to doughnuts that's the White House," Tommy muttered. "Ottawa will stop saying 'Whose country is this anyway?' in case they get an answer they don't like."

Tabitha came back and shrugged on her coat. "Do you ever wonder why our allies hate us?"

"No," I said.

"I've got to get back to the Galaxy. I'm flying out with them."

"The air force is leaving?"

"Let's hope it looks that way," she said. Tommy didn't seem surprised. "What's the mood on planet Canada?" she asked him.

"I ordered a banking scan on Leclerc," he said, "so some of them will be happy with that. But there are people in Ottawa who've been covering that bastard's ass for years and getting rich on the fees he kicks their way. They will not be happy."

"Works for me," Tabitha said. She turned a weary glance to me. "Poutine my ass," she said, picking up her keys. I watched the Tahoe with the two-star plate pull out of the parking lot and vanish down the hill.

40

D on't give me that look," Tommy said, taking out a small tablet and setting it up on the table.

He thought I resented him conspiring with Tabitha. But somebody's always pulling your strings in our business. At least we both knew who it was.

"So Leclerc's in play?" I said.

He jacked in two sets of earbuds and handed one to me. He called up a video and hit the play button. "The Canadians cleared me to go up to Montreal and take a whack at him."

It was a measure of how desperate we were that Tommy had reached out to them at all. Tommy and Tabitha were high-fiving each other about what a pair of smooth operators they were. But it's never a good idea for your neighbors to know how much you're spying on them, and if they let Tommy go up and slap Leclerc around, they were getting something for it.

The picture was razor sharp. I could even make out the tiny sunglasses design printed on Leclerc's Salvatore Ferragamo tie. I glanced at Tommy, and he tapped a button on his shirt. "Super micro," he said. "Latest high-end optics."

In the video, Leclerc wore a white shirt and a charcoal-gray suit that fit him like a glove.

"Deputy assistant secretary of the Treasury," he said, glancing at Tommy's card. "I'm not sure how I can possibly be of use."

"We'll think of something," Tommy said.

Leclerc let his smile drift away and waved Tommy to a corner of the huge office, where a pair of sofas faced each other across a coffee table. He looked pretty cool, considering the notice he'd been given. None. Tommy had appeared on the forty-third floor of Place Ville Marie with a uniformed officer of the RCMP, who'd handed the receptionist an official letter from a senior officer requesting the meeting for Tommy. Given Tommy's rank, it's possible Leclerc didn't expect an extremely large Black man in a bowling shirt.

"It asks here," Leclerc consulted the letter, "that I assist you with an urgent matter. Perhaps you could elaborate?"

"Sure," Tommy said. "Basically I'm looking for information on one of your clients. Liliana Ostrokhova, a Russian citizen currently with landed-immigrant status in Canada, resident here in Montreal."

There was a long pause. "I beg your pardon?" Leclerc said finally in an icy voice. "I must have misheard you."

"Liliana," Tommy repeated slowly, "Ostrokhova. She's your client."

"I heard what you said, Mr. Cleary. I'm dumbfounded that you said it. Even the suggestion that I would reveal the slightest detail of a client's affairs is an appalling affront to me not only professionally but also personally." There was a moment's silence while Leclerc arranged his face so Tommy could see how appalled and affronted he was, before he added, "I'm not affirming in any way that the person you mentioned is a client of this firm, or that, in fact, I have even heard of her before this moment. Now, I don't know how they do things in your country, but I received you purely as a courtesy."

"Uh-huh," Tommy said. He snapped his briefcase open and thumped a stack of paper on the table. "Let me show you how we do things in my country." He spread out some pages. "What we do is, we identify banking targets we think will elucidate certain relationships we want to understand, put all those bank accounts into the computer, and see what the National Security Agency can tell us. What they give us back is this—banking trails that show exactly how the targets move their money around."

"I don't see what this has to do with me," Leclerc said, but he leaned forward to take a closer look. Hard to resist. If he was laundering his clients' money, Tommy was showing him a diagram of the machinery.

"I'm sure this is all very important to you, Mr. Cleary, but a stack of uncertified paper documents"—he picked up a page and studied it—"a document purporting to be banking records, as I believe you're suggesting." He let the page slip back onto the table. "Well, again, I hardly see what this has to do with me."

"I'll tell you what it has to do with you," Tommy said. "These are all numbered accounts. You set up the companies behind these accounts. You opened the bank accounts. You have power of attorney to move money in and out of them as directed. We think there's a good chance some of that money comes from criminal activity. Ostrokhova is of particular interest to us at the moment, but I think we're going to find some Chinese connections in there too, when we take a harder look. So that's where you come in. You tell us who owns the numbered accounts, and we"—he picked up a paper and consulted it—"we agree to keep this one to ourselves." He handed the page to Leclerc.

"What's that?" I said.

Tommy stopped the playback. "A Liechtenstein account. That new algorithm we have figured out it's where Leclerc put his private stash."

"And that remark about the Chinese?"

He shrugged. "Spur of the moment. Hey, it's a fake. We see what happens."

He hit the play button, and the video resumed. Through the plate-glass window behind Leclerc, the trees on the slopes of Mount Royal blazed in the autumn air. Here and there the gray stone gable of a mansion peeked from the foliage. It was a great view, but at the moment one hundred percent of Gus Leclerc's attention was laser-focused on the paper sitting on his coffee table. Finally he looked up at Tommy.

"Are you making a record of this conversation?"

"If it'll make you feel better," Tommy said, "frisk me."

It would make him feel better. Leclerc buzzed, and a young heavy in a blazer came into the room. Tommy stood up, and the kid patted him down. Full-service law firm.

When they were alone again, Leclerc leaned forward and said in a cold voice, "Are you threatening me?"

Tommy sighed. "Come on, Leclerc. Lawyer to lawyer. Why do you think I came up to Montreal? Of course I'm threatening you. I'm giving you a get-out-of-jail-free card if you cooperate. Think of this as a discovery meeting. I'm showing you some of my case. You know what the penalties are. We see if there's some solution that works for both of us."

Leclerc laughed. "Case?" he said. "What case? I don't know where you went to law school, but if you had any kind of case—and I don't even know what crimes the case would allege or who the defendants would be—I wouldn't be hearing about it from a stranger with a briefcase full of banking records probably obtained illegally by unauthorized foreign government actions."

"Yale," Tommy said.

"Eh?"

"That's where I went to law school. So I take your point about procedure. If I were still a prosecutor in New York, where we specialized in hunting down guys like you, I'd have come better prepared. But the work I do now, sometimes we cut corners."

Leclerc studied Tommy with a detached expression. I had to hand it to the guy: he didn't try to smile or make a witty remark to show how cool he was. He was cool enough just saying nothing. Then he put his finger on the buzzer, and the door opened.

"Show this gentleman out," he said. "He seems to have wandered into the wrong country."

"You never thought he'd cooperate," I said when we were heading out to Tommy's rental.

"He's in too deep. He has to fight it out."

"You went up there to make him panic."

Tommy opened the door of a Toyota Corolla and crammed himself in behind the wheel. The driver's side sank and swayed as he struggled to get the seat belt fastened. It must have been the last car left in the lot. We scraped onto the road and headed down the hill.

There was a hump in the pavement near the floatplane dock. We hit it hard, and the car made a sickening crunch.

"Leclerc's guy patted you down pretty well. I get that he wouldn't have found the camera, but where was the wire?"

He rolled the piping on his shirt between his thumb and forefinger. "In here. Minnie's idea. It's something she invented." His face wore an arid look.

"Minnie invented a sophisticated clandestine recording system?"

He kept his eye on the road and didn't answer.

"And the target was you," I said.

He tried to make a casual wave with his hand, but Tommy was nuts about Minnie. It must have hurt. Plus the humiliation when he'd had to report it to Tabitha. But a very cold feeling came over me at that moment, and it wasn't because I felt bad for Tommy's battered heart.

"How did you find out she was bugging you?"

"I was in the office when the techs were doing the monthly sweep. They picked it up."

"Uh-huh. And when was that?"

"I wanted to tell you."

"Jesus Christ, Tommy. You son of a bitch. When did you find the wire?"

"Three days ago."

We drove through the city. Heavy traffic kept us creeping from light to light. There wasn't much to say. The people I worked for had let Lily and me walk into a trap. Fan knew we were coming. Beijing would have warned him. At the meeting in Tommy's office when we'd watched the video of the convoy, the Chinese had listened in on Minnie's wire.

"Alex," Tommy began, but I cut him off.

"Spare me, Tommy. I know how it goes. Tabitha thought that if I didn't break into the warehouse, the Chinese would figure out we'd found the wire. You didn't tell me because Tabitha wants to keep the channel open so you can feed misinformation the other way. I understand how it works."

We drove in silence for another couple of blocks before I thought about Leclerc again.

"Back to the lawyer. You went up there to spook him. Did it work?"

"Five minutes after I left his office he was on the phone to George Wu."

"Christ—Wu? That means Leclerc is working for the twins too. Wu will assume that Lily rolled on Leclerc and that maybe we're coming after Fan too."

"Fine," Tommy said. "Fan panics. Let's see what he does."

I'd been sitting on my anger for too long. "Will you fucking *try* to think more than one step ahead! Who's just gone to Vancouver? Lily. The person Fan already thinks is conspiring against him with his sister."

"Settle down, Alex. How does he even know where Lily is?"

"Oh, for Christ's sake. He has eyes at the airport. If poutine girl could find out when Lily left and where she was headed, I think Fan might be able to match the intelligence coup."

I called Luc and told him Lily was arriving in Vancouver that afternoon. I thought Fan might try to grab her. The Canadian security establishment didn't like us much, but they liked the Chinese less.

"I'll get somebody on it," he said, and hung up.

41

The Black Hawks came low up the bay, as pale as fish. They made a sound like a scythe swishing through the air. Tommy stood on the terrace watching. His chartreuse bowling shirt flapped in the cold gusts that blew in from the bay.

"Black Hawk UH-60s," he said. "The stealth model. That silver finish makes them hard to see on radar. Same with that modified tail boom and the hubcap thing on top of the rotor. That's the chopper they used on the Bin Laden raid. The Pakistanis never even knew they were there."

The helicopters sank out of sight and landed noiselessly behind the trees.

"So the Galaxy leaves, and with it goes the appearance of American control," I said. "But we offer tactical support to keep our foot in the door."

"Something like that," Tommy said. "We provide the choppers, and Canada provides the muscle. Win-win."

Muscle for what? The Canadians don't want to act openly against the twins. They already wish they'd never touched the sister."

He laced his thick fingers together and leaned on the railing, watching the girl with the blonde hair pull her kayak from the back of a pickup and carry it to the edge of the little lake. "The official line—it's a policing action. Ongoing murder investigation, so need to have another look at the site. But that's just for starters. Drilling without proper environmental approvals. Commencement of exploration without plant and animal census."

"You are kidding me."

"Amigo"—Tommy shook his head—"you should see the regulations. A woman from Fish & Game came over to Luc's office to brief us. Fan's guys should have counted every fish and bunny rabbit within a stipulated radius. That's so they can put them back when they're done."

A skirt of ice glimmered by the shore. The girl laid the kayak on the ground and stripped off her thick pants to reveal a black wetsuit. She pulled on a black wool cap, picked up the kayak, and high-stepped into the lake, breaking the ice as she went. When she was up to her knees, she smashed a space with her legs and put the kayak in the water.

"The Chinese will know it's all about screwing with Fan," I said.

"Sure they'll know. Who cares? The Canadians have deniability. The Galaxy leaving is great optics for them. They can say they put their foot down and the bully backed off. Plus they get a boatload of banking material on Leclerc. Plus we're letting the sister go."

"You mean we're dropping the extradition?"

"She's as free as a bird."

"So the Canadians get everything they want, and we get to fly their cops out to issue, like, parking tickets?"

He spread his shovel-sized hands. "Who doesn't like to be a good neighbor?"

The girl climbed into the kayak and drove herself through the thin ice, smashing her paddle hard through the crust and forcing a channel out into the open water. Her blonde hair shivered behind her with each powerful stroke. Shards of dripping ice flew from her paddle and slithered across the frozen surface. Her breath came in white puffs, and the faint sound of tinkling ice chimed in the cold air.

My phone vibrated. I checked the screen: Luc. We went inside, and I put the phone on speaker and set it on the coffee table.

"We missed her," he said. "That flight had already arrived when you called. We ran the surveillance tape from the arrivals level. She was waiting outside for an airport limo. A black Navigator pulled up, and she got in."

"Can you track it?"

"It belonged to the twins. We've had a team on that house they own in Vancouver. The Navigator got back an hour ago."

"Could they see Lily?"

"Smoked windows. But I think we have to assume that's where she is." I could hear Luc pacing back and forth in whatever dingy office he was using. "Maybe it's time for you to tell me what her status is." He sounded irritated. "She's your agent, right?"

Lily was never really anybody's agent. Lily worked for Lily. Even when I had her flipped against the Russians, Lily had never performed a single act from which she couldn't extract an advantage. But everybody makes mistakes, and for sure she'd made one now.

"She has no official protection, Luc."

He opened a drawer and slammed it shut again. "So we won't get an official request to help her. Translation: the US government never heard of her. Even for a cold-hearted bastard like you, that's shitty, Alex."

"Yes, Luc. It is."

I heard him open a door and mutter a few words. The door shut again.

"OK. We'll do it off the books. You're going to owe me, Alex. Meet Cedric there. I'll notify Vancouver," he said and ended the call.

Tommy and I sat there looking at the phone for a minute.

"I should have told you about Leclerc's call to Wu earlier," he said.

"Yes."

"I'm sorry, Alex."

"They'll kill her."

For a brief moment, I could feel her in my arms. Lily ruled herself from behind a glamorous exterior, applied and maintained with care and resolution. Only in the heat of passion did I ever catch a glimpse of the lost child she'd been. In those moments she clung to me, and I loved her.

42

We came in on a looping path over the Pacific. The setting sun slashed a golden sidelight on the coast. Ferries etched their wakes on a copper sea. Cedric handed me a small backpack. I zipped it open just as the wheels squeaked onto the runway. My MPX.

A bright-yellow box truck waited on the apron in front of a deserted hangar. It had a flashing orange light on the roof and the logo of British Columbia Power on the door. A square young man with Asian features stood beside the vehicle. His blue power-company shirt had the name "Hal" stitched on the breast pocket.

"Evening, Staff," Cedric said.

"Evening, sir," he replied, deep-sixing for good the fiction that Cedric was a constable.

"Staff Sergeant Chen is field leader for the Vancouver ERT," Cedric explained to me. The Emergency Response Teams were the RCMP's tactical units—highly-trained specialists with advanced weapons. "Mr. Turner is a friendly," Cedric said, introducing me. "It's his associate we're going to extract."

"Yes, sir," Chen said. "Perhaps we should start with a situational." He banged his hand on the side of the truck, and the back door sprang open. Inside, a communications unit with two flat-screen monitors and a phosphor green map of Vancouver glowed on the right-hand wall. An operator in a headset sat in front with her eyes on the screens. Three guys and a woman with pigtails pinned tight to her head sat on a bench against the other wall. They all wore street clothes—jeans and beat-up cargo pants, old sweatshirts with the sleeves ripped off at the shoulders. They weren't wearing what they usually wore to work: head-to-toe black tac suits and the Mounties' gun of choice for their elite force—Heckler & Koch MP5A3 submachine pistols. Still, you wouldn't mistake them for the pizza guy.

I wondered what weapons they had. Maybe the question was written on my face. The one sitting nearest to me looked a few years older than the others. He tugged up his sweatshirt. He had a SIG Sauer P226 in a quick-draw rig. He let the shirt fall back and pulled up one leg of his jeans. He had a black KA-BAR knife in a ballistic sheath. The model they call the Warthog. Six-inch blade.

"Sergeant Cox is team leader," Chen said. He stuck out his hand, and Cox gave him a tablet in a metal case. Chen tapped in a code, and a map of West Vancouver popped up. Marine Drive paralleled the shore of Burrard Inlet.

"The target house is here." Chen tapped a finger on the screen at a point on the shore. He tapped again, and the map dissolved to an aerial view of a large house. What looked like a gatehouse guarded the entrance to the driveway. The house was about a hundred feet in from the road. Behind the house, lawns and gardens faced the water. A flight of broad stone steps led down through flower beds to a wharf and boathouse on the shore.

"A marine unit is watching the water side. We have surveillance on the gatehouse. Ostrokhova is assumed to be inside. Fan is visually confirmed on the property. The gate is steel. We gain entrance by pretext. Power to the house has been intermittent for the last three hours."

"So they're expecting you," I said.

"They're expecting the power company," Chen said. "Power will be cut again one minute before we arrive, so no lights and no cameras. At the same time, our people on the water simulate engine trouble and put in at the dock."

"Drawing off security from the house," Cedric said.

"Correct."

"What about the twins?" I said.

"We subdue them," Cedric said. "It's an extraction of a kidnap victim. We don't anticipate an official complaint from the Xis. If we are wrong and she's not there, it was a bungled robbery by persons unknown."

The twilight was thickening around us. It would be dark by the time we reached the house. Cedric changed into a shirt like Chen's. He would ride shotgun in the front. He handed me my bag and a Kevlar vest, and I climbed in the back. They shut the door and we drove off.

I put on the vest and opened the bag in the dim green light from the screens. I took out the MPX. I screwed on the silencer. Cox made an approving murmur and asked for a closer look. He hefted it, snapped out the clip, clicked it back in and passed it around. The back of the truck relaxed into a companionable chat about gun weight and rate of fire and the merits of short-stroke gas-operated action. Then Cox inspected my face.

"That's some shiner," he said. "I guess this isn't your first date." He gave me a fist bump and handed me a headset.

A dry, steady voice called off our progress. On the dimly glowing map, the blip that was our truck moved through the city. One of the monitors was locked on a view of the gatehouse, the steel gates, and the thick hedge that concealed the property. The other showed the view from the water—the floodlit dock and the steps leading up to the house. The voice in my ear had just announced ten minutes to target when a dark SUV appeared inside the gate.

"Vehicle exiting target," a different voice broke in. "Apprehend?"

"Wait to see who it is," Cedric said.

The gates swung open. The camera closed in on a tighter shot. An SUV drove out and turned down the road in the direction of the city.

"ID?" Cedric said.

"Negative. Tinted windows."

"Alex," he said. "We'll put a tail the SUV and proceed with the operation. Agree?"

"Yes," I said. If we stopped the vehicle and Lily wasn't in it, we'd have tipped off the house.

At one minute to go, the monitor showed the house suddenly plunged into darkness. Sixty seconds later, our flashing orange light appeared out of the pitch-black night and pulled up at the gate.

43

With the power cut, only the emergency light glimmered in the guardhouse. We strapped on night vision goggles as the guard opened the gate. The truck drove through and stopped. I watched the monitor as the guard came out with a clipboard and gestured for Chen to open the truck for inspection. Chen hopped out of the cab. The guard stepped toward the back, and Chen clamped an arm around his neck and heaved him off the ground in a choke hold that squeezed the carotid artery and cut off the flow of blood to the brain. The guard flailed briefly and then sagged unconscious. Chen cuffed him with plastic ties and gagged him with a strip of duct tape. We tumbled out of the truck and headed for the front door.

The house was a sleek, modern structure of cedar and glass. It had a single floor at the front that became two floors at the back, where the land sloped down to the shore. Cox flattened himself against the wall beside the door. The sound of harsh voices came from the other side of the house—distant, down by the dock. The second unit was creating its diversion. Cox made a signal, and the cop with the pigtails stepped forward with a rubber vacuum disk. Tall panes of glass flanked the door. She pressed the rubber disk against the glass, and quickly incised a line around it. She tapped the rubber, and the glass broke neatly with a light pop. She pulled it out, and Cox reached through the hole and opened the door.

We slipped inside the house and fanned out into the foyer. Two men peeled off to the right and vanished toward some bedrooms. I followed Cox and pigtails into an enormous room that took up the rest of the first floor. The seaward wall was an unbroken expanse of glass. As we moved, the room seemed to capture our shadowy presence and repeat it in the glass; not as a reflection but as a shiver in the light—as if the aqueous quality of the ocean filled the room and we rippled through it like a school of barracudas.

The room was sparely furnished. Groups of leather-and-chrome sofas and matching chairs. Carved Chinese figures in pale stone hid their hands in their sleeves and watched with horrified expressions, like palace mandarins caught in a barbarian invasion. As we swept through the room, our feet made a light patter on the polished surface.

No sign of Fan or Mei. The first floor checked clear, and we made our way quickly to a staircase that descended at one side of the room. Suddenly Cox raised a hand. I heard the sound of a glass door sliding open on the floor below, followed by whispering, and the door swishing shut. Cox pointed at the floor below and made a circling motion, and two of the team slipped away.

We faded back from the stairs. After another whispered exchange, the men below started to come up. By then the two officers had circled behind the house. One of them tapped lightly at the closed glass door. The pair on the stairs whispered again and went back to check. After that the only sounds were the glass door sliding open and the guards stepping out and getting throat-punched.

I followed Cox and pigtails down the stairs. Her hair flew out behind her as she dashed down a hall to the left to check the rooms on that side. A gunshot sounded from the dock, and Cox signaled to me he was heading down to check it out. I pointed to my eyes and then down a short hall to the right, and the only remaining room. He gave me a thumbs-up and disappeared. I crept down the hall to the door and put my head against it. Nothing. I threw it open, dashed in low, and rolled to the side.

The smell told me I'd found her. It pierced me like a knife. The sweet smell of Lily's skin, and overpowering it, the stench of urine. But the room was empty. There was some apparatus, not clear in the blurry green imaging of the night lens.

I heard a generator kick on somewhere in the bowels of the house. Emergency lights flickered on and cast a dim light into the room. I took off the night-vision goggles. When my eyes adjusted to the low light, my heart went cold.

A gurney stood in the middle of the room. Armatures stuck out from the sides. It looked like an execution bed in a death chamber, the shape of her body pressed into the stained sheets.

The grim shape looked like what it was, an instrument of terror. The work Fan had wanted to perform at the warehouse, he could accomplish here at his leisure. Everything was laid out neatly. The same instruments he'd had on his desk at the airport. Needle-nose pliers, small knives like scalpels.

Something brushed against my ankle, and I leapt away.

Meow, said Brutus.

Mei swished in and closed the door behind her. Her tiny eyes peered through the thick glasses. Her face was haggard. She seemed shaken. Strands of hair escaped from the blue hair clips and drifted in front of her face.

"Where is she?" I snapped.

"He's taking her up to the Barrens. He thinks Mitzi Angel is keeping the location of the real discovery secret, and that Lily knows where it is."

"What kind of shape is she in?"

She stared at the instruments. She pressed her lips tight and shut her eyes for a moment. When she opened them again she looked at me.

"I stopped it."

"But not before it started." A patch of red stained the sheet.

"I tried to protect her," she said tightly. She pushed her glasses up and pressed her knuckles to her eyes. "He hates her because she cheated us when we bought Russian diamonds. All he thinks of is revenge. All this," her face recorded her revulsion as she stared at the gleaming instruments. "He doesn't have possession of his mind."

Her eyes were red and her cheeks were wet, but when the glasses were back in place her eyes were as steady as flecks of mica.

"But you do have possession of your mind, and you stayed with him."

She was a woman used to mastering herself, but the struggle to do so now was twisting her face into a mask of loathing. Her eyes burned and her lips trembled and her mouth turned down. I didn't know if the rumors about incest were true, or whatever private outrage her twin might have committed behind a locked door. But I could see, stark and horrible, the trail it had left behind.

"I hate him," she hissed.

Pigtails appeared in the door. I shook my head. She gave me a thumb's up and stepped back into the hall.

"Mei. We don't have time. I need to know what there is between you and Lily. Because Fan is going to kill her for it."

She nodded and took a deep breath, lowering her gaze for a moment to compose herself. When she spoke her voice was steady.

"Lily and I—we have a business arrangement. She understands the movement of large amounts of rough, and has helped me understand that.

Mitzi Angel too—I have an understanding. Mitzi is not reliable, but she's smart." It was as if she were talking to herself, thinking through a business calculation, the emptions of a moment before silenced and locked away. "Fan will not kill Lily," she said, "until he finds the true diamond pipe. But he might harm her."

"Does Lily know the location of the pipe?"

"No."

Pigtails poked her head in the door and tapped her watch. "We have to go. Are we taking her?"

"Give us one more sec?" She nodded and slipped back into the hall. I heard her radio crackle as she went outside. I turned back to Mei.

"Why are you even here? The extradition—it's been dropped."

"What did you expect me to do?" she said harshly. "Run?" Her eyes blazed with sudden fury. "I protect my property! The property of my investors! This is a trust. I don't run away from it."

"I'm not writing this down for your profile in the *Wall Street Journal*, so spare me the noble bullshit. If you're staying it's because China Hard Asset told you to stay."

Her eyes narrowed. "You're an American government agent. They pay you to think like that." She squared her shoulders, and as she lifted her chin defiantly I saw the red mark on her throat. Fan. "But a company is not a country. Your own citizens buy shares in our properties."

"I'm sure they'd all be grateful to know that the assassination of Jimmy Angel and the seizure of his property and the attempted murder of his daughter were all in a good cause."

"Don't fool yourself, Mr. Turner. If it affected their dividends, most of them would close their eyes." She caught up a lock of stray hair and clipped it roughly into place.

I heard a motor growl to life down at the dock, and then the sound of a boat heading out into the inlet. Cox and the other team must have finished. They would be heading back up now. Pigtails gave me the throat-cut motion to show that we were done.

The cat meowed. Mei looked at me with her mica-chip eyes. "You'll have to kill him."

"It will be safer to make the interception at Yellowknife," Cedric's voice crackled in my earpiece. He was up front. I was sitting in the back of the truck, watching the screen that showed Fan's SUV exiting the main road and entering a corner of the airport through a guarded gate. "If the pursuit team tries to take him now, she could get hurt in the crossfire, or he might kill her. We have lots of time to get snipers into position in Yellowknife."

"Agreed," I said.

Fan's SUV pulled up beside Fan's jet. He got out and boarded with the waif. Tinkerbell and the kid with the tats opened the back of the truck and pulled out a crate shaped like a coffin and loaded it in the cargo door.

44

There wasn't any rescue at Yellowknife. There wasn't anyone to rescue. The snipers packed away their rifles and stood down.

"Fan's jet filed a flight plan for Yellowknife," Tommy told me as we stood on the windswept tarmac when I got back. "They stayed on course until they were on final, then they turned off their transponder, dropped below radar, and we didn't know where they were until an AWACS picked them up."

"And by then they were landing at Ekati," I said. It was a smart move. Fan had already worked out a deal with the diamond mine to use their strip, so he was cleared to come right in. From there it was only ten minutes by helicopter to the camp at Clip Bay. That's where he'd move her first.

The airport hummed with purpose. I stood with Tommy in a small group, looking at the Reaper drone. Its blunt nose poked out into the dawn light. It crouched on its spindly legs, most of its thirty-six-foot length inside the hangar, looming over the soldiers who were arming it.

"Hellfire missile," I said.

"New type, though," Carstairs said. "No bang-bang." He glanced at me with a self-satisfied expression. The office weapons nerd.

"R9X kinetic warhead," I said. "Excellent on soft targets." His face fell. The ground crew finished with the missile and wheeled the arming rig away. "I had you made for military intelligence from the first act of the bulldog show," I told Carstairs. "Please don't tell me MI is running this operation."

He shrugged deeper into his air force parka. "Officially it's NORAD."

We were standing in a corner of the airfield with the small group looking at the drone. Carstairs tugged his woolen hat lower. Tommy's concession to the biting wind was a thermal top under his indigo bowling shirt. It had the name "Elvis" scrawled on the front.

"Do we know where Fan is now?"

"No," Tommy said. "Today his crews staked four more properties and set up tent camps. They've been ferrying staking posts into the Clip Bay camp, and from there, out to the other camps by chopper."

"Is there any traffic that looks different from the rest—maybe only a single chopper?"

Tommy looked at me suspiciously. "We can't keep track of every flight. He could be holding Lily anywhere."

I shot a quick text to the priest. A Canadian army Chinook came in and landed behind the hangar. A file of soldiers debarked and assembled beside a concrete-block structure. They were armed with Heckler & Koch MP5s. Some with FN Minimi light machine guns, and a few Benelli tactical shotguns—Italian semiautomatic twelve-gauge guns that can carry seven shells. The helicopters might be stealth, but the quiet part of the operation was going to end the second those guys jumped out of the chopper.

"They're JTF2," Carstairs said. "Joint Task Force 2. Their top special-forces unit."

I pulled Tommy aside. "You've figured out that this is a decapitation, right? We dropped the charges on the sister. We got rid of the Galaxy. Xi Fan is a mad dog, so crazy even his sister wants him dead. So all this staking rush bullshit? It isn't going to give him cover. It's going to give *us* cover. It's going to give the *Canadians* cover. To kill him." I jerked my head at the drone. "That's why nobody shut down the depot full of posts. They want Fan out there dicking around. There is zero part of this operation that is about extraction."

"Alex, they've all been briefed on Lily. They know he has her. They know she's not to be endangered."

My phone pinged. I read the priest's reply. "Catch you later," I said, and walked away.

Closed to civilian traffic, the airport was a desolate expanse where nothing moved but the military vehicles patrolling the perimeter. Across the city, it was a different story. I watched another set of navigation lights blink across the sky as a Twin Otter lined up on the floatplane dock and sank from sight. It was the third bush plane in five minutes. I scrolled through my phone and found the bomb that Fan had just dropped on the market. Angel Minerals had made a diamond strike in the Barrens. The staking rush was on. Exactly the cover Fan wanted. The more activity, the better his chances of moving undetected as he hunted Mitzi Angel.

Tommy caught up with me in the empty passenger terminal.

"Don't you have a career to run, Tommy?"

"Hey." He clamped his hand on my arm and made me stop. "I have a job to do. It's not the same as your job."

"I doubt you have a clear idea of what that job is at the moment. You seem to think that planting agents behind my back and letting Tabitha enroll you in her schemes makes you the shadow master." I took his hand away and headed for the exit. He lumbered after me. "Here's the scoop," I said. "You're not running anything. They're running both of us. This has been a Pentagon op from the get-go. They needed someone to help put Fan in the crosshairs, so they could browbeat a weaker ally into taking action. You think we're going to find Chinese missile-silo kits hidden in the equipment shed like IKEA flat packs?"

The priest was waiting in his crumbling Econoline outside the terminal. His head was bent to the little black book that contained the liturgy of the hours—the prayers that Catholic priests say every day.

"It must be hard for you," Tommy said to me as I pulled open the van's sliding door. "All this time you thought you were working for the Boy Scouts of America. Now you've found out that we are bad and devious people, and our only excuse is that 350 million US citizens depend on us to keep them from being annihilated by bastards like the people Fan works for."

I tossed in my bag and started to close the door, but Tommy stuck out his arm and held it open.

"You're going after her," he said. It wasn't a question.

"They're going to kill her. She'll be collateral damage. She won't even show up in the report."

Tommy reached in, moved my bag aside, and climbed in.

"This is not your fight, Tommy. I don't need you."

"Bullshit," he said. He held up the sat phone. "Eyes and ears, muchacho." He slid the door shut with a bang.

45

We drove out of the city and took the highway south. "Silver Bird One, this is forward base dispatch," a voice from Tommy's phone said against the background chatter. "You are clear. Proceed to target."

Thirty seconds later the first Black Hawk appeared above the trees and went whispering across the highway heading north.

"Silver Bird Two, advise when embarkation complete."

By the time we reached the turnoff for Behchoko an hour later, the Black Hawks were closing on Clip Bay. The AWACS planes had jammed the camp's communications. We listened to the laconic voices of the Black Hawk pilots, reporting their positions as they came up the inlet fast, low on the water.

We drove through the village and pulled up at the wooden church. The priest went inside. He returned a few minutes later with his hockey bag, a small black leather case, and a couple of extra parkas. We drove down to the water and across the little bridge and onto the island.

The beat-up yellow Beaver with the black pontoons was moored to the stubby dock. The wind was picking up. Gray waves slapped against the plane, and whitecaps flashed in the channel. Pete had his hands shoved in the pockets of his overalls.

"This isn't fair," he said to the priest when we got out. "These guys are spies for the American government. Mitzi's business is Mitzi's business. I thought it was just going to be you. I agreed to meet because you said she was in danger."

"Pete," I said, "she's in trouble. I don't know exactly what she's planning, and I doubt you do. But if it involves cheating Fan, she picked the wrong sucker. Maybe you noticed the traffic on your way back here."

"We expected that. It's part of his plan. It's a staking rush. Of course it would happen. It's an area play. Anybody who can get a plane or helicopter and some stakes will form a little company and sell shares into a hot market." He glared at Tommy. "You have people all over town," he said to him, "asking about Mitzi and me. It's a small town, mister." He faced me. "I respect you, Alex, but we knew this was going to happen."

Tommy stuck out his hand. "Tommy Cleary," he said.

Pete tried to ignore it, but he wasn't that kind of guy, and reluctantly he shook hands.

"Got a laptop in there?" Tommy said.

Pete reached into the cargo deck and unzipped a bag and took out a grimy case. He opened it, and the screen flickered to life. Tommy tapped his screen and airdropped a feed from the command post at the airport. He unmuted the audio. The staccato exchange of military communications crackled into the cold air. Pete stared at the screen.

The map showed a square of a hundred miles a side. Scores of lakes, their rugged shorelines traced out in bright green against the dark background. In the center was Lac de Gras. Swarming like fireflies over the black expanse were winking dots of light, some in clusters, others blinking out over the Barrens on their own solitary paths.

"Some of these planes are carrying stakers," I said. "You probably know most of them. But one is carrying Fan and Lily. And they are not a staking crew. They're a hunting party. Lily is a hostage, if she's alive. Fan thinks she can help him find the person he is hunting, or come in handy when he finds her. See if you can think who that might be."

The priest hauled his hockey bag out of the van and lugged it to the plane.

"This is not some guy who took a flutter in diamonds and will lick his wounds and go away. This is the Chinese government playing for a foothold in the Arctic. They don't lick their wounds. They give you the wounds to lick."

Pete scowled at the screen and bit his lip.

"Jimmy salted the Clip Bay target, Pete. Mitzi knew. Don't pretend you were out of the loop. That's why we went up that night and hiked over from the container camp. She wondered what Fan was up to because she knew the pipe was a duster. When she saw that he was taking out a bulk sample to get an actual diamond count, I'm guessing she advanced her plans, because that count was going to be zero. So whatever she's got going, probably with Lily's help, got pushed up fast, and that's why she's disappeared."

Tommy had the sat phone pressed to his ear. "Guys," he said, "let me add something to the discussion." He slid the volume up.

"Base, Silver Bird One," a voice crackled from the phone. "First target has no foxtrot alpha mike. Repeat, no FAM present."

"FAM means fighting age males," I said to Pete. "It's military code for people they will probably have to engage. That's an elite force, and they're looking for Fan. You don't want Mitzi to be standing too close when they find him."

The screen cut to a satellite shot of the Black Hawk hovering in a storm of dirt. The site looked abandoned. The military dispatchers began to reel off the next coordinates. They had a list of Jimmy Angel's main exploration targets, places where Fan might go in his search for Mitzi. We watched as the screen reverted to the map, and the two Black Hawks left the camp and made their way into the dense clump of other blinking lights on their way to the second target.

"Fan is using all this activity as cover. His goal is to reach Mitzi before we can intercept him. He'll force her to give up the location of the pipe."

"He'll never find her."

"Pete. Wherever she is, you brought her there. The Chinese know about you. They might have tracked your flight."

He shook his head. "There's no transponder on this plane."

"They don't need to follow a transponder. We're not the only ones with satellites. Take a good look at that screen. There are people in Beijing watching one just like it, while we stand here buying them time."

"If they know where I flew from, why doesn't Fan just go straight there?"

"There's a Reaper drone above the Barrens. It took off from Yellowknife, so I don't think it's a secret. Fan won't go until he has some cover."

"I think he's getting it now," Tommy said. He zoomed the picture to the eastern sector of Lac de Gras. Two blips were leaving the main area of activity and heading east along the north coast of the lake.

"She's at the far end of the lake, isn't she," I said. "You have to take us there."

"Is that Fan?" Pete said, his eyes on the screen as the dots advanced across the eastern end of the lake.

"Probably not yet. He'll build up activity in the area first by ordering staking. When there's enough cover, then he'll go."

"Unless he's delayed," Pete said. "There's a low coming down from the Arctic. The weather's getting dirty."

"You know that won't stop him," I said.

He looked like a trapped man. But on the dock that morning, who wasn't? I was trapped by Lily. By what formed between us on nights when our only certainty was each other. Tommy was trapped too. I could see it when he wasn't guarding his face. Anguish that Minnie had betrayed him. I think that even now he hoped to save her from what would happen to her when we no longer needed her help with the twins. I don't know what trapped the priest—God or the awful weight of his past. Unless that was the same thing.

We cast off and taxied into the rough channel. We took off to the northeast, into a dirty sky.

46

Black cloud slid down from the north and clamped a package of evil weather onto the Barrens. We could see it ahead of us as we approached. Pete put the old bush plane into a slow descent. We were at eight hundred feet when he leveled off. Then we were under. The temperature dropped fast.

We reached Lac de Gras and flew east along the southern coast. Powerful gusts lathered the surface of the water. A dark funnel spiraled up out of the lake a mile to the left. The ceiling dropped again. We descended to six hundred feet. The inky water thrashed in the wind. The cabin got colder. The heater made a fitful effort and gave up. Icy fingers of wind pried their way into the plane and picked at our clothes. The sleet arrived with a hiss.

I sat beside Pete, watching the view ahead slowly disappear behind a film of ice. On the pilot's side, the defroster managed to gasp out enough tepid air to keep a patch of windshield clear. After about ten minutes, the altimeter needle began to inch around the dial as we lost altitude and sank closer to the tossing lake.

"Wings are icing up," Pete said. He pulled back gently on the yoke. The engine groaned, and the plane climbed slowly. "She's getting sluggish."

"Can we make it?"

He tapped the altimeter. "Normally I'd climb above the cloud to get out of the sleet. But then I'd have to come down blind. Where we're going—it's too risky. We'll have to stay under all the way and see how it goes."

I looked back into the cabin. "What's the action at the east end of the lake?"

Tommy shook his head. He had the device held to his ear. "Phone packed up. I lost the video feed. I can only hear scraps of the audio."

"What was happening before you lost the feed?"

"Two aircraft were heading to the east end of the lake."

"Any ID on them?"

"No. The Black Hawks were just finishing with the second target."

"Nothing?"

"No one there." He swiped his finger across the screen a few times. "I think they were going to check the third target." He frowned at the phone. "I'll try rebooting."

Jimmy's map had identified four main exploration targets. Clip Bay was the first. The next two were on the same side of the lake—the north side. If the Chinese had satellite surveillance of the lake, which I assumed they did, then they might know not only where Pete's plane had taken off from but also where the Black Hawks were. If our own satellite feed was breaking up because of extreme weather over the Barrens, probably theirs was too. But Fan didn't have to wait passively for reports. He could create his own cover by dispatching stakers to the east end of the lake. He could then cross the lake himself, a blip among other blips, and fly straight to the fourth of Jimmy Angel's targets. The one we were heading to now.

We droned along the shore. The side window was striped with threads of ice, but otherwise clear. Ice glistened on the rocks. Waves lashed a rocky beach. We lost another hundred feet.

"We're icing up fast," Pete said. He reached out to touch the defroster vent. "This is quitting." The little patch of clear glass on the windshield was filling in with ice. "If I have to come in hard, at least it's a good beach."

"We can't land at the camp. There's a chance Fan is already there. We need to get down where they can't see us."

Now the windshield was completely sealed by ice. Only the side windows were still clear.

"OK," Pete said. "I know a beach."

We entered a wide bay flanked by low hills. Waves rolled against a steep shore. Columns of white spray leapt into the air. At four hundred feet we turned slowly to the right and flew across the heaving bay. I looked down at the pontoons and the black water streaming by. Pete had his eyes locked on the instruments.

"You're going to have to put your head out the window. Tell me if you see a place with vegetation coming down to the water. Guys," he called into the cabin, "brace for a heavy landing!"

I slid the window open and snapped off my seat belt and leaned out. The sleet bit into my face. I held my hand up to shield my eyes. I caught a glimpse of red. The sleet wiped it away. Then it reappeared—a low, red hillside hurtling toward us.

"Three hundred yards!" I shouted.

The Beaver mashed down into the stormy water. The pontoons dug into the rollers. The nose dipped, and the sudden drag threw me forward into the instrument panel. We slewed sideways, and the big rollers rocked the ice-covered plane dangerously in the swell. Pete jammed his foot on the rudder pedal and powered the plane around to face the shore. When the pontoons ground against gravel, he gunned up onto a narrow beach.

It took an hour to crawl over the icy rocks. Tommy's face was fixed in concentration as he advanced across the frozen ground. We inched on our bellies the last few yards to the top of a rise and over the crest. The camp lay in a bowl of hills. Fan had got there first.

47

The tent was stiff with ice. It was pitched against one side of the bowl, its back to the hills. A thread of smoke curled from the tin stovepipe.

Two Jet Rangers rocked in the storm a hundred yards in front of the tent. Plastic sleeves protected the rotors from the sleet. Tethering lines secured the aircraft and the drooping blades against the wind. No one by the choppers or the tent. Beyond the tent was a structure made of two shipping containers placed side by side, and as I studied it, I caught movement.

The containers had garage doors installed at the ends. The doors were open. I took out a little sighting scope and looked again. Three men stood inside. Two of them wore flight suits. The third man stood apart. He had a hand resting on an Uzi slung from his shoulder. Even from three hundred yards, I could see the tats curling up his neck and read the sneer. The other two just looked scared. I handed Pete the scope.

"I know those pilots," he said as he peered through the lens. "They fly for the company that owns the choppers." He tracked around the site. "That's weird. No drill."

"Mitzi was drilling?"

"She said she was going to. The properties the Chinese invested in were all marked on a map. This bowl—Jimmy had marked it carefully. Mitzi thought it might be where he got the garnets." He checked the tent. "Flap zipped tight," he said, and handed back the scope.

A gust rattled the stovepipe. The weather-beaten canvas glistened with ice. The wind picked at the sides of the tent and made the guy ropes moan. Ice tinkled on the rocks. They wouldn't hear us coming.

The priest handed Tommy a nylon gun case.

"What did you give him?" I said as Tommy unzipped it.

"The Ithaca."

"The riot gun you gave Lily?"

He nodded. I didn't even ask. The man could find weapons. That was just the kind of flock he had. I helped myself to a Walther PPK from his bag. It looked exactly like the one the biker had aimed at me that night in the taxi. I shoved it in my belt.

"You're not shooting?"

"It's not my place," the priest said.

"What's in the small black case?"

"The last sacrament."

We made our plans. I rubbed the ice from my eyes. The slope provided cover as we circled around behind the camp. I had the MPX inside my jacket, and Pete had his Winchester out. Ice glinted on the barrel.

We crept down the incline, out of sight of the open ends of the containers. At the back of the tent, I put my ear against the stiff canvas. All I could hear was the rattle of ice and the ropes groaning in the wind.

I glanced at the priest. He nodded. Pete disappeared around the corner. He would move down the side of the tent away from the containers. I checked around the other corner, and then ran in a crouch across the open ground to the back of the first container. I lost my balance and slid the last few yards, smashing into the container. I scrambled into a kneeling position and aimed the MPX at the front corner. But the only sound was the steady drizzle of the ice. No one appeared.

I crossed the back and came down the side away from the tent. At the corner I stopped and listened. They were very close, stamping their feet in the cold and slapping their gloved hands together. I stepped into view and put a burst into the rocks, sending a storm of icy chips into the container.

"Outside and face down or I'll kill you right here," I said.

The two pilots gaped at me and then threw themselves onto the ground. The kid's face twisted with rage. He had a hand on the Uzi and looked like he was remembering a scene from a movie where the bad guy makes a quick move and gets away with it. I knew that scene. I shot the kid in the leg. He screamed and crumpled to the ground, and the Uzi went clattering across the ice.

Pete jumped out in front of the tent and aimed his rifle at the flap and yelled, "Go!"

The priest shuffled carefully into view with a hunting knife and went down one side of the tent, slashing ropes. The stiff canvas crumpled under the burden of ice. The stovepipe wobbled: the top broke off, and the rest of it slid inside the tent with a puff of soot.

Pete shouted at the tent that they were surrounded and ordered them to put their weapons out through the flap. I proned out the pilots and the howling kid and fixed their hands behind their backs with ties. I left them in the sleet and joined Pete. He nodded to the priest, who slashed the ropes on the other side too.

The tent sagged from its poles. Tendrils of black smoke were leaking from the edges of the flap. The air inside would be full of soot and choking fumes. There wasn't even a cough. The angular shapes pressed against the drooping canvas didn't look like people.

"They're gone," Pete said.

"Where could they go?"

He looked baffled. "Jimmy kept a tracked vehicle here. They could go anywhere. But why?"

We dragged the chopper pilots and the kid back into a container. I had a small med kit. I gave the kid a morphine jab, found some torn canvas, and tied off his leg above the wound. I asked him where Fan and the others had gone. He was starting to shake. He babbled something about maps.

"What's he talking about?" Pete asked the pilots.

"Jimmy was using NAD 27, and the Chinese guy found out."

Pete frowned. "That's crazy. Jimmy was a pilot. His GPS would have been NAD 83, or he couldn't even have navigated properly."

"I'm talking about the survey maps that showed his targets."

"Pete?" I said.

"Sorry. I'll explain. NAD 27 was the old GPS system. NAD means North American Datum. NAD 27 was based on reference points from 1927. By 1983, there was better data. The new system was called NAD 83."

I looked at the pilot. "If Jimmy was using an outdated map to disguise the location of his targets, wouldn't Fan's people know just by looking at the date?"

He shook his head. "Jimmy stripped off the version ID."

"So where are they now?"

"Mitzi was gone when we got here. They went after her."

"She took the tracked vehicle?" Pete said.

"I guess so. It wasn't here. It left a trail. They followed it on foot."

"How many?" I said.

There were six. From their descriptions, Fan and the waif, Tinkerbell, a man who had to be George Wu, and two heavies. Like the tat kid, the heavies had Uzis too.

"No one else? A prisoner?"

He shook his head. "They had a wooden box, like a long crate. There was a sled in here. The security guys put it on that and dragged it with them."

She had to be alive. Fan must be keeping her as a life to trade if he needed to. I pushed away the image of her lying in the freezing wooden crate.

The sleet was blowing into the containers. We dragged the pilots and the kid further in, out of the weather. I made sure the wrist ties were secure and tied their ankles too. Pete went to the back of the container and found some crampons. We were strapping them on when he looked around with a frown.

"The drill's gone," he said. "If she's not using it, this is where it should be."

"Could Mitzi have taken it by herself?"

"It was small. One person could run it. She could have towed it with the little Cat."

We looked at each other. "I guess she had an idea where the garnets came from after all," I said.

We went back into the sleet and followed the tracks out of the camp.

48

The track led uphill. It was easy to follow—tread marks cut into the icy ground. Not far from camp, the track curved and followed a passage between low hills. We made quick time with the crampons. The only sounds were the crunch of metal cleats on ice and the vast clinking of the sleet. In twenty minutes we covered about a mile. Ahead of us the track led over a hump. We were almost at the top when we heard the drill.

We fell back and crowded together on a patch of dry ground in the lee of a boulder. The sound faded in a gust of wind and then returned. The steady beat of a generator and the squeal of a drill boring into rock.

"What's on the other side?" I said. "Have they explored there before?"

"I've only flown over it," Pete said. "It's just a cleft between hills. I think there's an esker that runs down the middle of the gorge. I don't know why she'd be there."

"Pete, it is way too late for bullshit. You know why she's there. Replot the coordinates. Take the coordinates from the map Jimmy showed the twins—the old-version map—and put them into the new version. I'm betting it would put the target just over this hill."

He drew a deep breath. "Yeah, maybe." He thought about it. "OK, replotting to NAD 83 would move the target east." He looked at me. "It would put the target where she's drilling now."

The temperature was rising. Rain fell now with the sleet, making the ground even slipperier. We flattened onto the streaming ice and crawled the last twelve feet to the top of the rise.

They were gathered at the base of the glistening slope. It was a narrow space, about a dozen feet wide, between the esker and the slope. The little Cat had followed a switchback to the head of the valley and come down that way. They would spot us right away if we tried that route. We huddled for a short discussion. Our best bet was a surprise attack straight down the slope.

Mitzi operated the drill. Fan stood beside her in a black parka. The same long black scarf he'd worn before was looped around his neck. The waif stood beside him, wrapped in a long fur coat and holding an umbrella to protect Fan from the sleet. Tinkerbell loomed beside them. One of the two Uzi guys stood directly behind Mitzi. I put the scope on her. Her lips were pressed tight. She stared grimly at the drill. There was a red mark on the side of her face.

The generator puffed black smoke. The drill shaft turned. It looked like some strange nativity scene, where the drill was the god they had come to venerate. Even the two hoods with the machine guns seemed entranced by what was happening. Wu, the lawyer, was the only one not looking at the drill. He stood beside the tracked vehicle, his briefcase on the roof, only partly open, to protect the papers inside from the precipitation. He was scribbling furiously. The coffin lay on the ground beside him.

A plywood box, the lid held on with metal clips. Covered in a film of ice. Inside, Lily's body wedged tight in the freezing cold. A movement at the drill caught my eye.

Mitzi pushed a lever and idled the machine. Then she moved it again, this time in the opposite direction.

"She's pulling core," Pete said in a low voice.

"You mean a sample?"

Pete nodded. "The target must be under the esker. That kind of drill has a circular bit. It takes a core of solid rock into the circular opening and up into a tube. She's pulling that core out now."

"And then they'll examine it."

"That tray on the back of the little Cat," he said. "It has slots to hold the core. She'll carry it over and put it in there."

"That's when we shoot the guards."

The black core crept slowly out of the esker and up the angled frame of the drill. The drill revolved, and the metal squealed, and the generator poured black smoke. When the core of rock was fully extracted, Mitzi idled the drill. She opened the safety cage that surrounded the shaft, very carefully lifted the length of core from the drill, and carried it to the back of the Cat. Wu leaned over and snapped pictures with his phone. Fan and the waif watched closely as she laid the core into a slot in the box. Tinkerbell towered behind Fan. The Uzi guy on Mitzi was close behind her, the other one to the side.

"Are you worried about deflection in this weather?" I said.

"It's just shooting in the rain," Pete said. He levered a bullet into the chamber and lay flat out on the slick ice.

I realized I was soaked, and that the breeze was pushing warmer air against my face. The ground felt softer under the wet ice. The tinkling sound had changed to the hiss of rain. I handed the MPX to the priest.

"When we shoot, fire off a mag. Maximum confusion," I added, but he didn't need an explanation. He'd been there.

"I'll take the one on the right," I said, taking out the Walther. "As soon as we shoot, we all head down the hill."

Not the best plan in the world, but better than what happened.

Tommy's bad knee was giving him a hard time in the cold, and it was worse now in the rain. He wanted to be ready for the charge. He raised himself slightly to shift the weight onto his good leg, and his crampon detached a piece of melting ice. He lurched off balance and sprawled headlong. The Ithaca discharged with a boom, flew from his hand, and clattered down the hill, with Tommy slithering behind it. I got off two quick rounds at my target, who had started to swing toward Tommy. I caught him in the arm. The Uzi bounced on the ground, and the guard fell down screaming. Mitzi spun around at the sound, blocking Pete's line of fire on the second guard. Tinkerbell spotted us immediately. He grabbed Mitzi by the hair and used her as a shield. He stepped out, snatched up Tommy's Ithaca, and kicked him in the face. Fan screamed at the remaining guard.

"Show yourselves!" the guard shouted, pointing his Uzi at the box. "Or we kill the Russian!"

I shoved the Walther under my coat and gestured for the MPX. The priest passed it to me. When I had it, I stood up in full view and made a show of throwing the gun aside. Pete did the same with his rifle.

"If I make a move on the hood," I said to Pete, "grab the Walther in my belt and shoot the big guy."

49

We started down the steep slope. The dark overcast was sliding south. A soft, misty light flowed in behind it. The rain loosened the scree. Our crampons dislodged the icy cover, and we slid and scrabbled to the bottom.

Tinkerbell watched us spill from the slope, his face impassive. He pushed the shotgun barrel up under Mitzi's chin. The wounded guard writhed on the ground, screaming. His partner threw a panicked look at Tinkerbell. "Gun," roared Tinkerbell, and the guard jammed his Uzi into my ribs.

Fan's eyes flicked to me. Lipstick smudged his chin. The waif gave me a wan smile. Her lips parted and the umbrella wavered, and the rain poured down on Fan's now unprotected head.

"Dopehead bitch," he barked, striking her in the face with the back of his hand. She stumbled away and fell into the mud. "You can do nothing," he sneered at me. "Stupid. You show up with guns. You think this is a cowboy movie? Americans ride in to kill the bad Indians!" He chuckled, drooling a few more strands of red onto his chin. "It's mine, now. Mine."

The priest pushed in and fell to his knees beside the coffin and fumbled at the icy clips. I took a step to join him but Wu caught my eye and gave an almost imperceptible shake of his head.

"You want the Russian cunt?" Fan sneered at the priest. "Take the Russian cunt. I cooled her down for you." He tittered to the waif, back in place with the umbrella. "Wake up, guy," he said to me. "You think Canada gives a fuck who owns this? I give them an extra point on their shit royalty—hey, suddenly on my side!"

"Mitz," Pete called.

"I'm OK," she said in a strained voice, her head tilted back from the barrel of the shotgun.

"You're OK when I say you're OK, asshole." Fan smirked. "Or you end up bear food, like Jimmy." His eyes darted around the site. "Nobody fucks with me."

The waif planted a dreamy kiss on his cheek.

"We'll take them for a helicopter ride," he whispered to her in a stage aside, and she gave him a rapturous smile.

The priest grasped a clip on the plywood crate and snapped it open. He moved to the next clip, bumping the guard. The guard smacked the side of his head with the Uzi.

"Leave him," Wu said angrily. He snapped a terse Chinese phrase at Fan, who stepped to the Cat and took the proffered pen. He scribbled his initials on a document and threw the pen into the briefcase with a flourish.

"Hello, diamonds!" he sang in a falsetto, striking a diva pose and fluttering his eyelids at the waif.

"We have completed the transfer of this property to its rightful corporate owner," Wu said in a severe tone, as if trying to restore some order to the scene. "So you understand the import of this," he said to me, "this property is now an asset of Angel Minerals, whose owners include the investors you are allegedly here to protect."

Fan rattled a Chinese phrase at Wu, then seized the waif and did a clownish tango back to the drill.

Wu said in a low voice, not looking at me, "The woman is alive, but he means to kill you both."

I wondered if that meant Wu planned to intervene in some way, but at that moment the priest snapped the last clip open and was wrenching at the coffin lid. I knelt in the muck and hammered my fist on the crate, smashing the coating of ice. I heaved off the heavy lid.

All she had on was the red leather jacket and her jeans. Her arms were folded across her, as if she'd been hugging herself for warmth. The bandage had been ripped from her cheek, and a fresh, neat cut was incised beside the ragged wound. Frozen rivulets of blood clung to her gray skin. A strip of duct tape covered her mouth. I leaned in and grabbed her icy body, lifting her out and placing her on the lid.

The priest grasped a corner of the duct tape and peeled it away. He opened his little case and placed it on the ground. With his left hand he took out a tiny dish of oil. He dipped his right thumb into it and drew a cross on her forehead, mumbling something, and put his ear to her blue lips. They didn't move.

The guard shot a nervous glance at his partner, now blowing pink bubbles and choking on his own blood. Distracted, he let the barrel of the Uzi shift. I grabbed it and yanked it down. The mud exploded in a burst as the guard fired the whole clip. I grabbed his hair and slammed his face into the side of the coffin. Pete dove in and yanked the Walther from my belt. Fan shrieked. Tinkerbell swiveled the Ithaca away from Mitzi's chin and was aiming at Pete when Mitzi leaned down and sank her teeth into his wrist. The shotgun fell to the ground, and he struck her in the face. She stumbled backward, crashing into the rig.

Tommy scrambled to a crouch and planted his crampons. Tinkerbell caught the movement. He leapt around, landing nimbly on his feet with his hands held out like a martial artist ready to repel an attack.

Tommy got to Tinkerbell pretty quick for a guy with a bum knee. Tinkerbell shot out a kick. Tommy's face was already banged up from the first kick Tinkerbell had given him, but here's the thing: In pro ball, pain is the business they're in. The main outcome of the kick was that it just made Tommy madder. He cannoned into Tinkerbell and grabbed his ears in both hands, twisting hard.

Tinkerbell roared in pain, and they went bowling into the drill rig, smashing it loose from the mount and sending pieces clanging to the ground. Fan leapt back, raising his arms. It was the classic pose of someone in alarm. As I guess he was, because a Black Hawk rose up from behind the esker. Silver in a silver sky. Silent in the swish and hiss of the falling rain. The door slid open and Carstairs appeared, standing behind a soldier who had his eye to a short, thick scope. Carstairs leaned over the soldier, pointed down at us, and a small red dot popped into place on Fan's chest.

"No!" I yelled, waving my free arm like a maniac. Mitzi and Tommy were only feet from Fan. "No!" I yelled again. But even if Carstairs had heard me, he wasn't the one who was going to launch the Hellfire missile. It was the sergeant in that room in Cheyenne Mountain. He and his partner were the ones flying the Reaper. I couldn't see it, but it was out there in the rain, and the targeter kneeling in the Black Hawk's open door had planted the crosshairs squarely on Fan's chest.

Pete saw what was happening. He hit the guard with his Walther, dug his crampons into the muck, and threw himself at Mitzi, tackling her to the ground.

"Down," I bellowed at Tommy, and he hit the dirt.

The missile came out of the rain with a banshee wail, the blades already spread into a horrifying claw. Fan had lost his footing in the mire and was falling, his arms flung outward. The only one standing was the waif.

A blade clipped off Fan's right arm, just above the elbow, and dropped it neatly in his lap, beside the waif's head. Her face still bore the euphoric expression she'd taken with her into eternity. Fan gaped at her, then started squealing—high, piercing squeals as he lay on his back in the rain, his stump gushing blood. Tinkerbell tore off his jacket, scrambled to Fan, and wrapped the bleeding stump. I swaddled Lily in my parka and held her freezing body in my arms.

"You have to be super gentle with hypothermia," the medic from the Black Hawk said. He'd just finished tying off Fan's arm and giving him a jab to stop the screaming. Now he was trying to slide his arm slowly between me and Lily. "Sir? You're holding her too hard. Let go, OK?"

"Alex," Tommy said gently. "He's got her." He pried my fingers off, folded his hands over mine and levered my arms away.

The medic took her from me and laid her carefully on the blankets he'd put in the back of the Cat. The rain had stopped. He tented Lily in silver foil. He cut her clothes off quickly, the jeans and the red leather jacket, without disturbing the position of her body. He wrapped her in a fleece blanket, put on his stethoscope, and listened to her heart.

"Wow," he murmured. "That's some engine."

The medic was tending to the wounded guard when Lily opened her eyes. I helped her sit up so she could swallow some of the warm tea the medic had brought from the Black Hawk.

"Small sips," I said. She swallowed and closed her eyes. Her skin looked pinker, almost flickering with a rosy hue that seemed to come as much from the air as from Lily. When she opened her eyes again, she whispered something I couldn't make out. I put my ear against her lips. I could smell the tea on her breath as she whispered again. "The hill." And I turned.

The rain had washed the slope clean. The garnets glowed like the embers of a banked fire. Thousands of them, tens of thousands. They filled the valley with a rosy light.

50

Every operation comes to the same moment. When it's time to shuffle everything away and put it in a folder and send it downstairs to a locked room in the basement. Before that can happen, there's a meeting to get the story straight and decide what lie to file it under.

I walked all the way downtown from Ninety-Fourth Street. Through the park to Columbus Circle, over to Ninth Avenue, down to Hudson Yards. Then onto the High-Line, the old elevated railway made into a park. When the wind blows off the Hudson River, it's the cleanest air you can get in New York City. I took a good gulp. There wasn't going to be any at the meeting.

At Gansevoort Street I got off the High-Line and cut over to Greenwich. Fifteen minutes later I was on Clarkson Street, iris-scanning myself into the office.

I was early, so I spent a few minutes catching up on Fan. The Black Hawks were US Army. They never let him out of their custody. An army jet came up to Yellowknife and medevacked him down to Joint Base Lewis-McChord, near Tacoma. They kept him in the hospital there for five weeks. You have to ask yourself if the antibiotics and the morphine were the only drugs in the IV bag, because they got everything they wanted out of him.

The Chinese kicked up a fuss, and finally the army packed Fan up, and the air force took him to Osan Air Base in South Korea and let his bosses come and get him.

Then I read through the last emails and went upstairs.

Tommy's face still looked plowed up. Tinkerbell had kicked him hard. The plastic surgeon in Yellowknife had set his nose and popped the busted cheek back into place. "Zygomatic arch," she'd said. "I should give you guys a volume discount." She'd insisted Tommy come in again before he left, and when he did, offered him some tips on reconstructive surgery. She'd handed him a file. "Just give this to whoever you see in New York. You'll be good as new."

"Thanks, sweetie," Tommy said, "but I'm not much uglier now than I was before."

Tabitha was swiping her way through some documents. A slingback dangled from a toe as she sat swinging her leg. She glanced up when I came in, and puffed a tangle of auburn hair from her face. It fell back down. She put her phone on the desk and shot her hair back with both hands.

I gave them a rundown on the new mine. Development had just started. The pipe was under the esker. In the Barrens, prospectors were used to looking for diamond pipes under lakes. The soft rock that contained diamonds was gouged out by glaciers during the last ice age and then filled with water when the glaciers melted away. This time the glacier hadn't covered the gouged-out pipe with water but with gravel.

"That's the part I don't really get," Tommy said. "I was up there. It's all rock. I get that a melting glacier leaves water behind, but where does the gravel come from?"

"The ice sheet came further south than where Denver is today," I said. "The gravel could have come from anywhere."

"And Jimmy suspected the presence of a pipe because of all the garnets," Tabitha said.

"It had to be there. The hill was red with garnets. When the rain washed the ice away, we were picking them up by the handful."

"And Mitzi knew?"

"She knew that Jimmy had salted Clip Bay, and that the true target was at the east end of the lake. But not exactly where."

"How could she not know?" Tommy said. "All she had to do was plug in the right GPS coordinates, and she would have the right location."

"That's what she did do, but first she had to figure out what Jimmy had done to disguise the real location of the pipe."

A mineral discovery always sounds simple after the fact. The truth was that the old surveys identified all kinds of targets that geologists rushed out to investigate, only to find nothing. Planes flew back and forth across the Barrens towing instruments that recorded magnetic anomalies. Some of them turned out to be diamond pipes, some just turned out to be magnetic anomalies. That's how it goes. No one had ever found a pipe under an esker, just like no one had ever found one under a lake. Jimmy was the first to do both.

He'd probably discovered this one in the rain, hiking by on his way to somewhere else, and suddenly there it was—the whole hillside glowing like a ruby. That close to an esker, the garnets had normally been covered in dust and grit.

Tabitha checked her watch. A black Suburban was waiting outside to take her to the east side heliport. She'd moved up again. Someone else was writing the President's Daily Brief. Tabitha had a different reason for visiting the Oval Office now: Assistant Deputy to the Director of National Intelligence.

The decapitation of Fan had been Tabitha's operation. MI was the obvious way to do it. Although Fan had survived, the operation was deemed a success. The missile strike had crushed him. He hadn't been seen since we returned him to the Chinese as an emotional wreck. They were repaying him for his long service by stripping him of control of his companies and handing his share to Mei.

"I just need to dot a few i's on the Chinese position," Tabitha said. "Angel Minerals has a rich diamond mine. Who's going to run it?"

"Mitzi."

"I thought there was a clause in the original investment agreement that gave the twins control if Jimmy was out of the picture."

She gave a good imitation of someone swiping around among documents to locate important information she didn't already have.

"That's right," I said. "And Mei waived the right to exercise that provision. She says she's confident in the management of Angel Minerals. The management of Angel Minerals is Mitzi Angel. I'm sure you'll find it in there somewhere," I said, pointing at her phone, "because I sent it to you yesterday."

Tommy tilted his chair back and was examining the ceiling. Tabitha took a deep breath and exhaled slowly. "I think you know there's something we have to discuss. I'm sorry if it's personally awkward for you."

I'd had a pretty good idea she'd get straight to Lily.

"Are you asking me about the $2.5 million cashier's check from the Montreal lawyer that ended up in George Wu's account?"

"If it's not too much trouble."

"Sure," I said. "The way it worked—Fan was always jealous of Mei. She was the real business genius. He hated her for it. When we got the Canadians to lock her up, he used the opportunity to seize total control of their operations. He ran it like a triad gang. Maybe even crazier, because he'd developed a nasty crack habit by then. Mei was helpless. She had no access to funds. She asked Wu for help. But Wu thought she was finished. She needed to prove she was still a player."

"They call it 'show money,'" Tommy said to Tabitha.

"Thanks," she said in a lethal purr. "I think I can keep up."

"Mei had already met Lily in Montreal," I said. "Even though Lily had cheated her when the twins were buying Russian rough, Mei recognized how much Lily knew about diamonds, and went to Montreal to consult her about the investment in Jimmy Angel. So they had a connection before Mei was arrested on our extradition warrant."

Tabitha's phone pinged. She glanced at it, dropped it in her slim black Montblanc document case, and snapped the catches with a look of satisfaction. There were throats to cut, and she was in a hurry.

"I'm afraid this is bad for Lily," she said, deftly wriggling her foot back into the dangling shoe. "Helping Mei was the same as helping China Hard Asset. We really don't have any choice but to report this to the Canadians."

The idea that Luc didn't have Lily pegged was the laugh of the day. What Tabitha really wanted was to force me to bargain for Lily. She would then control not Lily but me.

"Before you strike the Canadians dumb with the news that Lily does business with the Chinese, Tab, take a quick peek at this."

I handed her a plain brown manila envelope. She sat there looking at it for a moment while the machinery in her head whirred through the possibilities. She darted a quizzical glance at me, tore the envelope open, and slid out a couple of the eight-by-ten screen grabs. The quality wasn't good, but good enough to recognize Tabitha and Mei as they came out of the restaurant, their heads bent together in conversation.

She slid the black-and-whites into a side pocket of her case, smoothed her skirt and got up. A blush stole up her throat, but that was probably anger rather than embarrassment. She kept her expression blank.

"The flight to Montreal?" she said.

"That's right," I said.

She closed her eyes and opened them. A slight frown creased her forehead as she tried to figure out how I could have found her. She wasn't going to ask. In the end she just gave a little shrug, picked an imaginary piece of lint from my lapel, and brushed the fabric lightly with her fingertips.

"You boys have a great day," she said.

"Ouch," Tommy said as he studied the copies I gave him. He shuffled through them slowly one by one. "How did you get them?" he asked, cocking his head and tilting a print to the light for a better look. I told him about the trip to Montreal that I'd seen listed in the flight log on the secretary's jet on the first trip to Yellowknife. He nodded. "And you were spending a lot of time in Montreal, and Lily was living there. You don't believe in coincidence, so you thought it might have something to do with you. You checked, and found the passenger was Tabitha. That gave you her arrival date in Montreal."

"Then it was just a matter of feeding her image to the NSA and letting their facial-recognition software rummage through Montreal."

"But you don't really have anything on Tabitha. So she met Mei and planned the whole operation to take out Fan."

"Even if she had the authority, how are her bosses going to like that a Treasury dick busted her so easy?"

We went outside. Tommy's Eldorado was parked in front. The October air was tart with the scent of dried leaves. A couple of kids on hoverboards came whizzing up the street, holding hands and grinning at each other. She puckered her lips and popped him a kiss. We stood there with our hands in our pockets, two guys with girl trouble, watching them go by.

"As soon as he knew Mei could still play, Wu made plans to dump Fan, didn't he?"

"Yes," I said. "Fan was pretty much out of it by then. The document he initialed at the pipe, it actually transferred control to Mei. Wu knew Fan wouldn't even read it."

Betrayal had been dished out all around. There was enough for everybody. When he wasn't guarding his expression, Tommy looked desolate. I didn't know exactly where he was with Minnie. We weren't charging her with anything. What would be the point? It would just tell the Chinese that we knew about the wire. One way or another we'd have to try running her as a double. Tommy would have to be part of that.

I knew how that went. Lily wasn't just a diamond thief. She had stolen from me. Not the diamonds she was still running—the stolen rough or the large gems with doubtful provenance. That's just the diamond trade. There has to be theft. It's part of what glitters. What she stole from me was something else. The shell that guarded me. That I had put together piece by piece from childhood. She chipped away at it with the intensity of her emotions.

Then came tenderness. The only tenderness I'd ever received had come from Lily. It took my breath away. And that's what lays you open. The tenderness. Now Tommy was learning what it cost.

51

No bathing suit this time. The ocean was too cold. Annie crossed the lawn in a wetsuit, ran onto the dock, and hopped down into the Laser. She tossed off the line and tacked out into the bay. When she was clear of the point, the ocean breeze caught the sail. The boat heeled, and she shot her feet under the hiking straps. She went tearing across the wind, the slender yellow hull bouncing over the waves in bursts of spray.

"She's strong," I said.

"You were pretty good yourself," Dad said.

"I had that old, gaff-rigged dinghy. It still had canvas sails. The centerboard weighed a ton."

"And you stood it on its side, just like she's doing now. If it was blowing a gale, so much the better." He grinned and shook his head. "Your mother was petrified. She could barely watch."

This was a new development. The happy family past. I'd already glimpsed scenes from this fairy tale. Annie would mention some event from my golden childhood in African diamond camps. I let it go.

I have no complaint about how I grew up. There were good people along the way. Maybe a little rough. They gave me what I needed. My parents were too busy with their own misery. I wasn't hearing that part from Annie.

We went back inside and sat down at the bench in his little lab. I opened the Ziploc and dumped the garnets on a sheet of clean white paper.

"These were all collected by Jimmy?" he said.

I nodded. "They're from the lab he had on his houseboat. They're the same as the ones I showed you last time."

He plucked one with his tweezers and placed it in the middle of the sheet. Then he opened a drawer and took out a clear-plastic tray with about a dozen garnets in it. "These are from the new mine," he said, his eyes alight with the interest that only a mineral could put there.

The garnets flared and shimmered in the sunlight. He picked one up with the tweezers and placed it beside the first one. A field lens hung from his neck on a long cord. He angled a powerful light onto the desk and studied each stone through the lens, one after the other. When he was through he put them back, Jimmy's on the paper and the one from the new discovery in the plastic tray.

"Take a look at this," he said, swinging the screen of his iMac around and tapping with two fingers at the keyboard. A deep red garnet flamed into view on the screen. "I took this with the microscope. The violet, purple, and ruby tints come from the high chrome content." His voice had a gentleness it never had at other times. "That's why some of them look like rubies. Chrome is what gives rubies the same bloodred color. The actual compound is chromium oxide. It indicates the stone's origin in a high-pressure zone in the upper mantle. The same high pressure required to squeeze graphite, or any other form of carbon, into the carbon form we want—diamond."

He tapped a key and the image disappeared, and he turned back to the garnets on the bench.

"I don't have to test these," he said when he was through examining them. "There's nothing like these garnets anywhere. The stones you took from the houseboat are the same as the ones from the new mine. There was only ever one target. That silly map of Jimmy's with the exploration targets marked." He waved his hand. "Baloney."

"And the garnet with the soil?"

He stared at the stones for a minute. When he looked at me, his worn face had crinkled into the bitter smile it was used to.

"Really, Alex, am I so decrepit?" He picked up a pair of tweezers and tapped the plastic tray. "That was from Clip Bay. Jimmy put it there. He salted the target."

"I didn't tell you the garnet was from Clip Bay. How did you know that?"

He was an old man now, but his blue eyes still had a cutting edge. His glance took a slice at me. I could feel the air on my cheek as the blade swished by. He got up and put the cover on the microscope, switched off the iMac, and put away the plastic tray of garnets from the mine. He used a tin diamond scoop to gather up the garnets I'd brought, poured them into the Ziploc, and handed me the bag.

He wasn't as tall as he'd been, had a slight stoop now. But he was all sinew and hard edges, and in his summer uniform of starched white shirt, khaki pants, and blue canvas shoes, he looked as spare and tough as ever. He stuck his chin out and let me have a good look at the expression that had tormented my childhood.

"It didn't take a genius to put it together," he said scornfully. "The word was out that Jimmy's remains had been discovered at Clip Bay. You were investigating his disappearance. Then you show up here with a bunch of Jimmy's garnets and give me that one with a bit of dirt. Where else would you have got it?"

"And you knew it couldn't be from Clip Bay because it didn't match the soil?"

"Oh, please." His voice was like ice. "These were the best garnets anyone has ever seen, and you found one in the heart of the original discovery zone? That area was explored with a fine-tooth comb. It had to have been put there."

"Mitzi said that target had been missed, because the shape of the pipe was concealed by its location at the edge of the inlet."

He gave me a pitying look. "I'll bet she did."

We left the lab and went out the side door. As we came around the side of the house, the wind snatched the field lens dangling from his neck and whipped it out behind him. He grabbed the cord and tucked the lens in his shirt, and we watched the gusts tear off the whitecaps and fling them downwind.

Annie sat well back, trying to keep her bow up, but it was rough, and as we watched she plowed into a trough and the Laser flew up and she dumped.

"She's OK," I said.

Dad held up a hand to shelter his eyes from the glare. "She'll stand on the centerboard," he said, "and haul it back up." By the time three big waves had rolled by she'd righted the boat and heaved herself back in and was bashing through the water, the Laser heeled right over to drain the water from the cockpit.

"You think Mitzi knew Jimmy salted Clip Bay?" I said.

"I think everybody knew but you."

Annie was headed straight in now. The wind was right behind her. She had the sail out like a spinnaker. The mast bent with the strain and her hair lashed in the wind. It was a sight that should have filled me with elation. Instead, something more familiar crept into my heart.

"It wasn't Jimmy who brought the garnets, was it."

"Jimmy had his own lab. He would never have asked anyone's opinion. Not about G10s that good. He was too obsessed with secrecy."

He turned from watching Annie. He had something even more enjoyable to look at, and he wanted to make sure he didn't miss it. My face.

"I can tell you now. It was Mitzi. And she wasn't alone. She brought someone else along."

A wave hit the seawall, and a gust whipped the spray into our faces. He never even blinked. His eyes bored into me.

"Lily," I said.

And for the first time, his smile was one of real joy.

Annie put the top up on her Miata before we left. "We don't want to yell all the way back," she said, although she looked as if it wouldn't bother her—hair in a mad tangle, salt crystals sparkling on her skin.

Dad made a big show of saying goodbye to Annie. I ignored the hand he offered me. We were through the village and crossing the causeway before I could shake his gloating expression from my mind. Annie had been shooting me meaningful looks since we left.

"Someday you are going to have to put the past behind you, Dad."

"Absolutely."

She pulled out and shot by a line of cars slowing for the Greenport turnoff. "I know Grampa wasn't always the best father."

But I wasn't thinking about him anymore. I was thinking about somebody else's dad. Mitzi's. And the tears she'd shed as we sat on the ridge while the crime-scene guys picked up Jimmy's bones. Who was she crying for?

They were all running a play. Jimmy was setting up the twins; the twins, each other. We were drawing a bead on Fan while the puppet masters in Beijing were twitching the strings on us. Mitzi probably thought her dad was going to blow it again. Outsmart himself by trying to cheat an investor. She'd worked for a discovery too. Every summer of her life. The long sampling months in a tent camp pitched by the latest diamond target. I knew what that felt like. Did she hate him? I don't know. But she grabbed some garnets and made her own deal on the side.

The straightest arrow in the game was Lily. All she wanted was diamonds.

"This can't just be me talking, Dad," Annie said, breaking into my reverie. "This is an opportunity for us, for a father and daughter, to really communicate."

"Yes," I said.

With that out of the way, she launched into a passionate lecture on sustainable fashion. I hung on as long as I could, but my fingers couldn't bear the combined weight of recycled ocean plastics and Lily's betrayal, and I slipped off into my bleak world.

If Mitzi had brought Lily to Dad's lab, it was because she had to. The question was: Why? What possible motive could Mitzi have for including Lily in such a closely guarded secret as the phenomenal garnets? When I'd visited Dad the first time, he'd said the garnets had come to him about a month before. When I thought back, I remembered a short trip Lily had made to New York around that time. I needed a way to connect the different events. The best way to do that was to arrange them in chronological order.

I already had some reliable dates from Montreal surveillance tapes, the log I'd looked at on the plane, and my own trip to New York when Tommy told me about Jimmy's disappearance. So I made a provisional list:

Tabitha flies to Montreal to meet Mei.

Lily goes to New York.

Mitzi and Lily visit Dad with garnets.

Obviously, a link was missing. Something had to happen between Tabitha's meeting with Mei and Lily's trip to New York. Something that accounted for the trip. It wasn't hard to understand what that had to be. A meeting between Lily and Mei.

"Dad," Annie exclaimed as we cleared Riverhead and got onto the Long Island Expressway, "this is, like, literally, a matter of life and death! Fashion is a trillion-dollar industry and one of the biggest polluters in the world. In America, we throw out the weight of the Empire State Building in clothes *every year*. That can't go on!"

"No."

"It's the responsibility of every human being on this planet!"

"Yes."

We came down the length of Long Island with Annie sketching out a life designing clothes that helped to heal a sickened planet, and me trying to find a way to fit Lily and Mei into the jigsaw puzzle of events. We were passing LaGuardia Airport by the time I got it. It had been clear since their meeting in the courthouse that Lily was Mei's essential partner. I should have drawn that connecting line back to the beginning.

If Tabitha had pitched Mei on a plan to take out Fan, Mei would have needed assurances that Tabitha couldn't give. The main assurance was that a viable diamond target existed. China Hard Asset would not have agreed without it. They wanted Fan erased, but not their foothold in the Arctic. How could Mei find out for sure what Jimmy had? Do a deal with the daughter.

The only problem was—Mitzi might try to deceive her too. Mei needed someone who knew the diamond business. She already knew that person. She and Lily had met before. The fact that Lily had a criminal past, and that Mei had been among her victims, wouldn't have bothered Mei. Lily's crooked past, as much as her access to cash, made her the ideal partner for Mei. Moreover, this time it wasn't Lily who would control the asset. It was Mei. Lily's job was to make sure that the asset was there. That was why she had shown up with Mitzi and the garnets, to hear what the world's foremost expert had to say about them.

A plane took off over Long Island Sound, its lights winking into the gathering night. We crossed the Triborough Bridge and got onto the FDR. The reflected lights of the city blazed on the East River. The traffic was slow, so Annie got off at 116th Street and treated me to a bravura demo of how adroitly she could thread the Harlem traffic. It didn't even interrupt her scathing account of the fashion business.

"You are so evasive, Dad," she said later, turning onto Central Park West. "You just let me talk and talk. It's like your secret tradecraft, where you get the other person to talk so you don't have to say anything." When I didn't respond immediately, she said, "See?"

She parked in front of Lily's building. The doorman started out, but I waved him away.

"I mean, what about Lily, Dad? At first she's living in Montreal, and now, suddenly, she's living *here*." She snapped her fingers to indicate the speed with which Lily had teleported herself from Montreal to New York. "I mean, if this is a thing now, and Lily is going to be my stepmom, I think I should know."

"Yes," I said.

"Yes what? Yes, Lily is going to be my stepmom?"

"Can you have a stepmom when you still have an actual mom?"

"Dad! Of course you can! Are you trying to duck the question?"

"Yes," I said. But we didn't say goodbye until I'd agreed that the three of us would sit down to what Annie called a "family dinner."

"I'll email you some dates," she said when I got out. Then she popped the clutch and shot away.

52

W hat does she like to eat?" Lily said, padding around the terrace in bare feet, a gardening apron pulled on over shorts and a T-shirt.

Antique carriage lanterns cast an eerie, orange light. The black night-time sea of Central Park stretched out below, its winding paths picked out by lights that glimmered in the trees. The lake shone like a mirror.

"Barbecue!" Lily said, waving her secateurs. "All Americans love barbecue."

The apron had special pockets for knives and tiny saws and a pronged, swallowtail instrument for digging weeds. Lily was proud of these tools and used them indiscriminately, seizing one and flailing at the soil, jamming it back into the apron and snatching another. Lumps of dirt lay scattered on the tiles. The secateurs flashed again in the lamplight as she made her way along a row of flower boxes, deadheading the chrysanthemums. She gazed at the flowers with a murderous look, pausing to fish a glass of frothing liquid from where she'd parked it among the blossoms. She took a loud slurp. A pitcher of the tawny mixture stood on a table. I could smell the vodka blended with the coffee. Lily called it *café à la Russe*.

"Pour yourself one," she said in her raspy voice as she dug back in with the shears. "Barbecue—that's the answer!"

I gulped one down and poured another and finished that one too. It didn't make me feel any better. I put the new list up inside my head:

Tabitha flies to Montreal to meet Mei.

Mei meets Lily.

Then Lily goes to New York to meet Mitzi.

Mitzi and Lily visit Dad with garnets.

From there it all made sense. Everybody was lined up for a payoff. Only one key thing they had to do. Get rid of Jimmy. Fan would take care of that. All he had to do was find him. That's where the bad feeling inside me was coming from. And maybe I should have let it go. I didn't.

"Have you ever wondered how Fan's hit men found Jimmy Angel?" I said.

Lily stopped what she was doing. She stared at the carnage of decapitated blooms. Petals clung to her hair, and a sprig of leaves perched on her shoulder. Her hair shivered in the warm breeze. Her eyes darted quick glances at me. In the orange light she looked like a forest sprite. Her lips tightened, and she squinted as if in pain.

"Why, Alex?" she said, jabbing her secateurs into the dirt. "Why are you doing this? Can you never let go? It's all over. Haven't we been through enough?" She gave me a pleading look. "Can't you just love me? Must everything be an interrogation?"

She picked up her glass, like someone grasping for relief. The liquid slopped on her hand, and the slippery glass fell from her fingers, smashing on the tiles. With a sob she yanked the swallowtail weeder from the apron and brandished it in the lurid light.

"Why don't you just stab me in the heart," she shouted, beating her chest with the fist that clenched the weeder. Her eyes filled with tears. "I give you my passionate love, and this is how you respond! The very *second* you are in the door," she cried, as if that were the really bad part of my behavior and not my question about Jimmy Angel, "the very *instant* you appear, the suspicions, the probing—it all begins again!"

She plunged the blade into the earth and, with a surprisingly graceful golf-stroke kind of swipe, scooped a chrysanthemum from the flowerbox and sent it flying against the penthouse wall. The clod of earth still caught in the roots exploded on impact, and the heady aroma of rich soil and *café à la Russe* filled the warm night air.

She seemed to feel better after that. We leaned on the smooth stone that formed the top of the parapet and stared out at the dark gulf of Central Park. Half a mile away, on the other side of the park, the facades of the apartment buildings on Fifth Avenue rose from the trees. The breeze picked at Lily's hair, and the pointy tips of her ears poked through. An ugly scrawl of red scar marked her cheek, and the tiny nicks from spraying Plexi hadn't completely healed. But I reminded myself that this was Lily. She had come out of everything that happened with a $100 million triplex on the Gold Coast, as this part of Central Park West was known. She had come out of everything that happened with an exclusive sales deal for the production of a fabulously rich diamond mine. And part of everything that happened was the murder of Jimmy Angel, who was guilty of crimes himself, for sure, but none for which the penalty was death.

She leaned against me, and we stood there for a while. The spectacle of New York City washed over us—the scent of trees from the park, the sounds that clamored through the streets in a kind of wind. The heartlessness. Just beyond the bottom of the park a phalanx of new, super-slim towers, like the sabers of a charging cavalry, stabbed the sky above Manhattan until only a handful of stars were left alive, bleeding their feeble light into the viscous luminescence of the city.

"You spoke to your father," she said.

"I knew you were involved with Mitzi. All that interest in garnets. What I didn't know was how far back it went."

Lily leaned on her elbows and laced her fingers together. Her skin had an ashy pallor. The weeder-brandishing and the chest-smiting—I put that down to the *café à la Russe*. She was running on the fumes. The physical injuries, the hypothermia, her mutilation at the hands of Fan. It had drained her dry.

"Fan had Jimmy followed with that special radar in that black plane," she said.

"Oh, stop it, Lily. The Caravan hadn't even got to Yellowknife when Jimmy flew out to Clip Bay. Mei knew that Fan had to find something important to make him want to move fast. That's what would expose him. Mitzi tipped them about Clip Bay. The problem was, Jimmy was still there."

It wasn't a carefully executed operation. It was an operation that was off the rails from the start. Even Mei had underestimated how quickly Fan would act.

"I don't know why the Chinese didn't just kill him," Lily said. "That's what Russians would have done."

"He was too famous. The hip new face of China. They don't get a lot of good press. So the magic twins on the front page with the world's golden people—that part they liked. But Fan just got too unpredictable. They wanted him gone."

Solution: tee him up for the Americans. The only real bad break they caught was that Fan survived. At Lewis-McChord we tapped him like a sugar maple.

Before Fan got on the down elevator with the waif, he'd been a real player. Mei ran the money, but Fan had the mugger's instinct that makes a great entrepreneur. He picked a target, Mei scoped the finances, the generals wrote the check. At Lewis-McChord, Carstairs built up a good picture of how the twins invested their way into strategic businesses in the West, with Beijing on board all the way. He wouldn't let me talk to Fan myself, but he put a few questions for me. That's how I knew how they'd found Jimmy.

Diamonds are supposed to stand for the permanence of human love. The forever stone. But love can wear away. A diamond doesn't. If a diamond represents any human quality, that quality is solitariness. The quality of being alone, as every person is.

A diamond is a xenocryst—literally, a stranger crystal. Formed in a violent sea, captured from the molten depths by a volcano and brought to the surface.

Not every diamond survives that journey. Most are changed back into graphite from the turbulence of the ascent. But some of them make it all the way—stranger crystals, not formed the way the rocks around them were. Eternally apart from the world. And that was Lily.

"I feel closer to you now," she murmured as we watched the city murdering the night. "I feel as if we are returning to the love we had."

But we were not returning to the love we had. We'd never left it. It was the love we'd always had. The love that everybody gets. The love of a stranger.

ACKNOWLEDGMENTS

The translation of Li Po's "The Long War" appeared in the August 1926 edition of *Poetry* magazine, and I am grateful to the translator, Cheng Yu San.

Thanks to Kathy and John Cormack for a close reading of the plane-chase scenes. John was a bush pilot who flew Twin Otters in the Arctic before becoming a long-haul captain for Air Canada; and Kathy, my niece, grew up in Yellowknife, and was no stranger to flying in the Barrens. The gas-contamination twist came from Stephanie Wright, who flies everything from 727s to helicopters, and her father, Greg McDougall, a former bush pilot in the north, who went on to found Harbour Air Seaplanes in Vancouver, BC, and later (still not satisfied!) invented an all-electric version of the iconic Beaver bush plane.

For the account of G10 garnets and the nature of the Arctic diamond pipes, I relied on the many friends I made reporting on the original diamond rush, in particular Eira Thomas, who was twenty-five when she drilled through dangerous, melting, Spring ice on Lac de Gras and made the discovery that became the Diavik mine.

For advice on indicator minerals, claim-staking, and the change to the GPS navigating system—many thanks to my friend the great diamond explorer Chris Jennings, and to geologist Ken Armstrong, CEO of North Arrow Minerals, whose targets include a cluster of pipes on Hudson Bay (where exploration drilling has produced tantalizing orange microdiamonds!)

Thanks to my nephew Peter Reardon, an ICU physician, and his wife, Aisling Fitzpatrick, a plastic surgeon, for how to repair a fractured zygomatic arch, and with other medical mayhem.

My dear friend Mary Lou Finlay read the galley and offered valuable feedback. To my implacable editor Leslie Wells, to Jessica Case at Pegasus, and to my agent Michael Carlisle—my enduring gratitude.

As always, I owe most to my wife, Heather Abbott, who has mastered of the art of making reassuring noises while never losing her place in the *Times*.